THE
TENTH
VIRGIN

THE TENTH VIRGIN

A NOVEL
GARY STEWART

A
Joan
Kahn
BOOK

St. Martin's Press   New York

Production Editor: Amelie Littell
Copy Editor: Elisa Petrini

Library of Congress Cataloging in Publication Data

Stewart, Gary.
    The tenth virgin.

    "A Joan Kahn book."
    I. Title.
PS3569.T4644T4   1983   813'.54   83-9645
ISBN 0-312-79122-4

First Edition

10 9 8 7 6 5 4 3 2 1

*For Larry
and for Diana*

". . . if any man espouse a virgin, and desire to espouse another . . . and they are
virgins . . . he cannot commit adultery with
that that belongeth unto him and to no one
else.

"And if he have ten virgins given unto
him by this law, he cannot commit adultery, for they belong to him, and they are
given unto him; therefore is he justified."
—Revelation to Joseph Smith,
First Mormon Prophet, 1843

THE
TENTH
VIRGIN

I

It hardly ever rains in Salt Lake City. And all that sunshine has been known to drive people crazy. But it is a magnificent city to fly into. The grand rugged mountains on the one side and the eerie turquoise lake on the other provide placid counterpoint to all the geological upthrusting.

As we approached the airport the city stood in relief against the mountains. The Mormon Temple has long since given over its place on the skyline to the skyscrapers, with the Mormon Administration Building standing preeminent, almost doing battle with God's mountains.

I was flying into the city to do a favor for a woman I hadn't seen in almost twenty years. She wouldn't tell me over the phone what it was but had assured me I would be well paid for my efforts. She also assured me she would be as happy to see me as she somehow knew I would be to see her. We had gone through high school together, the posh east side high school. She had attended by birthright—the family name was Young and her father was a Mormon Apostle. They owned a big house up on the hill. I had attended because my uncle ran a grocery store in the area. We lived in a small apartment above the store.

Since it was early in the day, I asked the taxi driver to deposit me in the middle of town. I wanted to get a room and clean up before I went to see Linda Young Peterson. I confess I wanted to look and smell my best for this old flame that had never quite extinguished itself. It rankled for many years that she had chosen David Peterson and not me.

And while I still told myself it was because David had much better prospects—Harvard Law School and a leg up in the Mormon establishment—I had gotten old enough to stop telling myself the most obvious lies.

My hotel was across the street from Temple Square, and the room had an excellent view of the assemblage of buildings that were the heart of the Mormon religion. Those remarkable old granite and sandstone structures stood as mute testimony to the strength and idealism of the founders of the Church. The men who built the Tabernacle and the Temple believed in themselves and their vision of the world. They were men willing to take significant risks for an idea.

The hotel was a squat, red brick building that looked barely respectable in the shadows of the corporate skyscrapers hovering overhead. It was a poor cousin to the elegant old Hotel Utah standing white and imperial in the afternoon sun just down the street. But my room had recently been redone and was clean and comfortable. The lobby shared space with the Trailways bus depot, but I liked that. It helped me feel a little as if I was home in New York City.

While I unpacked I flipped on the television set, curious about how Salt Lake City thought of itself these days. And sure enough, I couldn't have been anywhere else. I recognized from a long time ago the mellow, resonant voice of Amos D. Jensen, prominent Mormon Apostle, who was holding forth from the great podium in the Tabernacle across the street on the importance of families in the eternal scheme of things. He was an impressive, white-haired man who looked to be in his mid-fifties. I knew he was over seventy.

I sat on the bed for a few minutes, fascinated by the mixture of Old Testament fervor, backwoods horse sense, big-city lawyer savvy, country boy humor, and absolute self-assurance. And damned convincing. Must be hard to be single out here under Amos D. Jensen's shrewd, all-seeing eye. He had made a career, I knew, out of a combination of up-with-family and down-with-promiscuity sentiments, had preached all over the country, and had written half a dozen books published through the Mormon press. I turned off the set when I started feeling guilty about my recent divorce.

I showered and shaved and put on my best jeans and a smart Spanish leather jacket I had bought on sale. I even polished up my Black Lizard cowboy boots. I stopped at a coffee shop on the corner to get a sandwich and read the *Salt Lake Tribune*. The headline read POLYGAMIST DOCTOR SHOT TO DEATH. I was back in Mormon country all right. I read down the column, noting that it probably had something to do with interclan warfare among two Fundamentalist offshoots of the Mormon Church. Apparently there was a chief suspect who had escaped successfully, but there was no name given. There wasn't much else of interest in the paper. I had seen the line scores in the *Times* earlier in the day.

The cabbie deposited me at the foot of a steep driveway that led to one of the biggest houses I had ever seen. All wood and glass and native stone, it hugged the side of the mountain and looked out over the valley like some perching monster with great dark glasses. The citizens of this city were determined to conquer the mountains one way or another. This house was built on an incline that had intimidated me as a young hiker twenty-five years before. You do get a different perspective on the world being up high looking down rather than living in the valley looking up. You have a sense of owning everything you see down there. I still prefer the valley.

Linda greeted me at the door, all pink and fresh and blond. And she smelled terrific. Either she was always at her visual and olfactory prime at four in the afternoon or she had taken some trouble to prepare for my visit. I liked to think the latter. She stayed back in the shadow of the hallway and she appeared not to have aged even five years— she was as trim and as tidy as at twenty. I was even more nervous than I had expected to be. I felt awkward and a little dumb for not having a corsage in my hand.

"Come in, Gabe."

I walked into the front hall wondering whether to embrace her, shake her hand, or stand staring at my boots. She hesitated, too, but in a few seconds moved toward me and hugged me gently, careful not to muss her hairdo or to let me too close to her mouth. Through all the perfume and expensive soap penetrated the faint smell of alcohol. She took my hand and led me into the living room.

"Would you like something to drink? Fruit juice? Pop? I have a little instant coffee tucked away in the back of the cupboard. We don't have liquor in the house—David won't allow it, not even for company."

Then she turned to me, a little sadly. "I suddenly realize I don't know anything about you, Gabe. Twenty years ago I'd have known just what to fix you."

She stood staring at me from the doorway to the kitchen. She looked older as my eyes grew accustomed to the interior. There were worry lines around her eyes, a hard edge around her mouth, and the grooves from her nose to her chin were pronounced and ineradicable. Still, she looked very good to me. And I hadn't improved a lot. I had most of my hair and my teeth were still good, but I was wrestling with a paunch and my shoulders were rounding into a typical Utley stoop.

"How about a Seven-Up," I said.

"Fine. I'll be right back."

We drank our 7-Ups while musing a little on the superficialities of our present lives. We just built this house. David is away a lot. Salt Lake is growing very fast. Stuff like that. I told her I liked living in the East, that I enjoyed my work, that I didn't really have family anymore. Eventually we had to get to the business at hand. I got us there.

"I know you didn't spend all that money to fly me out here because you've missed me—though I'd like to think that."

"It's Jennifer . . ." She paused. "But you don't know Jennifer, do you?"

"No, I don't."

"Jennifer is our daughter. She turned sixteen last March."

"What about Jennifer?" I said.

"She's been gone a week. I don't know where she is." Linda paused, got up, and paced back and forth a couple of times, straightening her hair, clasping herself as if it was cold in the room. She looked like a woman who needed a drink. Then she stopped behind the couch and went on. "I think she may have been kidnapped!"

"What do you mean you *think* she may have been kidnapped?"

"She ran away before—a few weeks ago."

"And you don't think she ran away again?"

"Last time she came back after four days."

"Why don't you think she'll come back this time?"

Linda came and sat down again; she was crying. "I received a note. It came in the mail three days ago."

"Well, can I have a look at it?"

She dabbed her eyes with a fresh pink handkerchief. "Gabe, I know this all sounds stupid, like I've dragged you all the way out here to find some troubled child."

"Do you know where she went last time?" I asked.

"I know where she told me she went. She said she and a friend went to Las Vegas . . . to have a fling."

"A girl friend or a boy friend?" I said.

Linda looked startled. "Why, a girl friend, of course. She's only sixteen."

Perhaps sixteen-year-olds were younger out here. "Can I see the note, Linda?"

"Oh, yes, I'll get it. It's in my desk. Just a minute."

Linda seemed more in control when she returned with the note. I sensed she'd gone out for more than the note. I took the plain white piece of notepaper from her hand and read it. The message was in three parts. The first had a more than vaguely scriptural ring to it: *And have I not commanded men that if they were Abraham's seed and would enter into my glory they must do the works of Abraham.* The second was a cryptic piece of advice, not vague at all: *Don't try and find me!* The third was a simple drawing of a human eye. The note wasn't signed.

I asked Linda what she thought the reference to Abraham meant. She looked at her hands for a moment, as though she knew but didn't want to tell me. She asked me a question instead.

"You know who Abraham was?"

I said I did.

"You remember his significance for Mormons?"

"He had a lot of wives," I said, beginning to get the picture.

Tears were filling Linda's eyes again. "Gabe, I'm afraid she's been kidnapped . . . by the Fundamentalists."

"The note doesn't sound like she was kidnapped," I said. "Isn't it her handwriting?"

"I think so. But she had to be forced. She wouldn't go off willingly like that. She knows what those people are like. My God, did you see the paper this morning? One of them got killed, shot, right in his own living room!" She got up, distractedly, and started to pace again, clearly wanting this conversation to be over, wanting me to get on with the search for her daughter, wanting me to stop asking questions.

"I don't even know where to start on this, Linda. I really doubt I can help you much."

She turned sharply to me. "Is it money, Gabe? We have plenty of money. That won't be a problem."

"No, it isn't money, Linda," I said; trying to sound significantly less offended than I was. "It's a problem of not having enough information even to get started. I haven't been in this state for almost twenty years. I haven't any idea how the system works. I wouldn't know a Mormon Fundamentalist if he bit me on the leg. Why don't you just give this to the police? They'll know the polygamist underground; at least they'll know where to start."

Linda drew herself up to her full height, determination in her eyes. She looked directly at me for the first time. "I don't want the authorities in on this, Gabe. They mustn't know."

"Well, how the hell do you think you're going to keep a kidnapping secret from them?"

"That's part of your job, Gabe. You must do this without involving the police or anyone who might leak this to the press. I called you in precisely because you don't know anyone here. And no one knows you."

"What about David?" I asked. "What does he think about all this?"

She looked at me coldly. "David doesn't know about this."

"He doesn't know you called me?" I said, my incredulity mounting.

"He doesn't know Jennifer is gone."

I just sat and stared at her for a minute before I could tumble out a response. "David doesn't know? . . . Jesus Christ, Linda. David doesn't know? His daughter's been gone a week and he doesn't know?"

She hung her head. "No, I haven't told him. He has a lot on his mind right now. I couldn't worry him with it. Not yet."

"Well, when do you plan to tell him?" I asked. "Christmas morning when Jennifer doesn't show up to open her presents?"

"I'd like it to be after you find Jennifer."

"Good God," I said under my breath.

"That has to be part of the deal, Gabe, that you not talk with him. I can't make him go through this." And she looked soulfully at me with her marvelous eyes. Why didn't I just get up, stalk out the door, and get on the next plane home? My every instinct told me I'd better. This was insane. But I sat like a dummy while Linda went on. "David does care, Gabe. He cares a lot about Jennifer. But he can't be involved."

"Why not?" I asked softly, entirely suckered by her brown eyes.

"David has worked very hard, he's made a lot of money, and he has a prominent position in the Church. It's just possible he might be an Apostle in another couple of years. He's Amos D. Jensen's protégé, and you need to know that Elder Jensen feels very strongly about close family ties. Any hint that David hasn't raised his daughter properly and his career in the Church would be seriously compromised."

I shifted awkwardly, grasping in my mind for anything that would get me out of this. Then Linda said, "You'll help me, won't you Gabe?" And I was done for. I breathed heavily and asked my next detective question.

"Who was the girl Jennifer went to Las Vegas with?"

Linda smiled thank you and said, "Her name was Susan Whitesides."

"What do you know about her?"

She paused, thinking. "Nothing really. I don't even know who her parents are."

"Where she lives?"

"No. Not that either."

"Well, how did Jennifer know her?"

She looked puzzled and guilty, as if it was just occurring to her that she didn't know very much about her daughter's life. "I don't really know. She met her at school, I think."

"And that's all you know about her?" I said, trying to stay calm and keep from saying something like, Jesus Christ, I'm surprised you even remember your daughter's name.

"I do know she was a year or two older than Jennifer."

I thanked her, folded Jennifer's note into my pocket, and walked to the front door, beating back an impulse to have myself committed to the psychiatric ward of the Latter-day Saints' hospital. And to get away from those damn eyes. Jesus, Utley. Dumb son-of-a-bitch.

But Linda caught me by the arm before I could escape. "Thank you for coming, Gabe. I didn't know what else to do, who else to go to."

"How did you know I'd be a sucker twenty years later? And how the hell did you track me down?"

"I didn't have to track you down."

"What?"

"I've kept track all along. Doris. You remember Doris."

"Your sister," I said.

"Doris lives in Westchester. You're in the Yellow Pages."

More than I could hope for. An adolescent's dream come true. I just stared dumbly at her.

"Gabe. You haven't told me where you're staying."

I told her.

"Thank you, Gabe." And she gave me a kiss on the cheek.

I told her it was okay, that it was great to be back in Salt Lake, and that I was looking forward to meeting all sorts of interesting people. Then I got out fast before I offered to mow her lawn.

II

Back at the hotel, I lounged against a bank of pillows and tried making some notes about what I needed to find out and how I might possibly find it out. I didn't do that long; I kept getting reminded what a dunce I was. So I turned on the TV to the local news, poured a stiff drink of bourbon, and picked up the Salt Lake telephone directory. I turned to the *W*s and wrote down names, numbers, and addresses for all the Whitesides who lived even close to the East High School area. Then I proceeded to call each of the seven numbers I had found and ask for Susan.

The first three calls yielded no Susans; the fourth brought a giggly five-year-old to the phone. My fifth call prompted a long pause, then, "Who is this, please." It was a rather formal woman's voice.

I told her I was from the school and that I needed to talk with Susan. The only thing I knew about the girl was that she probably went to school.

Another pause, and, "Susan isn't here right now. She may not be back for some time." Then she hung up.

Since Mrs. Whitesides was the closest thing I had to a lead, I decided to pay her a visit. I put on my jacket and was about to turn off the television when a voice thrust itself into my consciousness, a voice I recognized from the past. On the screen appeared the face of a kinky-haired middle-aged man, looking impishly at me, telling me I should attend a production of a play called *What the Butler Saw* by a group called Theatre Genesis. The voice on the commercial was that of a young man I had known well in high school. The face could have been a forty-year-old version of his face. His name was Jerry Calabrese, and he had been a very good friend. Most interesting to me right now was the fact that Jerry had, twenty years ago, introduced me to what there was of Salt Lake City's lowlife.

Jerry's face, if it was his, disappeared, fading back into the handsome vacuous face of the anchorman. I picked up the telephone directory again and turned to the *C*s. Jerry wasn't listed. I determined to go to the theater later in the evening, after I visited Mrs. Whitesides.

The address listed in the telephone directory for M. A. Whitesides was in an older neighborhood, just below a steep hill on Eleventh East Street. This hill in my time had been the dividing line between the privileged and the not-so-privileged. The haves lived on top, the have-nots down below. My uncle's store had been right at the bottom of the hill.

As I got out of the cab, I saw that the Whitesides residence didn't do anything for the neighborhood. The lawn was long and brown with lots of dandelions. The house was old and frame, somber and peeling in the twilight. I knocked on the door.

Several knocks later, the door opened a few inches.

"Mrs. Whitesides?"

"What do you want?"

"Mrs. Whitesides, I'd like to come in and talk with you for a few minutes."

"What about?"

It was hard having a conversation with a three-inch-wide shadow and a wary eye, but I persisted. "I'd like to see you about your daughter Susan." I hoped Susan was her daughter.

There was a long pause, then she opened the door and silently motioned that I could come in.

I don't know what I expected inside—a small witch's cave, perhaps. But I was surprised to find a very homey room, colorful and smelling of fresh-baked bread. Everything looked handmade—the braided rug on the floor, the drapes, even the furniture—handcrafted and right out of the nineteenth century. The woman herself was right out of the nineteenth century. She had on a long dress with sleeves to her wrists, the collar buttoned to her throat, and she wore no makeup. Her long hair was braided in a single strand. She was wearing a black armband.

"I shouldn't let you in, but you asked about my daughter."

"Susan is your daughter?" I asked.

"Yes. And I've been worried about her. She didn't come home last night." She paused and indicated a handsome rocking chair. "I'm sorry. I'm not being very polite. Won't you sit down? Would you like anything? I have some tea brewing."

I sat down and told her I would love some tea.

The tea brought back memories. It was made from local herbs, red clover and mint.

"Now, Mr.—"

"Utley, Gabriel Utley," I answered.

"What a nice name. I know some Utleys," she said as she sat down. "Do you know something about Susan, Mr. Utley?"

"Not really. But I'd like to. Actually I'm trying to find a girl named Jennifer Peterson. She's been gone about a week. I understand she and Susan were friends, that they went away together for a few days not long ago."

Mrs. Whitesides tensed. Her big black eyes narrowed into suspicious marbles. "Are you with the police?"

"No, but I am a private investigator, and your daughter is the only person I know who may know where the Peterson girl is."

Mrs. Whitesides stood up abruptly. "I knew I shouldn't have let you in." She walked to the door and opened it. "You'll have to leave now."

I stood up, but I made no move to go. I conjured up my best whipped-dog look. "I really need your help, Mrs. Whitesides."

She softened a little, pushed the door closed.

"Who brought you into this?" she asked skeptically.

"I'm working for Mrs. Peterson."

"Not the Mormon Church?"

"Not the Mormon Church. Mrs. Peterson doesn't want the Church brought into this at all. She's simply worried about her daughter."

The woman relaxed, though deep strain was still apparent on her face. "I'm sorry to be rude, Mr. Utley. It's been a very hard few days. It's not like Susan to be away so long, not without telling me. And then . . ." Her voice trailed off as her hand went absently to the black armband.

I waited briefly then said, "Someone close to you died?"

She looked at me, a little startled, her hand fluttered away from the band. "Yes . . . yes. Someone close. A cousin. A cousin I loved very much."

I dropped that subject quickly and pushed on with my question. "Do you know where your daughter and Jennifer went?"

She looked as if she was close to opening her mouth to tell me. Then, as though a veil had descended, her face closed against me. She opened the door again. "I'm sorry, Mr. Utley. I truly am. But I can help you no more. I wish you well in your search. . . . But I must tell you nothing more." And she ushered me out the door. My one lead had dribbled away into nothing.

I stood on the corner down from the house, strongly tempted to get on the next plane to New York. I didn't recall ever knowing so little about so much. We establish our contacts, find our grooves, set up ways of solving whatever problems come our way. Being in the middle of a network of people with whom we have superficial contacts gives us a fine and secure sense that we are important in the scheme of things. In New York I had only to pick up the phone and I could find out almost anything I wanted to know. Right now I was a little zero in the middle of a big zero. It seemed that the only person who might lead me anywhere was that mischievous face on TV. I pointed my boots toward Theatre Genesis.

III

I walked by the theater twice before I saw the inconspicuous little sign hanging on the inconspicuous little building. The marquee couldn't have brought in many patrons. I walked in and saw that outside appearances were somewhat deceiving. The lobby was smallish but adequate. No one was in the box office.

I was just ready to push open the door to the theater proper when it burst into my face, and a skinny young man in a leotard and Levis came prancing out. "Oh excuse me. I'm always going places too fast."

I caught him by the arm before he could go the next place too fast. "There's not a play on tonight?"

"No. We don't open until tomorrow. Can you come back then?" he said cheerfully.

"Maybe," I said. "But right now I'm trying to find someone."

"Oh! Do you think it could be me?" He fluttered his eyelashes at me. A very aggressive gay, or a smart ass. Or both.

"Sorry, I'm engaged right now, to a lovely boy in Soho." I said. "But if it doesn't work out, you'll be the first to know."

He shot me a disappointed look, though the wicked sparkle in his eyes stayed in place. "Well, you'll have to see the play anyway. I play a bellboy who changes back and forth between a boy and a girl. Very stimulating."

I gave him an amused look. "Hard to be ambivalent in Salt Lake, is it?"

"A bitch, honey. But as I say, stimulating. If you can keep ahead of the police. Buggery's a capital offense in this state. Watch out for men in dark polyester suits and mirror glasses."

"Look, if you can attach your feet to the floor for half a minute, I'd like to see if you could help me find someone."

"For you I'm a statue, Cowboy." He posed appropriately.

"Thank you. Do you know a man named Jerry Calabrese?" I asked in my flat detective voice.

"Jerry Calabrese? No. Can't help you. Why do you think I should know? Is this a test by the vice squad? A setup?"

15

"No setup. I saw him on television last night, plugging your play. Fortyish, kinky hair, big blue eyes."

"Oh," he said, the light switching on, "you mean Jerry Romero, the bad-ass Mexican bandito!"

"Is that who I mean? Is he around?" I asked.

"No, he's not around here much, not lately. Sometimes he'll act a role but he's been scarce since he got a real job— well, sort of a real job." He eyed me a little more admiringly. "You know Jerry?"

"I used to know Jerry, when he had another name. Do you know where I can find him?"

"It's hard to tell with Jerry. He doesn't stay put very well. Like me."

"Well, how about a clue?" I prompted.

"He has an apartment just up the street." He told me where. "But more likely you'll find him over at Maizies."

"Maizies?"

"Yeah. It's a bar, kind of a disco bar. 'Course, disco's passé, even in Salt Lake. Call it a bar where people dance. It's across from the Salt Palace. Jerry's girls should be doing a show soon."

"Jerry's girls?" I was beginning to sound like a question machine. Put in a quarter and I repeat an important word in your last sentence in the form of a question.

"He works with Sally Walpole; they run a talent agency. Jerry hustles clients. His girls do a fashion show in the bar twice a night."

I thanked the boy, assured him I'd try to see his show, and told him I'd be happy to find him a place to stay in Soho if he ever came to New York. Then I headed toward the Salt Palace.

Maizies was not subtle in its greeting. A great flashing neon sign right out of the 1940s invited me in. I couldn't get in, however, until I paid a $20 membership fee. Any Utah bar that serves something stronger than 3.2 beer at your table has to be a private club. You want a strawberry daiquiri, you become a member or you come in with a friend. I decided to try to find a friend.

The agency was next door and looked busy, so I walked in. Young women in garish makeup and in various states of undress were running about, obviously preparing for something. No one noticed me, so I stood for a while admiring the women and looking casually about the place for Jerry the Mexican bandito. I saw him helping an attractive young blonde with her makeup on the other side of the room.

It looked to be the same Jerry, but a Jerry who had had a rough twenty years. There was still a definite Mediterranean cast to his features, or was it now Latin American? He had always had a large head but his hairdo emphasized it, and great blue bulging eyes served under the arched Mephistophelean eyebrows to give him the look of an enormous surprised pixie. His eyes were constantly darting about whatever room he was in, looking for something he seldom found. On one of his periodic absent scannings of the room, his eyes focused on me. They settled, squinted, moved away, then quickly came back again. Something there he recognized.

He handed the girl the makeup brush he was holding and staggered his way through the room toward me. Jerry had always staggered when he walked, like an ebullient drunk. But if anything he staggered less when he was drunk. We eyed each other hesitantly, not quite sure. Then we knew, and Jerry's great warm body opened up and embraced me. He remembered. I had a friend in this damn foreign city—at last.

"Gabe?!" he announced and asked at the same time. "Gabe Utley?"

"You have a hell of a memory for names." I embraced him back.

"Jesus Christ! Gabe Utley. What are you doing in town. The New York cops finally deport you?"

"I'm here for a few days. Can I take you to dinner later?"

"I've never turned down dinner, a drink, or a pretty girl or boy in my life." He was halfway across the room again, this time toward a ripe, thirtyish brunette with fashionable makeup that made her look like a Las Vegas hooker. "C'mon over and meet Gail! Gail, come here. This is Gabe Utley, my best friend. He's back in town, from New York. Gabe and me kept West Second South alive when there wasn't any West Second South." West Second South Street was famous for its prostitutes and illegal gambling.

And Jerry took off again. He was flying around the room, patting models on the rump, bussing them on the cheek, getting them primed for this fashion show, introducing me to everyone. I hadn't the heart to tell him I didn't really want to be introduced about. It was not likely, however, that anyone would remember. Jerry had always attracted every stray dog who came down the block. Strangers in the midst of Jerry's entourage were not uncommon. So I nodded a few nods around the room and tried to look anonymous.

Jerry dragged me into Maizies and pulled me up to the bar with him. We had front row seats for the show. The girls came out one at a time onto the small square floor to the neo-disco beat of the music and the coordinated throbbing colored lights. They were modeling some of the ugliest clothes I had ever seen. But they did it with wit and style. Gail was the favorite with the crowd and with Jerry as well, and I could see why. She was a good dancer, she could make the ugliest dress ensemble look passable, and she had a mock come-hither look that could harden a celibate's privates. Jerry turned to me after she left the stage.

"Gabe, I'm in love."

I nodded as if I didn't believe him.

"No, I'm serious, Gabe." The man had an uncanny ability

to make you seem really his best friend, party to all his innermost secrets. I felt it was yesterday and we were hitting the pool halls on South State. "I really am in love with that bitch."

"Gail?"

"Yeah, Gail."

"You're welcome to bring her to dinner too."

"I was hoping you'd ask." Then Jerry's darting eyes picked up someone who had just come in. "Hey Mona! Mona!" he shouted across the room. He shouted a lot across rooms. "Come over here! Someone I want you to meet!"

Mona looked a touch embarrassed. She was with a guy. But she started to wind her way through the crowd to the bar.

"Wait till you meet this lady. Amazing broad. You'll love her."

I must confess that if I didn't love her just yet, I certainly liked the way she looked. She was probably half Chicano and all class, about thirty-five and tall, with a lovely self-aware smile.

"Mona, this here's Gabe Utley. Back in town from the Big Apple for a few days. Gonna take Gail and me out to dinner after the show. C'mon and join us." Sounded like we'd have to hire a hall for this intimate dinner. I smiled and held out my hand. Mona looked at me, sizing me up. You never took Jerry's friends at his word. You had to make your own assessments.

She took my hand and looked approving. Apparently I'd passed some sort of test. The guy behind her had had more trouble than she picking his way through the crowded bar. He had a dark suit and tie and looked uncomfortable, a little like a Mormon missionary in a whorehouse lobby. It turned out I wasn't far from wrong.

"This is Howard Peterson," Mona said. "He works with me on the paper—the *Deseret News*. He's fashion editor, among other things. I brought him here to cover the show.

Looks like we're late." She smiled wider at me. "And I will take you up on dinner."

"Fine. Have any other friends or family you'd care to bring along?" An hour ago I'd felt alone and friendless, but this was getting ridiculous.

"Oh don't worry about Howard. He has a church meeting. He and his big powerful voice announce for the Tabernacle Choir. It's rehearsal tonight . . . Well, shake hands with the man, Howard," she said, as if talking to a nine-year-old. Howard held out his hand.

"Pleased to meet you Mr.—" Howard announced in his big beautiful voice.

"Utley," I said, as I took his hand. "You *Deseret News* types spend a lot of time hanging out in bars?" I asked. The *Deseret News* is the Mormon newspaper.

Howard gave a snorty laugh. "Sometimes we have to mingle with the gentiles in order to get a good story." He laughed again in the way that people with no sense of irony laugh. "Mona dragged me down here against my will. But I try to keep up with fashion. My readers expect it." I couldn't imagine he'd give the show a good review—too much peekaboo. But Howard sat at the bar, ordered a Fresca, and began to take notes.

Out of curiosity I leaned over to Jerry and asked if Howard was related to David Peterson.

"He's his younger brother."

My God, I thought, some undercover detective. Half a day on the case and I'm sitting between my client's brother-in-law and a Mormon newspaper reporter. I had somehow expected Jerry to lead me to shadier underworld types. I was surprised he even knew any Mormons. But I settled down, sipped my bourbon, and enjoyed Gail's second number and the warmth of Mona Whatever-her-name-was pressed against my arm at the crowded bar. I just wouldn't tell anybody who I was or why I was here.

Of course, if I didn't, I wouldn't find out anything.

IV

The number for dinner stayed at four. Still I felt as if I was on a double date—I found myself missing my old Studebaker. Jerry guided us to a French restaurant across from the police station, jogged us there actually, in his awkward, jerky stride. I was exhausted as I slid in beside Mona at our booth. It wasn't exactly that Jerry was into physical fitness, it was more that he raced everywhere. After we sat down, he jumped back up to get our drinks. In Utah restaurants you have to buy liquor at the counter; no table service, they only bring setups. It apparently keeps the local religious establishment feeling good about controlling other people's vices.

Before we had a chance to empty our minibottles into our setups, Jerry slipped each of us a benny—the explanation for some of his energy. Certainly not all, however; he'd always been like that. I pocketed mine, and I noticed Mona did the same, though this Mormon reporter did order a discreet Smirnoff vodka to pour into her tomato juice.

Finally we were settled, picking at our snails and ready to get to know each other. They started on me. I told them as little as I could get away with. Gail couldn't believe there were still such things as private detectives, and she asked a lot of questions that I answered very vaguely. Midway through the onion soup, Jerry spotted some friends across the restaurant and disappeared. The other three of us sat silently, as though the source of energy had gone from the party. My monosyllabic answers had somehow discouraged Gail, and Mona hadn't said three words since we arrived. Finally Gail got up to "powder her nose"—actually to track down Jerry—and Mona and I were left together. She lit a Benson and Hedges.

"Why are you here, really?" she said. The lady was direct.

"I'm investigating a case."

"We don't have detectives in Salt Lake?"

"I'm sure you do," I said.

"Some pretty good ones. So why should anyone reach out two thousand miles for one?" She didn't know I was asking myself the same question, and with a good deal more intensity.

"Let's just say it's kind of a favor to an old friend."

Mona looked at me skeptically. "Doesn't your friend know that detectives kind of have to know the scene before they can do anybody a favor?"

She had me on that one. "Would you believe it if I told you I am a fast learner?"

She smiled her very nice smile. "Well, if it's something simple, maybe it won't matter. 'Course, if it was something simple your friend wouldn't have taken all the trouble to bring you here, right?"

"And you're going to tell me that maybe you can help out," I said.

"Why not?"

"Well, in detective school they teach you to ask questions, not answer them. Especially those of newspaper reporters . . . even very attractive ones."

"You're a sly bastard, you are," Mona said.

"Just careful. I don't want to be printed up in the afternoon paper."

"That important, huh?"

Why was I feeling like a fly being led expertly into a web? "Probably not. It's just that my client insists on keeping everything very subdued. It's a private family matter."

"So, why don't you try me? See if I can't help. I can keep a secret, and I read a lot of mysteries. I love Ross Mac-Donald. Or do you plan to do whatever you're trying to do through telepathy?"

"People important to me could get hurt. You can understand my being a little skittish—especially with a newspaper reporter with marvelous eyes."

"I have a nice personality too."

I laughed with her. "That'll take longer to find out," I said.

Mona stretched like a docile pussycat and smiled very warmly at me. "Get me another drink and I'll tell you anything you want to know." Contented as she looked, I knew I should have paid more attention to the devilish gleam that never left her eye. But I got up to get the drinks—two for each of us—and noticed that Jerry and Gail had joined a very noisy party in the next room. Same old Jerry. I told the waitress to deliver their main course to them in there. Then I rejoined Mona at the table.

"Might as well get on with it, I guess. What I really need is to be put onto someone who can lead me around in the Mormon Fundamentalist underground."

Mona looked at me sideways, sipping her Bloody Mary. "And you don't really know who I am?" What was that cat-got-the-canary smile about?

"All I know is that you're Mona who works for the *Deseret News* and who is a friend of Jerry's and who has nice eyes."

"You really don't know much, do you?"

I thanked her for the compliment.

"No, I mean you don't know that my name is Ramona McKinley and that I just did a series of articles on Mormon Fundamentalist sects."

"Jesus, you're right, I don't know anything." My ignorance really was primary.

"I'd say you'd better be a fast learner—and a fast runner—if you're messing around with the polygamist cults," Mona said. "I'm tired as hell tonight because I've just spent all day checking out the Lawrence Alger murder. My story headlined the *Deseret News* this afternoon."

"My apologies. I read the *Tribune*."

"Most people do," she sighed. "Most tourists, anyway."

Mona's eyes had gotten very shrewd in the last minute and a half. But even shrewd I liked them. "You investigating anything to do with the Alger murder?" she asked.

"Not as far as I know," I admitted.

"Well, what are you investigating?" She was getting a shade impatient with me.

"This sounds dumb, especially now, but I can't tell you."

"You ever solve anything in New York?"

"I'm considered pretty good in New York."

"Well, you'd be a lot safer back there investigating the Mafia than out here looking into the polygamists. Certainly with your rather staggering gaps in knowledge."

Before the spider proceeded to chew off something vital, I decided to tell her as much as I felt I could. "Okay, I will say this. I'm investigating a runaway teenager. She may have run off to join some polygamist group."

A pause. Then, "That's all you know?" There was great wonder in her voice.

"That's all. A pisser, isn't it." I reached into my pocket and brought forth the unsigned escape note and handed it to Mona. "This is all I've got."

She studied the note with agitated interest, then said, "The quotation is from a revelation the Fundamentalists claim John Taylor had, in 1886. John Taylor was the third Prophet of the Mormon Church."

"I know." It was the first time I remembered saying that since I got off the plane. "Can't live in Utah twenty years and not know that."

"See?" she said, looking up from the note. "You do know a few things. You just hide it well."

"What else does the revelation say?"

"It's a strong defense of plural marriage. A powerful argument that it was not meant to be given up by the true Church. Jesus Christ and Joseph Smith were supposed to have appeared to Taylor and told him that. The Fundamentalists use it to support their claim that the L.D.S. Church has apostatized."

"What about the drawing of the eye?" I said.

"It's a symbol one of the cults uses—the all-seeing eye of God."

"Which cult?"

She shook her head from side to side as she answered this question, as though she thought I wasn't quite bright. "It's called the Church of Unity in the Lamb of God. It's presided over by a family named Kimball. And if your little runaway is mixed up with those folks, you'd better hire a SWAT team to go along with you. That's a mean bunch."

"You're very reassuring," I said.

"Better tell your friend where to send the body."

"There is one other thing," I said.

"I'm almost afraid to ask."

I told her about my visit to Susan Whitesides's mother.

"Mary Ann Whitesides?" Mona asked.

"We didn't get on a first name basis, but she was listed in the directory as M. A. Whitesides."

"And you say you don't know whether you're looking into the Alger murder?" Mona's great skeptical eye was even sharper now.

"I beg your pardon," I said.

"Mary Ann Whitesides was one of Lawrence Alger's wives."

A few things were coming together in my foolish head. Susan Whitesides was the dead doctor's daughter. Jennifer Peterson was in a good deal more trouble than I had thought. And Mona McKinley was a very lovely woman.

Mona went on before I had a chance to tell her how lovely she was. "You've bought yourself a lot of trouble, Gabe Utley—or someone has bought it for you. I hope you're getting paid well, because nobody out here would do what you're doing for a mansion in the sky. I've been on the Kimball hit list for three months now. I've changed phone numbers four times, moved twice, had my dog killed, and I get incredible amounts of hate mail where I work. All because of a few newspaper articles."

I stared somewhat helplessly across the table at Mona. She was out of breath. We both were grateful I'd gotten two drinks. Then I said, "Well thanks. The picture is a lot clearer now. And you've made it appropriately scary."

"Scary enough, I would think, to get you on a plane before morning."

"Wouldn't you miss me?"

Mona's eyes softened. That made me feel good. I'm glad something did. "I don't even know you, Gabe. And if you stay out here, I don't think you're a good bet. I can get a lot of stupid men."

"I'm very persistent," I said, intending the double meaning. "And I always have had a penchant for getting myself into messes. But I have a reputation for following through. I expect I will on this, too."

She took my hand across the table. "Well, I certainly wish you luck, Gabe Utley. You're going to need a lot of it."

V

I woke up at eight o'clock the next morning and made my list for the day. There were more things I knew on it this time. At least I knew the nature of the problem. Jerry hadn't helped much, at least not directly, but as years ago, he always seemed to be in the middle of the action. I made a note to look him up this morning, take him out for coffee, and see if he could lead me to any shady underworld types. He obviously had some drug connections. At the top of my list was getting over to the *Deseret News* and taking Ramona McKinley to lunch. I had some more questions for her. And I just wanted to take her to lunch.

After a shower I dressed and walked downstairs to the coffee shop. I picked up a *Tribune*—the *Deseret News* was an afternoon paper—and settled myself into a booth with a cup of coffee and an English muffin. I opened the paper and found a very pretty face frozen in a graduation photo staring out at me. The headline told me the girl in the picture had been murdered. Her body had been found about two this morning in front of a small memorial chapel in a place called Memory Grove. Her throat had been slit from ear to ear. The caption told me her name was Susan Whitesides.

I left money on the table, bolted out the door, and ran the three blocks to the *Deseret News* office. Mona McKinley was not there. I was told by a rather unfriendly older woman with white hair and a frilly blue blouse that she was out on assignment.

"Can you tell me where? It's important I know."

"It's not our policy to divulge where our reporters have gone."

She had orthodox Mormon written all over her, so I leaned ingratiatingly on the counter that separated us and said, "I appreciate the rule, but I know Mona is on the Susan Whitesides case and I have information that may help her." I got even more confidential, as if we were sharing a secret. "I'm a detective and I'm on the trail of these Fundamentalists myself. This killing last night might be our way to get them."

The woman was obviously as antagonistic as the next good Mormon woman to the polygamists. She took off her glasses, looked around, then whispered, "She was in fifteen minutes ago, to get some things. She just came back from Memory Grove and has gone down to the police station. Police Chief Neff has scheduled a press conference."

I patted her on the cheek, hurried out the door, and caught a taxi to the station.

The grand beige complex that housed the judicial and police establishments demonstrated convincingly that Salt Lake City took its law enforcement seriously. Inside, the place was as busy as a big cubed anthill, with police and other official types running everywhere. I followed in the direction most of them seemed to be heading and found the press conference just getting under way. My beefy manner and official New York Private Investigator card got me into the crowded little auditorium. I leaned against the back wall listening to the police chief's opening remarks and scanning the room for Mona McKinley.

His statement was brief, to the point, and completely devoid of useful information. The girl's body had been found at 2:00 A.M. She was a student at East High School. Her throat had been cut. There were no leads.

The question-answer session was much more polite than on similar occasions in New York City, where all reporters assume the police are lying and there is a lot of shouting and accusation-throwing. Here the surface was calm, but emotions were boiling underneath. No one called the chief a liar, but no one doubted he was telling only part of what he knew. After the opening statement hands shot up all over the room.

The first was a difficult rhetorical question from a clean-cut young man with a newscaster's voice. "How long are the police going to sit back and allow these polygamist killings to take place?"

Chief Neff was clearly annoyed and contemptuous of the questioner. "We are doing, sir, everything in our power to solve the Alger killing. And so far we have no proof that the Whitesides girl's murder was part of that or any other so-called polygamist incident."

A young woman with very short hair was next. She asked, "Don't you find the way she was killed significant in this regard? I mean this was a popular mode of blood atonement in Brigham Young's day."

The Chief warmed a little to the young woman, if not to the question. "Miss Wixom, I know what you're saying and I appreciate what it seems to point to. But there simply is no proof."

I felt a hand on my arm and turned to see Mona leading me toward the door. "Come on. You'll get nothing here. Buy me a cup of coffee."

I couldn't argue with either suggestion, so I followed her out and across the street to a fast food place with a big goofy plastic clown weaving to and fro in front.

I bought the coffee and slid onto a plastic bench across from Mona. Awful stuff, the coffee. Utah has terrible coffee. "You've had a busy morning," I said.

"God, but ain't that the truth," she said.

"Find anything out up at Memory Grove?"

"Not really. I saw the body. Brutal."

"Seems a little extravagant, taking out a seventeen-year-old girl. Got any ideas?" I probed.

"Nothing beyond what anybody who reads the papers can figure out."

"Do most people know Susan was Dr. Alger's daughter?"

"No, I guess they don't."

"Do the police know?"

She looked at me slyly. "I guess they don't, most of them. There's a young lieutenant who helped me a lot on my articles. He knows."

"Then the police know," I said.

"One thing you have to understand, Gabe, about this town. There are two very definite points of view about how to handle the polygamy issue. Probably three points of view, come to think of it. A large group would just like to leave the whole mess alone—let the true believers fight it out among themselves. I think Lee Neff is one of those at heart. There are others, led by the current mayor, who would like to launch a full-blown frontal attack, slam them all in jail on immorality charges and throw away the key."

"Good solid Bill of Rights types," I quipped. "And the third? One usually saves the favorite for last."

She smiled. "This lieutenant—Dale Olander—probably has kept his secret because Neff and his troops wouldn't do anything, and the mayor and his would get out the machine guns. Dale figures the best way to achieve anything is to work inside somehow. He's been trying that angle for five years now."

"Any luck?"

"Not much, frankly. Secrecy seems this people's number one obsession in life."

I took a sip of my coffee and appraised my chances of getting a name inside the Fundamentalist establishment that could help me. "Can I read your articles?"

She was one jump ahead of me. "You won't find anything in them that'll help you."

"You changed the names."

"I changed the names. Some of them. The ones that mattered."

"Terrific. And you're not going to give me a lead."

"I'll make a deal with you."

"What is it?" I asked, figuring I already knew the answer. I did.

"A name for a name. Tell me who you're looking for."

I got up and moved toward the door. She caught me with her voice.

"Gabe."

I turned back. "Yeah?"

"No deal?"

"That's right. No deal. It's sad, how two people can screw up a promising relationship over a conflict of interest."

"Yes, it is." She looked at her coffee and I walked out the door.

I had done a lot of walking in the last twenty-four hours. I kept looking for a subway entrance. No luck. The buses seemed to run about every three hours. Taxis were fine but expensive, and just now I felt like walking anyway so I headed myself east, deciding I would try to see Susan's mother again. Maybe circumstances would have made her a little more welcoming this time. Later in the day I would look up Lieutenant Dale Olander.

The Whitesides house looked even worse in the bright sunlight. I had knocked at least five times before there was any response, and that was behind me. A voice from the bottom of the porch steps asked, none too politely, "What do you want?"

I turned and found myself looking at an extra large young man in overalls and a green flannel shirt. He was blond and quite good looking, and he had on a tractor hat that said STINSON SHEEP. He was chewing on a toothpick, the old-fashioned kind.

"My name is Utley. I talked with Mrs. Whitesides yesterday. I'd like to see her today. Is she in?"

"No, she ain't."

"Well, when do you expect her?"

"I don't."

There were a number of lags in the discussion. The lad hadn't been trained in the art of good conversation. "Do you know where she's gone?"

"Yup."

"But you're not going to tell me."

"Nope."

I decided on a more emotional approach. "Was that your sister killed this morning?"

The lad's big shoulders tensed, his face got hostile, but it did prompt his longest sentence so far. "You mind your own business, mister."

"It is my business, kind of. I'm looking for a friend of Susan's. Someone who might be in trouble."

I could see that the young man was getting out of his depth. His short answers weren't adequate anymore and he was starting to get itchy. "You just better get on out of here, bub. I don't know nothing. Nobody here does. And—I just want you out of here. What happened to Susan is none of your business!"

"So you do know the girl who was killed." I was good at making fast appraisals.

"Damn it! Quit this. I told you I won't talk about it!" He looked ready to charge up the steps at me, to throw me bodily out of the yard. I was quite sure he could if he wanted to. I lumbered on, perhaps foolishly.

"How about if we work a trade? I won't call the police in if you tell me about Susan."

That was too much. The tractor cap came lunging up the stairs, two very muscular arms raised to do mischief. I ducked, then danced to my right. He crashed into the screen door, ripping the wire mesh from its wooden frame. I was up and ready for a second charge when the door itself opened, and a very angry-looking older man dressed for farm chores came out and slapped the blond guy on the side of the head, sending him scampering into a corner. Next he turned to me, hands on hips, and asked the same question the other guy had. They both seemed to have limited conversational graces.

"We got nothin' you want, bub."

"What I want is to talk with you for a few minutes. I'm not the police and I don't want trouble. I'm looking for a young girl. A young girl who was a friend of Susan Whitesides." The big blond guy was still hovering in the corner.

"Susan's dead," the older man answered.

"I know. That's why I came. I don't want the other girl to be dead."

Before he could refuse to answer in yet another way, the man saw something out of the corner of a well-trained fugitive's eye. I saw it too—a police car a block and a half down the street. "Come inside the house!" he shouted. "Both of you!" And I was shoved rudely into Mary Ann Whitesides's living room. We waited until the car drove past, then the man reached down into his boot and drew out a nasty-looking steel hunting knife. He advanced a step toward me.

"Bub, I'm only going to say this once more, then I'm

going to open the door and send you on your way. We know nothing that you want to know. You're wasting your time. So take my advice, which is all I'm giving, and get out of here. None of it's your business." He opened the door for me.

I walked out into the sunlight and kept on moving down the street. I don't ever recall being thrown out of the same house twice in two days before. I was getting some visceral sense of how tough it was going to be to penetrate the Fundamentalist society, and I was gaining respect for Mona for writing about them. Since I didn't know where to go next, I decided I would trot on down to the library and read her articles. Maybe there would be something helpful there. Anything. Right now I wasn't fussy.

VI

As I walked back downtown—the wandering pilgrim come to Zion—I figured that it was time to telephone Linda Peterson and urge upon her the seriousness of her daughter's situation. I didn't know exactly what to advise her. But it still seemed a little self-indulgent to have a New York detective who didn't know anybody in town chasing down your daughter who might be murdered at any minute. She should hire someone who at least knew the street numbers.

I went into a restaurant called Rex and Irma's and ordered a cup of what turned out to be pretty good coffee, put my coin in the telephone box, and dialed the Petersons' number. It took twelve rings to get an answer from a distant, dopey-sounding Linda. It took her thirty seconds after I said who I was for the comprehension to sink in. She sounded as if she was answering from deep in the ground. I spent the first two minutes leading her out of the valley of shadows. Finally I jolted her awake.

"You know, Linda, that Susan Whitesides was murdered early this morning!"

She started to cry on the other end.

"Don't you think it's time to call in the police?"

"We . . . we . . . can't, Gabe. We can't," she said through her sobs.

"Isn't it getting late to worry about David's career?"

"Oh, God, Gabe. I'm so confused."

"Why don't you let me talk to someone at the police station. I know of a lieutenant who can keep secrets," I said, hoping I was telling the truth.

"No, Gabe. You can't. I won't let you." Linda was emerging from her blurred journey through the nether world. "I hired you to find Jennifer. I'm paying you a lot of money to find Jennifer. Now, if you can't do it, tell me and I'll get someone else!"

She was stinging me where it matters. I knew, if she didn't, that I would keep trying. I think she knew it too. She knew I was a persistent bastard. But I did at least feel it was time to bring Jennifer's daddy into our exclusive little club.

"Have you talked with David since you found out about Susan?" I asked.

"No I haven't. I can't disturb him with it."

"I'd like to talk with him," I said. "He'll hate us both if anything happens and he doesn't know."

She paused, thinking this one over. Then she said, "I guess it's only fair. We'd better let him know."

"Will you call him? Or should I just drop by?"

"You'd better let me call him. He hates surprises."

So I had gathered. "Tell him I'll be by about three o'clock."

"All right," she answered weakly.

"The Church Office Building?"

"Yes."

"And, Linda—"

"Yes, Gabe?"

"Stay away from the booze. It'll kill you!"

She hung up on me.

I walked to the city library next to the police station, thinking I would invite Dale Olander to lunch later, and checked out microfilm copies of Mona McKinley's series on polygamist cults. After fifteen minutes threading the damn machine, I sat and rolled my way through each of the five articles.

In the first she outlined the beliefs all the Fundamentalist world shared, doctrines that separated them from Ortho-dox Mormonism. They all agreed that the Mormon Church was in a state of apostasy and that true Priesthood authority was vested in one or another of the offshoot groups. These were big stakes—the claim to be the one true church of God on earth—and the cults apparently fought bitterly for the honor. To me it seemed an awful burden to fight for. But then I liked my God ambiguous. That better reflected the world as I knew it.

The two doctrines that caught my attention particularly were those of Celestial Marriage and Blood Atonement. The first was the obvious injunction that a righteous man ought to have more than one wife, and Ms. McKinley cited the supposed revelation to John Taylor. I recognized the quote.

The second doctrine was not so obvious in its reinforce-ment of what I knew about the Mormon Fundamentalists—the doctrine of Blood Atonement. These people believed that the righteous should kill sinners. The scriptural sup-port for this came from no less a source than Brigham Young himself.

There are sins that men commit for which they cannot receive forgiveness in this world, or in that which is to come, and if they had their eyes open to see their true condition, they would be perfectly willing to have their blood spilt upon the ground, that the smoke thereof might ascend to heaven as an offering for their sins.

The image of that sharp steel hunting knife hung in my brain. I was grateful I hadn't tried any heroics.

It was interesting that the three top sins that would justify having one's blood spilt were murder, adultery, and something called sinning against the Holy Ghost. As far as I could tell, this last sin had something to do with leaving the one true religion, a broad and vague range of crimes. One would have to be very careful in that world not to offend. Apparently there had been a lot of offenders recently.

I had to get up and take a drink of water and a couple of aspirins before I continued.

The next two articles were explorations of the day-to-day life-styles of typical polygamist people. Here all the names were undoubtedly changed and most of the subjects seemed peaceloving enough. They had lots of children, raised their own food, made their own clothes and household furnishings, and generally lived in benign communes. While the principle of plural marriage informed their beliefs, the principle of living healthy, productive lives seemed to inform their day-to-day existence.

Mona would have us believe that there were polygamists all around, in the city as well as on the farm. And while many chose the basically rural model of the nineteenth-century frontier, a significant number lived—outwardly—typical Mormon lives. Doctors, lawyers, teachers. Hard to tell from superficial signs that they were different from anybody else on the block. Lawrence Alger apparently had been one of these.

The fourth article was an examination of what Mona had already summarized for me—the attempts by state and local authorities to control polygamy. She concluded it was a hopeless task. For while the official Mormon Church and the Fundamentalist sects were ostensibly at odds with one another, the real network of below-the-surface familial ties

kept open warfare at bay. Almost everybody had a polygamous relative.

I rolled to the last article, which was probably the main
reason she had gotten into trouble. Here she named names.
She focused on two of the biggest and most important polygamist cults. The one led by the recently deceased Dr.
Lawrence Alger seemed to claim the most members and was
called the Church of the Covenant. The sect looked to con-
sist of many well-to-do types, many of whom lived incognito
right in Salt Lake City. Mona even claimed that the sect was
very wealthy. She also said they were basically peaceful, seldom prone to violence.

The second group was at the other end of the spectrum.
They were called The Church of Unity in the Lamb of God,
and they were poor and scattered about through the rural
mountain west and Mexico. They had a history of violence,
with three brothers vying for supremacy. One brother had
been murdered in Mexico three years ago; another was in
hiding, probably somewhere in southern Utah; and the
third, the apparent victor in the family squabble, was almost
everywhere, trying to unite all the Fundamentalist sects under his leadership. His name was Jedediah Kimball. Kimball—my God—the all-seeing eye.

I had known a Jed Kimball in high school. A big, scruffy,
ingrown kid who lived in an old house not far from my
uncle's store at the bottom of the Eleventh East hill. Of
course there were a lot of Kimballs in Salt Lake City. Still,
this tall kid with cold blue eyes and a big chip on his shoulder stayed in my mind. Was I getting familiar enough with
the territory to have hunches about it? A first hint that
maybe I had a rabbit's chance on this case.

I took back the nasty little rolls of microfilm and walked
across the parking lot to police headquarters. It was 11:45
and I figured I would have a jump on Dale Olander for
lunch.

I was wrong. When I arrived at his office he and Mona

McKinley were just walking out, obviously on their way to eat.

"Hello," I said to Mona.

"Hello, Gabe," and she introduced me to Lieutenant Olander, a look of Viking triumph in her eyes. "We're on our way to lunch."

But the "Will you join us?" I hoped for never came. I could grow to hate this woman. I think I would have been well on the way if she hadn't come to me, taken my arm affectionately, and asked, "Want to do dinner tonight?"

I thought about playing hard to get but decided against it. Her Viking glint had mellowed into a Latin glimmer. She really wanted to do dinner. So did I. But I wasn't letting them go now until I had to.

"Just read your articles . . . very good work," I said.

"Find anything?" she queried with a superior smile.

"No contacts. You were right about that. But I did see an interesting name."

"You did?" Her smile went from superior to good.

"Yeah." And I looked right at Dale Olander. "Jedediah Kimball."

Olander flushed and Ramona answered, "Well he's hardly going to be a useful contact, Gabe. Unless you have very good radar and you want your throat cut."

I continued looking at an uncomfortable Lieutenant Olander. "He's your prime suspect in the Alger murder, isn't he?"

He pondered his polished shoes, then turned to Mona with a who-the-hell-is-this-guy look.

Mona had to laugh. "This is a private detective from New York City, Dale. He's here looking for someone and he won't say who. He hopes to entrap you into helping with his little treasure hunt."

Lieutenant Dale Olander drew himself up to his full five-feet-eight height, oozing pomposity. "We're not allowed to give out that information, Mr. Utley. It's confidential."

Mona apparently cottoned to pomposity about as much as I did. "Oh, come off it Dale. Everybody in town who's read a newspaper in the past three years knows." She paused, looking at me, not unfriendly at all. "Besides, he's a good guy."

Dale looked prudishly at me, letting out a great breath of hot air. He was not charmed by Mona's interest in me. The gold ring on his finger probably wouldn't allow him to be anything but not charmed. He wasn't in Mona's league. But then I was strongly doubting I was.

Finally Dale talked, though he was still obviously not convinced I was a good guy. "Yes, Kimball is our prime suspect. But you're to keep that confidential. And may I see your license."

I showed him my license. "Any leads?" I asked.

Dale gave me a disgusted look, then took Mona's arm and walked her away. Mona shot me a see-you-later smile over her shoulder, and the two of them were off, walking toward the big plastic clown. I couldn't believe Dale was going to take Mona to lunch there. Still there was a 25-cent special on hamburgers, and policemen, even lieutenants, don't make very much money. Neither, come to think of it, do reporters. Maybe that's why they're stingy with information.

VII

After a passable enchilada and a bottle of 3.2 Budweiser at a Mexican restaurant in the middle of town, I retired to my hotel room to put up my tired feet, sans boots, and bring my what-I-know list up to date. A little progress. At least I knew people I could say hi to on the street.

At 2:45 I walked over to the Church Office Building at 47 East South Temple Street. This cold and forbidding building with abnormally thick gray granite walls had been built

in the early twentieth century after the Mormons had decided to concentrate on their corporate rather than their
religious image. It looked like a very safe bank and revealed
nothing of the Mormon people's remarkable past or of their
current aspirations. It must have been reassuring to the
faithful in one way, however. They could believe that their
souls were securely tucked away in great divine safety boxes.
It was a hard building to get into. It would be a harder
building to get out of.

I made my way past at least three suspicious secretaries
and went up a flight of stairs and down a hall to David Peterson's office. The interior of the building was rich and
solid and dim and provoked the feeling that there were a lot
of secrets hidden there. David's secretary was polite, efficient, and dressed to the nines. She buzzed and announced
I was there, then told me to have a seat.

While I was leafing through a slick Church magazine,
skimming an article urging men to spend more quality time
with their families, a short, spindly man in a white shirt and
blue tie came in and sat on the secretary's desk. He picked
out a blue jellybean from the jar on the desk, then turned
and stared at me, smiling wryly. He hadn't the face of most
people in this building and I was more than a little surprised when he spoke.

"Your name's Utley, right?"

I must have looked startled because he began to laugh.
His eyes twinkled when he laughed, and his mouth was a
little crooked. "Don't worry. I won't tell."

"It isn't so much who you might tell I'm worried about, as
who told you," I said.

He laughed again and reached for another jellybean, blue
again. "I'm a friend of Mona McKinley," he said.

"She keeps some secrets better than others," I said cryp-
tically.

He leaned forward as though he were hard of hearing. "I
beg your pardon?"

"Nothing. A little joke between Mona and me."

As he reached for his third blue jellybean, I noticed something peculiar about his eyes—one of them was brown and one of them was gray. He saw me staring. "A birth defect," he said. "Too much inbreeding among upper-class Mormons."

"You an upper-class Mormon?"

"My uncle's president of the Church," he said. "I'm a shade too perverse to be in this building on my own merit. Name's Arvin Smith IV."

"What are you, the house detective?" I asked.

"No. You're the detective. I'm assistant director for public relations. I help present our image to the world. Undoubtedly I'll never be director for public relations. My view of the world is a little twisted. But I'm useful. I also oversee some of the Church security operations—the sensitive part."

"You seem good at finding things out," I said.

"Things that might be troublesome to the Church."

"You figure I might be troublesome to the Church?"

"I am a little curious as to why you're in town." Another jellybean, a red one this time—red for commie? "Mona says you're trying to find someone."

"How about my lost youth, the person I used to be?"

Arvin Smith IV scooped out a handful of jellybeans and walked over and sat down by me on the couch.

"How about Jennifer Peterson?" Arvin said as he handed me a green jellybean.

I gave Arvin my fishiest look. He popped another jellybean into his mouth and read the fingernails on his left hand. After another bean, he said quietly, so David's secretary couldn't hear, "You needn't worry about me. My job is to keep Church secrets, not trumpet them about. Mona's a bitch, won't quit digging until she finds out what she wants to find out. I'm pretty good at knowing what goes on inside this building and all the little Mormon satellites out there.

That's another reason they keep me around. Need people like me to make sure people like him"—he pointed at David Peterson's closed door—"don't go and do something stupid. Besides, on my mother's side I'm a descendant of Porter Rockwell. That's where I get the gray eye."

Just then the buzzer on the secretary's many-buttoned phone sounded, and I was told I could go in now. No cordial greeting by an old friend out in the waiting room. I was being summoned. I got up and walked to the heavy oak door with the burnished brass plate that read DAVID R. PETERSON, FIRST QUORUM OF THE SEVENTY. Before I went in, I turned to Arvin Smith IV, who was calmly nibbling on a black jellybean.

"How about you being around when I get through here?"

He raised his arms. "Where would I go? I'm your faithful servant." Then he took off his wire-rimmed glasses and proceeded to polish them on his shirttail as I walked into David Peterson's office.

I hadn't seen David Peterson in twenty years, and he greeted me as if he hadn't seen me in twenty years and hadn't minded. But he did stand up and thrust out a hand, very politely.

"Hello, Gabe. Nice to see you." He didn't sound like he meant it at all. "Won't you sit down?" I did.

David was one of those executives who placed his desk in front of a window, so you had to look at him framed in it. He got all the advantages of the lighting. I could hardly see his face. Still, I could tell he was immaculately dressed and groomed down to his cuff links, which were little question marks, obviously real gold. I meant to ask him about them. David had always seemed much more likely to have answers than questions. But perhaps I was carrying a twenty-year lingering misjudgment of him.

"What can I do for you?" David asked as he rearranged some papers on his desk, looking at the papers rather than me. "Linda said you wanted to see me." When he finally noticed that I was simply sitting and staring at him, he went on—someone had to keep the conversational ball rolling. "It was stupid of her to get you involved in this."

By now I was squirming in my chair. I'm afraid all the glare from the window and the indifference behind the desk were getting to me. My answer was a little tart: "Just fine, thanks, David. And how are you?"

David stared at me blankly for a moment, as if he didn't get it. Then he smiled a little apologetic smile and said, "I'm sorry, Gabe, I'm behaving badly. It's just that it's been a rough day. I'm getting ready for a trip to Mexico tomorrow afternoon and I'm pulling some things together for Amos Jensen."

Amos Jensen. His name had come up twice in two days. But that shouldn't be surprising, not out here. He was one of the most powerful of the Twelve Apostles, the ruling body of the Church.

"Life's tough at the top, I guess," I said with a straight face. David went on past that as if he hadn't heard.

"Linda told me you were here. Said you've been in New York for several years. Sounds interesting. The wife and kids okay?" David was pushing things back and forth in his desk drawer on that line. The man was incredibly uneasy.

"I don't have a wife," I said.

"Oh, I'm sorry."

"That I don't have a wife?"

I was not helping him to be more at ease, I realized. But the part of David that was responding to me seemed like a programmed machine. He hadn't even seen me yet, not really.

He interrupted my thought. "Look, Gabe, maybe we'd better get on with what you came for. I have an appointment with Elder Jensen at three-thirty." He looked at his watch, rustled some more papers. I decided to get on with it.

"Has your wife informed you that your daughter's been gone a week?"

David took off his fashionable dark-rimmed glasses and swiveled around to look out the window. He didn't say anything, but he was clearing his throat a lot.

"Let me put it another way, David. A good friend of your daughter's, one she's quite probably spent a lot of time with lately, was found murdered this morning." I found myself talking loud, as if he were hard of hearing.

He swiveled back around and clasped his hands together, placing them in front of him on the handsome mahogany desk. His knuckles were white. He swallowed three times and struggled toward an answer.

"Linda told me just a few minutes ago."

I resisted an impulse to bring him the article on quality time and instead asked him one of my famous detective questions: "Do you have any idea why your daughter might have run away?"

"Didn't Linda cover all that with you?" he asked, impatiently.

"She told me a few things," I said. "Sounds like neither of you has much of an idea what's going on in your daughter's life."

This time David Peterson stood up and walked to his window. In twenty years he had become a very nervous man. "Look, Gabe," he said, as he stared out the window at Brigham Young's Lion House, the building that supposedly has one gable for each of his wives, "Jennifer is a sixteen-year-old girl. She has been well brought up and knows right from wrong." His hands were behind his back just now. He was shifting position on almost every word.

"That's all well and good, David," I said to his back. "But it's not much help in trying to figure where she's been for the past week."

All of a sudden David got angry, and like a spoiled child

he turned toward me, banging his fist on his desk. He barely missed spiking himself on his expensive pen set. "Damn it, Gabe! Linda and I have done the best we can. I haven't any idea where she might be. That's apparently what Linda hired you to find out. Now either get out and do it or get on back to New York where you came from!"

I don't think he knew how tempted I was to take him up on the latter suggestion. But I was working for Linda, and someone in the room had to remain calm.

"I'm working very hard at it, David," I said, as calmly as I could. "It's just that I don't have much to go on." I knew my next comment was going to affect him rather strongly, so I braced myself. "I suggested to Linda that we call in the police."

David almost vaulted across his desk. In fact, I wasn't sure he didn't. The next thing I knew he was standing directly in front of me, talking frantically into my face. "We can't do that! The police can't help us in this!"

I tended to agree with him, but I felt our reasons were different. I didn't say anything. He sat back on the edge of his desk, getting hold of himself. He started chewing his fingernails. God, he changed moods fast.

"I love my little girl, Gabe, and I'm scared to death about what might happen to her. But she's been unpredictable for years, never been easy to manage. My thought would be just to let it go. She'll come home. She always has." I was fascinated as I saw David relax and actually become affable. I was fascinated because he seemed to be doing it through an act of will. "Linda tells me you're good at what you do, Gabe, that she checked you out and found she couldn't have found anybody better, anywhere." I couldn't argue with him on that one. Flattery will buy the toughest of us. I became dubious about the compliment, however, as he went on. "Seems a shame you should come clear out here to look for some mixed-up kid. I mean, goodness, Gabe, it'll all work itself out in a couple of days. Jennie will come whimpering back home."

"Linda seems to think she may have been kidnapped," I said flatly, successfully fighting being bought by praise.

David went back behind his desk, changing from affable to troubled on the way. He was back to fussing with the much-fussed-over papers on his desk. "I frankly think that's silly, Gabe. I mean the girl has a history of running away from home, since she was nine."

"For a week at a time?"

"No, but overnight, for a weekend. Just a month ago she was gone four or five days."

"And you're not worried she might have been taken?" I said.

David looked at me directly for the first time. His posture was one of paternal concern. "Linda told me about the note, Gabe. Sounds like a conscious choice to me. I don't see anything that points to kidnapping."

"Except your wife's sense of the situation."

David shifted into a confidential tone with me and came back around in front of his desk. My God, he could change persona fast. Such a performance had to take a lot out of you. "Gabe, I'm sure you don't know this, but Linda's had a lot of nervous trouble the past few years. She's had to be on medication almost constantly. She has aberrations sometimes, you know, paranoias. I think neither of us should have any reason to believe this isn't one of those. Now why don't you let me buy you a first-class ticket to New York, pay you five hundred dollars for your trouble, and let's forget the whole thing."

I was almost convinced—but not quite. Susan Whitesides's graduation picture was too set in my mind. So were Mrs. Peterson's eyes, come to think of it. I thanked David and got up to leave.

"Gabe!" he said loudly as I got to the door. "I suppose I

can't stop you. You always were a stubborn son of a gun. But, believe me, this just isn't worth your time."

"I guess I'll just have to be the judge of that, David."

Without another word, David trotted around behind his desk, picked up those papers, and put them in his briefcase. "If you'll excuse me, Gabe, I have to get to my meeting. Elder Jensen doesn't like to be kept waiting." He clipped his case closed, picked it up, and brushed past me. He was running by the time he hit the outer office. He didn't bother to say good-bye.

I stood looking after him, an unfinished expression on my face, as if I'd seen half a good trapeze act and been left with one of the team in mid-air. I hoped David wouldn't fall. But I had my doubts about him. Mormon Apostles tend not to be fools, and David's ambition to be one seemed verging on hysteria. He was a very frightened man, a man who was trying too hard to be something he wasn't.

Arvin Smith came over to me and took my arm. We walked down the stairs together. "He's a little bit of an asshole, isn't he?" Arvin said.

"He was most likely to succeed at East High, Class of 1959."

Arvin smiled a little crooked smile. "Before the year's out the Church will send him on a mission to Guam and he'll never be heard from again."

"Is he always that tense?" I asked, as we emerged from the great gray vault of a building.

"Usually, he's too busy licking behinds to see what's going on around him. Amos Jensen has a very big behind."

We had continued walking as if we knew where we were going. I finally asked.

"How about the church cafeteria?" he said. "Pretty good range of soft drinks and juices. Not a great place to talk, but I have to think of my reputation. Can't afford to be seen in too many smoky bars with people like you."

*   *   *

In the huge tasteful plastic underground cafeteria, Arvin slipped into a corner booth with his carrot juice, and I slid in opposite him with a glass of highly peppered buttermilk. My mother had told me as I got into my teens that pepper stimulated your reproductive organs. Maybe I was being perverse in this atmosphere. Maybe I was looking forward to dinner.

I decided to get right to the point with Arvin. "You seem to know quite a bit about what I'm working on."

He pulled a jellybean from his shirt pocket and took it with his carrot juice. "It's my job to keep in touch with levels of reality in the official Mormon world."

"Do you know where Jennifer Peterson is?"

"Oh, goodness, no."

"Have you tried to find out?" I asked.

"I gather she's been hauled off by one or another of the cult groups."

"What makes you think that?"

"You, mostly. Mona told me where you were poking around. I just put two and two together. I'm good at that."

He took another gulp of carrot juice. He looked like he'd much rather have a gin and tonic in his hand. "I knew Jennifer was missing four days ago."

"How did you know that?"

"I keep track of important Mormon children. Jennifer Peterson's had trouble written all over her for two years. I mean, her boob of a dad is never home. He would hardly know her if he ran into her in a dark parking lot. Mom whiles away her day inside a vodka bottle. The kid's been messing with a bad crowd."

"What do you know about that crowd?"

"Kids from the Alger clan, mostly."

"Like Susan Whitesides," I said.

"Like Susan Whitesides."

I drank down the last of my buttermilk, accepted a proffered green jellybean, and asked if the Mormons ever mixed themselves up in things like this—with the polygamists.

"Not on a hot bet," he said. "One thing you need to understand, Utley, is that the gentlemen who run the Church don't even acknowledge publicly that people with more than one wife exist. Oh, there's an occasional conference talk that warns vaguely against Fundamentalist proselyting. The sects get to be a nuisance sometimes. But underneath it all the Brethren stay clear, don't meddle."

"Why not?" I asked.

"A couple of things. One is that they realize most people see the polygamists as fringe kooks. Best not dignify them with attention. Oh, we'll let an article on them go by now and then in the *Deseret News,* just to let people know we're concerned."

"What's the other thing?" I asked, figuring it had to be more interesting. Smith assured me by his increased intensity, by the flecks of saliva at the corners of his mouth, that I was right. He went on in confidential tones, as if he didn't much want to be overheard.

"We're really in the same bed together. There's a lot of residual guilt, at least in some of the Brethren." I assumed by "Brethren" he meant the Twelve Apostles, the Church presidency, and any others of a small group that ruled Mormondom. "I mean, it's hard to erase fifty years of history, and for fifty years the Church defended plural marriage as its central tenet. A lot of definitive statements were made by Brigham Young and others, statements that are hard to ignore, such as that God will visit his wrath on this people if they ever give it up. Stuff that's best not broadcast with a Tabernacle Choir concert. And there are a great many cousins out there who could be in trouble. Almost everybody in this damn state is related. Best just to leave it all alone."

I put my elbow on the table and rested my chin on my

hand. "I suppose this is a polite way of telling me that the Mormon secret service isn't going to help find Jennifer Peterson."

"Let me put it this way, Detective," Arvin Smith IV said through his wry smile. "You don't find a whole lot of sentimentality among those tough old birds who run the Church. Amos D. Jensen, the Amos D. Jensen who has written five best-selling books on childrearing, has a daughter who lives in a lesbian commune in San Francisco, a fifty-year-old son who spends all day cutting out paper dolls in a sanitarium just outside Fresno, and another son who stands on streetcorners downtown handing out Fundamentalist tracts. Now this man, compassionate as he says he is in his books, is not going to send out the avenging angels to track down the screwed-up daughter of a certified doodle."

"No, I guess not," I said, as I tried to scrape out the last of the pepper from the inside of my glass. "How about one more question, though?"

"I don't mind. You're good company. I don't get much chance to talk about this stuff."

"You're very trusting," I said. "How do you know this won't all appear in the *Tribune* tomorrow morning?"

"The *Tribune* would know better. And I haven't given you anything that anybody in town with half a brain doesn't know. Besides, you're not a gossip."

"No, I suppose not," I said. "But back to my question."

"Right."

"What can you tell me about Jedediah Kimball that I can't read in the papers?"

He pondered. "How about, he heads a Fundamentalist cult?"

Arvin Smith's confidential eyes had all of a sudden acquired a bureaucratic glaze.

"You're not going to tell me anything, are you?"

"I'm pretty good at sorting out what the public should or shouldn't know," he smiled. "It's what I get paid for."

"And what I'm getting paid for is to find Jennifer Peterson," I said.

Arvin gave me a friendly look. "And I wish you luck."

I got up to leave.

"Utley."

"Yes?"

"A couple of pieces of friendly advice?"

"Why not?"

"Don't count too much on getting paid. David doesn't give Linda any money."

"I'll consider that."

"And—"

"And?"

"Don't do anything that'll stir up trouble—newspaper trouble."

"How can I tell until I find out what I've got to do?"

"My uncle doesn't cotton much to troublemakers."

"I'll consider that, too."

"Do. I kind of like you. Most of my colleagues haven't much sense of humor."

"Maybe I'll see you around," I said.

"Count on it." He grinned.

"Oh, by the way," I said.

"Yes."

"You're really a descendant of Porter Rockwell?"

"That's right," Arvin said, with considerable pride radiating from his lively, mismatched eyes.

"He was Joseph Smith's bodyguard, wasn't he?"

"Yup. Had long braided hair, a fierce loyalty to the Prophet, and the most savage gun in the West. Made about any of your famous gunfighters look like Sunday School teachers."

"Didn't you fellows lose your strength when you cut your hair short?"

"Don't bet on it. Appearances can be deceiving. The Mormons haven't built a big economic empire through fine-turned sermons and aw-shucks affability, lest you forget."

"I won't forget," I said, and walked up and out into the late afternoon sunlight and a sculpture garden that looked like frozen images of the Osmond family dressed in 1950s clothes. There was no statue of Porter Rockwell.

VIII

It was a little after five when I walked into the city room of the *Deseret News,* leaned against the counter, and looked for Mona. It was early for dinner—in New York, at least—but I didn't have anything better to do. And I kind of wanted to have a little conversation with Howard Peterson.

Mona was on the other side of the room, leaning over a desk, talking with a chubby, intense young man who looked as if he was the dining-out editor and was probably the head sportswriter. She waved at me. As luck would have it, Howard was just coming out of the men's room and walked over to the counter when he saw me. He didn't lean on it, but he did rest his hands.

"Hello, Mr. Utley."

"Hi, Howard. How did the rehearsal go?"

"The rehearsal?"

"The Tabernacle Choir rehearsal."

"Oh, yes! I'd forgotten you knew about that." He lit up like a Temple spire. "It went fine. And I think my sermon is the best I've ever done." He spoke in his best broadcast voice. "Would you like to hear it? It's on spending quality time with the family."

The Mormons seemed to be obsessed with quality time. "Have you shown it to your brother?" I asked.

"I beg your pardon."

"Nothing."

He smiled a half-comprehending smile, then reached into his inside coat pocket and pulled out a three-page manuscript. "Here, you can read my original."

I held out my hand, palm toward him, refusing the honor. "I don't want to spoil it, Howard. I want it to be fresh Sunday morning."

He grinned a fatuous grin at me, repocketed the script, and leaned confidentially onto the counter. "I think you'll enjoy it. Do you have children?"

"Not anymore," I said.

"You're missing a great deal."

"I know." I'd forgotten how much I missed them.

"Arlene and I had our sixth last month," he said, reaching for his wallet.

"In my line of work, you're away from home a lot."

"Boy, do I know about that," he said. "I almost feel hypocritical giving such a sermon. I don't spend as much time as I should with Arlene and the boys. But we men have to be out building the kingdom." That last was meant to be a little joke.

"Yeah, it's tough," I said.

We both paused awkwardly—Howard because he'd about come to the end of his conversational repertoire, me because I was looking for a segue into what I wanted to ask him. Just before he got his wallet open and the pictures out, I said, "Howard, you remember the Kimball boys from East High?"

"You mean Jed Kimball and his brothers?"

"Yeah. What were their names, Orville and Aaron?"

"Sure I do. Real wild kids. Never bathed. Always picking fights. Mom wouldn't let us go near them."

"Yeah. Those are the ones."

"They've sure been in a lot of trouble since. Might have known they were Fundamentalists." He was shaking his head all this time. "One of them was killed, wasn't he?"

"Orville," I volunteered.

He was still shaking his head. "Sure shows what'll happen to boys who aren't well brought up. Start messing around in all that apostate stuff. Polygamy, murder, heaven knows what all else."

"Howard, do you know what ever happened to the rest of the family? Were there any sisters? Where are Mom and Dad?"

"Well, I suppose you know about Jed, most everybody does. And Aaron's gone into hiding; I think Jed tried to kill him. Then Orson—"

"Orson?" I said.

"Yes. Orson was the fourth brother."

"I didn't know there was a fourth brother."

"Well, he didn't exactly run with the other three," he said as he leaned in closer to me, as if he had a dirty little secret.

"What do you mean?" I goaded him on.

His face was practically next to my face by now. "He wouldn't exactly have been interested in being a polygamist, if you know what I mean."

"No, Howard, I don't know what you mean."

"He was a . . . ," and he dragged this last word out as if he was sizing up a foot-long hot dog, "Ho-mo-sex-u-al . . . you know. What do they say now, gay? In my day we called them queers."

"Gay, usually," I said.

"He was always hanging around the boy's john, you know? Trying to watch us boys pee."

I stood up straighter. "Do you know where Orson is now?"

"Gosh no. Haven't heard about him in years, not since he got out of high school."

"I take it he was about your age."

"Yes. We graduated the same year."

"That would make him?" I asked.

"Thirty-three," Howard said. "He was the youngest."

Just then, Mona, who had crept up on us unnoticed, broke in. "You two planning on a tryst later tonight?"

Howard quickly sprang, like a startled antelope, out of his intimate posture. His face was red, and his eyes a little frantic, as if he'd been caught peeking into a girls' locker room. Mona turned to me.

"You questioning Howard? He'll give you anything you want on the Tabernacle Choir."

I applied my best sphinx mask and said, "Howard knows a few things. Hang around a newspaper or a men's room long enough and you find things out."

Howard joined in the laughter. I meant him to. The one thing that annoyed me about this attractive, self-assured woman was her supercilious secrecy about information. I tried to be less ostentatious with my secrets, but then I could afford to be on this case. I didn't have any.

"C'mon Gabe," Mona said as she locked into my arm and started us both towards the door. "We have plenty of time to freak out on Cokes before I take you to eat a good dinner." She winked back over her shoulder at Howard as she pushed open the door.

I stopped, turned back, and said, "Thanks, Howard. You've been a help, really you have. And I will catch the broadcast Sunday morning."

"Nine-thirty!" he said loudly, as I went through the door. He had a smile on his face.

Mona moved me fast along the street, clearly headed somewhere. "C'mon, Gabe, I need a drink. What a hell of a day!"

I got into stride and followed her three or four blocks to a private club—translated, a nice bar—named the Green Cockatoo. It was very nice inside, but I had the uneasy feeling that elements of California chic were stretching their tentacles into Salt Lake City. I don't know why it bothered me. Maybe I'd have preferred if they had to import a style that they chose New York chic. I'd have felt more comfortable. But the woods were well chosen, the brass highly polished, the plants healthy, and the strawberry daiquiris looked ample and fresh. Mona ordered a margarita; I got a Wild Turkey on the rocks.

Mona leaned back in her side of the booth and stretched her very nice legs. The dark circles under her eyes and the tension lines around her mouth betrayed weariness and anxiety. She gulped half her margarita when it arrived and pushed the hair out of her eyes.

"Any leads in the Susan Whitesides case?" I asked.

She didn't even play games. "No, and it'll be hard. The murder style leaves little doubt that it was some Fundamentalist or other."

"Jedediah Kimball?" I asked, as unassuming as I could.

She drank the rest of her drink and ordered another. "I think it might be," she said, without any trace of superiority in her voice. "He seems to be on something of a roll."

"You think it could have been some of her own family?" I asked, thinking of the big hunting knife I'd encountered this afternoon.

She looked at me as if I might not have a bad question there. "I don't think so. They're not the violent kind. At least they haven't a history of violence." She paused. "Still when your leader gets shot in broad daylight, it might lead to some rethinking."

All of a sudden she put her face in her hands as if she was trying to hold her head together. When she seemed to have achieved that, she looked over at me through bloodshot eyes and said, "Look, Gabe. Do you mind if we don't talk any more about this?"

"Okay," I said.

It was while we were sitting, drinking, and pondering our respective anxieties that I saw the man in the navy blue pinstripe suit for the first time. I noticed him because he was very conspicuous and couldn't possibly have been an undercover man, not with his elegant head of well-coiffed gray hair, his ample height—maybe six feet five—and the peculiar olive green flannel shirt he wore with a white tie. The shirt was peculiar only in counterpoint to the suit. He was simply leaning against a lamppost in front of the saloon.

After she ordered her third margarita, Mona looked at me again. The dark circles under her eyes had deepened.

"Gabe."

"Yeah?"

"I'm scared."

"Who isn't?" I said.

She hesitated, decided not to stab me in the eye with her plastic cocktail sword, and went on. "I got a call today at the paper." She stopped there.

"Well?" I said.

"It was a man's voice."

"Did you recognize it?"

"No."

I waited. I was going to have to coax her into a confession. "What did he say?" I asked.

"He said I'd written my last article on the Fundamentalists."

"Is that all?" I asked, knowing that of course it wasn't.

"He told me I'd be dead before morning."

"Well, I think we're safe here," I said, still not taking the whole thing quite seriously enough. "I doubt that many Fundamentalists frequent a place called the Green Cockatoo. See, I am getting a feel for the case—at least for the kind of people we're dealing with here." I smiled at her, trying to bolster her sense of humor. "You've had threats before," I said. "You gave me a recitation last night."

"I know."

"You told me you're on their hit list. Whose hit list? Kimball's?"

"I assume so."

"Well?"

"Well, I guess that was before they'd killed two people."

I couldn't argue with that. "I see what you mean," I said, and we fell into pensive silence again.

A soulful-looking woman with long blond hair and a big guitar got up on a raised platform and began singing sad songs about lost love and innocence. She looked like a bummed-out Mary Travers, with glazed eyes that were turned half inward. I guessed she was looking back at Haight Ashbury, circa 1968. They'd have a more hip act later in the evening, but I enjoyed her. I could imagine Mona on the barricades with her a decade ago.

"How did you get connected with the *Deseret News?*" I asked.

She laughed a little bit.

"I mean, you don't exactly seem the type to be star reporter for the Mormon newspaper. Yours has to be the darkest face I saw in that office. And I doubt many of your colleagues jog frantically to the nearest bar after work for six double margaritas."

"Well, for one thing," she said, "the paper's getting better, and they tolerate a few questionable types—if they're good."

"And you're good."

"And I'm good."

"And for another thing?" I prompted.

"I'm good for Affirmative Action—on two counts."

"I see."

"There's more. My mother cleans house for the president of the Church every Tuesday and Thursday."

"I get the picture," I said.

"And I'm not really that unorthodox. I go to church, sometimes, even."

"I wouldn't have imagined your credentials were so good, not in those areas."

"And . . . ," she said.

"And?"

"And I've got something on almost everybody."

"Well, you're certainly discreet," I said.

"Yes, I am," she grinned.

I grinned back, not entirely convincingly. I decided at this point to slip in a fast one—couldn't hurt to try. "Do you know where I can find Orson Kimball?"

Her face went totally blank.

"Who?" she said.

"Aha!" I exclaimed. "Got you."

She looked puzzled. "I'm afraid you have—asshole." She was into her fourth margarita.

"Jedediah Kimball's brother."

"I've never heard of him, Gabe."

"Never turned him up in all your research?"

"Nope. And where did you hear about him?"

I was silent for a moment, enjoying it. Then I said, "Better learn not to underestimate old Howard."

"I'll be damned." Her reporter's eyes looked like black beads right now and were starting to sparkle. "What do you know about him?"

"What I don't know about him is where he is. I'd like to find him. About the only thing I do know is that he's possibly gay."

"Terrific," she said a little contemptuously. "That certainly narrows it down."

"Well, it kind of does in Salt Lake City, I should think. Any ideas?"

"All I can think of is maybe you . . . we . . . should talk with Jerry Romero. His roommate knows the scene." She gulped down the remains of her drink and got up. She was ready to go. "Maizies is a good place to start," she said. "This could be a real coup!"

I stood up and took her hand. "Look, sweetheart, this one's mine. You can tag along, but I do the interview. Understand?"

She looked a little chastised.

"Besides, you think you're in trouble now, wait till you start writing articles about Jed Kimball's gay brother."

IX

We checked out Maizies and the modeling agency next door. No Jerry. The agency was closed and Maizies' small dance floor was occupied by a few slow-moving young couples warming up for the evening. The band was a bland rock group warming up too, just going through the motions this early.

Mona said, "Why don't we get my car and drive out to a restaurant Jerry likes."

"Sounds good." And we walked the few blocks to the high-rise parking lot where she kept her car. We took the elevator to the fifth level and found our way to a red Toyota Land Cruiser with very big tires. It had been backed into place.

"This is what you call your car?"

"This is it. Like it?"

"It's beautiful. But it seems a little excessive for commuter driving."

She laughed, half of it still a margarita laugh, and said as she fished out her keys, "I like to get away, weekends. There's still some country around here where you can go and not see anybody. I just got back two days ago from Canyonlands. My pretty baby's still dirty."

"Could use a bath," I said. "Don't you ever wash it?"

Mona gave me the finger as she started to climb into the driver's seat.

"Mona!" I said, rather too loudly.

She was startled and a little cross. "What the hell's the matter? I'm not going to wash it right here. No hose."

"Were you really serious about that phone call today?"

"Serious?" she shot at me. "You think I make up things like that?"

"Come over here." I invited her over to the front of the Land Cruiser and pointed. "Have you opened the hood since you got back? Or been to a garage?"

"Jesus, Gabe, what is this? I haven't had five minutes since I got back."

"I want you to walk up to that end of the ramp while I check something."

"I'm getting sick of this, Gabe. Now what the hell is going on?"

I pointed to the fender and the hood. "Somebody's been messing about with your car, as you call it. Now if it wasn't you, it was somebody else. Follow? It's probably nothing, but we're both possibly going to be a lot happier later in the evening if I take the time to check. Now get over where I told you to."

She went, a little petulantly, and I opened the hood. There it was, enough plastic explosives to turn this tough little vehicle, the Mercedes to the left, and the Plymouth to the right into iron pilings. It was an amateur piece of work, crudely wired, but it would certainly have done the job. One spark and Mona and I would have been virtually unidentifiable. Novices always use too much dynamite. Very gingerly I disengaged the nasty blob, then motioned Mona back.

"Guess whoever called meant business," I said.

Mona gave me a hug.

"Want me to drive?" I asked.

"Would you?"

I folded the blob of explosives and the wires into a couple of day-old copies of the *Deseret News* Mona had and placed the lot inside a plastic thermos in the back of the Toyota. Then I drove down the ramp and up the street to the police station. I gave the container to the desk sergeant and told him it was for Dale Olander. "Just tell him this was a gift for Mona from the guy who makes obscene phone calls. And tell him not to plug it in anywhere."

After a nervous cup of coffee in the shadow of the big clown, Mona guided me to Jerry's restaurant, which was part of a Hispanic cultural complex on the west side. It was a very popular place, and the big dining room that looked as if it used to be a warehouse was crammed with people. It was the most cosmopolitan-looking group I'd seen since I got to town. There were young couples in rumpled jeans and muslin shirts wrestling their noisy kids around, truck drivers, professorial types, a lot of Hispanics, families, and singles. The pictures on the wall and the two priests presiding benignly over the enterprise told me the center was Catholic sponsored. Catholics are much more tolerant generally than Mormons, at least out here in Mormon country. But then the Catholics have been around longer, have had more changes in their attitudes toward people, and probably understand human nature a little better. Give the Mormons time. They'll learn.

Jerry was sitting in a booth not far from a small mariachi band playing quietly on a stage in the corner. Someone was opposite him at the table; I couldn't see who. As we approached, Jerry waved enthusiastically and got up to greet us. He gave Mona a big hug, then it was my turn. It was as though we'd never been separated. "Come and sit down. We just ordered. Jack brought a pitcher of margaritas. Mona, you know Jack. Jack Vigo, this is Gabe Utley, an old friend, my best friend from more years back than either of us can remember in our drug-addled brains."

Jack stood and held out his hand. It was the young man I'd literally run into at Theatre Genesis.

"Hey, Cowboy. Life is full of coincidences. Find what you were looking for?"

"Thanks to you."

"Glad to be of service to any friend of Jerry's. If you need anything, let me know, and all that." He smiled. It was a warm smile. But he was more nervous than he'd been yesterday.

"Say, don't you have an opening tonight?" I asked.

"Sure do. I'm here practicing the boy's part. Jerry helps me out. He likes girls better than boys. Especially now. Right, Jerry?"

Jerry rolled his eyes. "Oh Gabe, I'm so in love. God, I feel like a teenager." His hands were all over me, not intentionally; he was more like a great friendly Saint Bernard. Why had I slid in beside him? Mona had known better, she sat beside Jack. "Gabe, it's like—remember Dorothy Packard—I haven't felt like this since Dorothy Packard." He grasped his stomach. "Oh Mona, I'm in pain."

Jack drank down the last of his margarita from a water glass and made a face at me as if he couldn't abide Jerry's pain a moment longer. He leaned over toward him. "Hey Jerry, if you can come back to the world of the living, I've got to get to the theater. Don't you have something for me? I need it before I go on."

"Oh, sorry, Jack," Jerry said. "Got it right here." He looked around as he dug into his pocket, his big eyes scanning the room with a shrewdness that belied his adolescent performance of a moment ago. He slipped something he had cupped in his palm into Jack Vigo's hand. I saw that it was a small tube of pills. "There. That'll make you brilliant tonight, gorgeous. I got an aunt owns a drugstore, Gabe. Now give Jerry a big sloppy kiss—for luck." Jerry half stood and pulled Jack's head over to him and kissed him full on the lips. Jack pocketed the pills as he returned the kiss. Mona got up to let Jack out.

"You knock 'em dead tonight, kid," Jerry said, as Jack slid out of the booth. "Tonight Salt Lake, tomorrow a starlet in L.A."

Jack reached over and gave Jerry a too-hard pat on the

cheek. "You know I'm all yours, babe. And when you've got enough sense to throw over that cunt Gail, I'll be waiting in the bubble bath." He danced around the tables to the exit. He blew us all a kiss before he slithered out the front door. No one in the place seemed to pay attention to any of this.

We all sat back down. Jerry seemed to have shrunk and was sitting staring at the basket of tortilla chips in front of him. I had made sure I sat by Mona this time, looking her way. She smiled and shook her head as if to say, "Don't worry, it happens all the time." I remembered Jerry's mood fluctuations from the old days. But this seemed rather stark.

"You okay, Jerry?" I asked.

He looked up at me, pain in his eyes. "I'm so fuckin' much in love with that broad, Gabe."

"Well, why don't you just marry her and settle down and raise little Romeros or Calabreses or whatever?"

"She's already taken," he said. "The bouncer at Maizies."

"Well, have him rubbed out," I suggested.

"She loves him," Jerry said, without changing his expression. "And besides, he's already trying to rub me out."

Mona giggled. "What for, Jerry. Why would anybody want to rub out a lovable character like yourself?"

Still no smile from Jerry. "Because I owe him money. Five hundred dollars. Yesterday." Then, as if a warm front had moved over the inside of Jerry's head, his face lit up, his body became animated again, and he leaned right into Mona's face. "Hey, Chicano baby, have I got some stuff for you. Came in yesterday. Colombian. Best I've ever had. Best you'll ever have. We Latinos have to stick together. Give you the best, right off the top. For you, fifty bucks."

Mona took Jerry's face in her hands, planted a kiss on his forehead, and said, "Jerry baby, I've got a whole drawerful from your last terrific batch. Any more and I'll be burning the stuff in my fireplace. But you're nice to think of me."

He squirmed around toward me. "Hey Gabe. I got such stuff. Great deals on any medicinal wonders. Mix and match. My aunt's a walking pharmacopoeia. Wondrous bargains."

I leaned back to avoid too much contact, looking around the room for narcs as I did so. I noticed Jerry's eyes were scanning again. Street instinct kept him alert for all his dopiness. "On what I make, friend, I do well to keep in bad bourbon and Genesee beer."

Jerry sank back into place. "Yeah, times are hard." He was disconsolate again. He looked at me with big soulful blue eyes. "You think it's too late for me, Gabe?"

"For what, Jerry?"

"For a little cottage, a wife, kids. Maybe I could be a Mormon bishop."

I smiled. Jerry didn't. "You'd lose a lot of friends," I said. "I don't think you'd like a lot of the ones you'd gain. But life's full of reversals."

I had noticed out of the corner of my eye that Mona was getting restless. Her reporter's eyes were firmly in place, and she was ready to get on with it. She had more chance to banter with Jerry Romero than I did and wasn't enjoying herself anymore. She took this lull in the conversation to ask a question she knew I would have felt better asking myself.

"Jerry, we're—Gabe and me—trying to find someone. We thought maybe you could help."

"Try me," he said.

I cleared my throat, darted Mona a semithreatening glance, and carried on the questioning. She had that annoying posture of having got the jump on me. Life with her would be disquieting.

"Remember the Kimball family from East High School?"

"Kimball. How many goddamn Kimballs are there in this town?"

"Jed Kimball. Kid our age. We used to make fun of him a lot. Seems to be getting his revenge these days."

Jerry remembered. "Oh, yeah. You know I'd never really made the connection between that mad dog polygamist and that creepy big Jeddie kid. If you're trying to find him, I'm not exactly the fellow to come to, you know. I have enough trouble tracking down one girl friend. This dude has eighteen wives."

"How about his brother?" I said.

"His brother?"

"Orson, the youngest of the four brothers."

Jerry's eyes narrowed. "Why do you want to find him?"

"I'm a detective; I have questions," I said.

"He doesn't take much to strangers, Gabe. He hides out a lot."

"Is he in town?"

"I think so," he said. Jerry leaned back. I thought I saw dollar signs in his eyes. He folded his arms and grinned at me. "How much is it worth to you?"

"To help you pay the bouncer?"

"To help me pay the bouncer." He leaned forward, all intimacy again. "That fucker's gonna kill me, Gabe. I don't have five hundred tomorrow noon, he's gonna kill me."

"How about you tell me first, then I tell you what it's worth."

"You don't want to see your old pool room buddy dead in a ditch tomorrow, do you, Gabe?"

"I can get a short list of the gay bars in Salt Lake for a lot less than five hundred, Jerry."

"Maybe Mona'd go half . . . Would you, beautiful Chicano baby . . . sister?"

Mona gave him a look that said, "Fat chance."

"How about fifty bucks?" I said.

"Seventy-five?"

"Fifty."

"Aw shit," Jerry said, taking my hands in his and kissing them. "What are old friends for? Besides, I got long-range plans for you two. You're a lovely couple. And we need a good New York cop in town to help thicken the blood and ask good questions." Then Jerry got very close to my face. I hoped he wasn't going to kiss me. "And I've been trying to find Mona here a good man since that Mormon bastard kicked her out on her beautiful Latin behind."

Mona got furious. "You asshole!" she lashed out at Jerry. "You chauvinist asshole! Nobody threw me out! And nobody finds men for me!"

Jerry grinned his quirky smile, very pleased with himself, as if he didn't get the lady very often. Mona caught herself immediately, looking sheepish, as if she didn't get gotten very often but had this time. I was entranced by the whole spectacle, but I was also ready to get on the road in search of Orson Kimball.

"Orson Kimball?" I said.

"Oh yes, Orson Kimball." Jerry mused. "Orson Kimball. My best guess is that he'd be hanging out at the Golden Nugget Bar out on Redwood Road, this being Friday night and all."

"A gay bar?" I asked.

"A lot of leather out there. But it's mixed. Orson doesn't broadcast his sexual tendencies much."

"This isn't a good town to do that in, I imagine."

"That's part of it," Jerry said.

"What's the other part?"

"The other part is that Jed and Aaron and Orville took their baby brother out behind the barn just after he graduated from high school and cut his cock off."

Tough journalist Ramona McKinley turned white. I didn't know whether to laugh or to go somewhere and throw up. "You're kidding," I said.

"It's not much of a joke to Orson Kimball. 'If the little queer's gonna act like a girl, we're gonna make him into a girl.' I think Jed's manifesto went something like that."

"Jesus," I said. "Poor bastard."

"Yeah. Orson stuffs a sock in his pants when he goes out on the town now." Jerry leaned against the wall, his lived-in face showing all the years, all the drugs, and all the sadness.

He absently popped a white tablet into his mouth and washed it down with the remains of the pitcher of margaritas.

Mona stood up, ready to go. Her face was pinkish brown again. She didn't brood long over tragedy.

We left Jerry staring blankly at a young man in the mariachi band. I slipped a $100 bill into his shirt pocket before I went.

It was as we went out the door that I noticed the gray-haired man in the pin-stripe suit for the second time, sitting drinking an orangeade, staring at Jerry Romero. But then Salt Lake isn't all that big a city, I thought to myself, and escorted Mona out to her red Toyota.

X

We pulled into a pitted parking lot that completely surrounded a cheap cinder block building that had been painted white ten or fifteen years ago. The building had a small sign provided by the 7-Up people, which read GOLDEN NUGGET. There were a lot of cars and trucks around, mostly older models that looked as if they'd followed a great many sheep trails. There were no windows in the building.

We opened the door into a dim, smoky room cluttered with people and tables. A bar to the left was dominated by a Coors sign that looked like cascading water. The bartender was a beefy, scowling Indian with scars on his face. To our right was a pool table, illuminated by the second brightest light in the place, where two big men with beer bellies and cowboy hats were playing eight-ball. Two fortyish women who were trying to look younger were standing by watching.

The brightest light focused on a sad little country band

on a small stage directly in front of us against the back wall. The lead singer and guitarist was a man in his fifties who had drunk a lot of 3.2 beer. He was singing an old Merle Haggard song, "The Bottle Let Me Down." A few couples were dancing listlessly in a small space in front of the band. Most people at the tables were talking and laughing, not listening much to the music.

Since I didn't know who I was looking for, I went over to the bar, motioned to the bartender, and ordered a Coors. Coors is very good when it's fresh and cold. Mona stayed right with me, clinging; this was not her normal scene. She ordered a Budweiser. I leaned casually on the bar after my first sip and said, "I'm looking for a guy."

A little grim smile turned up one corner of the Indian's mouth. "The lady mind?" I was going to have to deal with a minor comedian.

"Only when I leave her out," I said.

"There are a lot of guys in here. Any particular size and shape?"

"I don't know," I said. "All I got is a name."

"A lot of names I don't know," he said.

"How about Orson Kimball?"

He screwed up his face as if he was trying to remember. Obviously he did but wasn't quite ready to tell me. I bought a 20-cent cigar and paid him $10 for it. His memory got better, and he pointed to a corner by the band.

"Try that man there, the one with the flannel shirt and the big black hat." He walked away to pour a pitcher of beer for one of the waitresses. Most people I noticed weren't drinking beer. There were a lot of bottles sticking their necks out of brown bags on the tables. Ah, Utah. The state liquor stores get the bucks, places like the Golden Nugget get the clientele. No wonder they couldn't afford to pave their parking lot.

I left Mona perched nervously on a barstool while I made my way through the crowded room to the corner staked out by Orson Kimball. The band was just finishing up a flaccid version of "Mamas, Don't Let Your Babies Grow Up to Be Cowboys." Orson Kimball was alone, very much alone. I decided to go right at it, so I pulled out a chair and sat down beside him.

"Hi! My name's Gabe Utley." The preppy approach.

"Who the fuck gives a shit?" he said without looking up from the drink he was concocting, which looked like a strong mixture of cheap Canadian whiskey and beer. "You wanna sit down, find another table, ass face." Our relationship was clearly not off to a good start.

I slowly peeled my cigar and lit it, then leaned back and looked at Kimball. I would try again. "I like your hat," I said. It was a nice hat, a big pheasant feather sticking up into the air.

He didn't respond. I thought maybe I was making headway and plunged ahead. "I've got a couple of questions."

With great fury and speed, Orson Kimball pulled a big switch-blade knife from somewhere, sprang it open, and stabbed it into the table between my thumb and index finger. He looked at me this time when he spoke. "Look, motherfucker, I don't answer questions. I don't talk to people. I just like to be left alone. So take a walk. I don't give a fuck about your questions."

I didn't move my hand. I simply sat and stared at him. He certainly said *fuck* a lot. And I would think he'd learned not to play with knives. He kept glaring at me. Finally I moved my hand and spoke. Softly.

"Look, I know you're Orson Kimball and I need some help from you." I paused. Orson didn't move, but he was very tense. There was a lot of rage stopped up just behind those eyes. I went on as carefully as I could. I had a hunch it wasn't a smart thing to say, but I said it anyway. "It's about your brother . . . Jed."

That's all I got out of my mouth. Orson erupted like a volcano, sending our table, booze, knife, and all hurtling into the laps of the people next to us. He grabbed me by my leather lapels and smashed me into the wall behind. All the air in my body rushed out and I slid to the floor. I looked up to see that Orson was just beginning his rampage, charging through the dance floor, knocking down patrons like tenpins. And then he was on the stage, breaking up an uninspired rendering of "Good Ole Boys Like Me." It was bad but not that bad, I thought, as Orson pushed the singer into the drummer and smashed the bass guitar into the back wall. In all his fury, Orson seemed unwilling really to hurt anybody, which I took to be a good sign. He wasn't so careful with property.

The big Indian behind the bar didn't see any of it as a good sign. He came angrily from behind the bar, a nasty sawed-off double-barreled shotgun in his hand. The two big guys from the pool table fell in step behind him. They brought their sticks with them.

Orson Kimball had just finished kicking in all the drumheads when the two pool players got to him. Using the sticks as clubs, they started beating him to the floor, until all he could do was cover with his arms whatever he instinctively felt was vital. The bartender stood back watching, shotgun ready. People in the bar were up and cheering as if they were at a bullfight. Mona, pale and drawn, had pushed to the front of the crowd, wanting to do something, but helpless.

When it became clear that the bulls were doing their job too well, I knew I would have to get involved. They were beating the poor bastard to a bloody pulp, and the crowd was getting mean. This clearly wasn't going to stop until somebody was killed, most likely Orson Kimball.

I saw that the shotgun was cocked and ready to shoot, so I decided to take care of that first. I leaped quickly into the fray, smashing down the gun barrel with a chair. It was indeed primed, and went off, discharging into the worn wooden dance floor. The noise of the blast in the enclosed room was enough to still the mob in an instant. Nobody breathed after the gun clattered to the floor. I picked it up, careful to keep it pointed down—there was undoubtedly another shell in it—and told everybody in the room to stay put. No moves! No sounds! I told the two bulls to get up on the platform with the band, after they dropped their bloody pool cues. They were surly, but they did as they were told.

Then I helped a battered Orson Kimball to his feet. Blood was streaming out of his mouth and nose and trickling out of his ears. He was a little surly, too, but he seemed to realize I was the closest thing to a friend he had in the room.

The Indian stepped forward—he knew I wouldn't shoot him—and pushed a finger into Orson's puzzled face. "Okay, troublemaker. This is the last time you show your ugly face in here. Next time we finish the job."

As we half led and half carried Orson Kimball out to the Toyota, I dismissed the possibility that the gray-haired man in the pin-stripe suit was sitting in the dark blue Ford LTD in the parking lot. This man had a hat on and Salt Lake isn't *that* small.

Mona drove while I ministered what little first aid I could to the big half-conscious man. I didn't get the sense that anything was broken, and he was alive and muttering incoherent obscenities. I caught a lot of *fucks* again. The address on his driver's license told us he lived in a place called Magna, in the Shady Pines Trailer Court. Mona knew Magna and proceeded to drive us there. It was a smelly mining town on the west side of the Salt Lake Valley. The Shady Pines took a while to locate, and we drove for twenty minutes along unpaved roads until we finally found it discreetly tucked away next to a junkyard.

When I started to fumble in the front pocket of Orson Kimball's Lee jeans for the key to his trailer, the big man came to life. He thrust me away from him and looked wild-eyed at Mona, then seemed to remember that if we weren't exactly friends, we weren't exactly enemies either. He turned to the door, inserted the key, and growled, "I'm goin' in now."

"Not without me, you're not," I said. "I've gone through too much trouble. Besides, I want to make sure you're all right under a proper light. You've just had the shit beat out of you, buddy."

The tough talk or something—maybe he just hurt too much to care—backed him down, and he didn't object to our following him into the small trailer. He went quickly to the filthy refrigerator, got out a beer, and sat down carefully on the couch at one end of the room. It was clear he didn't feel very well, but it was also clear that he would be all right. He behaved as a man who had been through many such homecomings.

When Orson saw Mona eyeing the magazines scattered all over the trailer, he muttered to me, "She ain't stayin'. Not havin' no fuckin' woman in here." His magazines were an assortment of volumes having to do with young boys, ranging from old issues of *Boy's Life* to hard-core pornography with titles such as *Hard Teen Lust.* "No goddamn cunts. You hear me?" He was adamant on the subject.

Mona looked at him, pondering what she should do, then at me with a growing defiance on her face. I glared at her—this was no time for offended womanhood. This poor bastard was living on the edge. Mona got the message. Probably her reporter's brain was concluding she would get more information from me later than from Orson Kimball now. She sashayed to the door and turned imperially to us. "See you boys later. Have a good time." She winked nastily at me and was gone.

As I got myself a beer from the fridge, I saw a half-full whiskey bottle on the counter and brought it over to Orson. "Here. You look like you need this." He took it from me without smiling, removed the cap, and swallowed a very healthy percentage of what remained in the bottle. I drank my beer, something called Lucky Lager, and sat looking at him.

Kimball shifted uncomfortably, took another slug of whiskey, and stared at the floor. Then he took out a dirty handkerchief, wiped at his blood-clotted nose, and finally said, "What the fuck do you want?"

"I'm looking for someone, Orson."

He looked at me hostilely. I was beginning to conclude that was the only expression he had, so I didn't take offense. Something behind the hostility wasn't forbidding. And clearly not too many people called him by his first name. He looked back down at his can of beer without saying anything. I went on.

"A young girl who's been missing over a week. She's only sixteen." I paused, bracing myself for this one. "And I have reason to believe she's been taken away by your brother Jedediah."

He didn't come at me this time. He merely squeezed the can in his hand until what remained of the beer was running down onto the floor.

"I thought you might be able to tell me where he is."

He answered this time, without removing his eyes from the can. He was holding it as if it was somebody's neck. somebody he didn't like. "How the fuck would I know where he is? Ain't seen him in ten years. And what the fuck do I care about some girl?"

"You have another brother, Aaron. Somebody told me he's in hiding. You keep in touch with him?"

Orson looked back up at me. His attitude had softened all of a sudden. He looked as if he was close to tears. "You know about me, don't you?"

I nodded that I did.

"How do I know Jed didn't send you? How do I know you're not some fuckin' Mormon spy tryin' to wipe out my family?"

"The only member of your family I'm interested in is Jed.

And all I want from him is to get the girl back. The rest of it's between him and the law."

"You're not the law?"

"Nope. But I am a private investigator and I've been hired to find the girl. Now what about Aaron?" I said.

"Aaron's the only one tried to stop 'em doin' what they did, you know. He told them they had no right."

"And you keep in touch with Aaron."

He nodded through his tears.

"Will you tell me where he is?"

"You won't hurt him?"

I said I wouldn't.

"You won't tell Jed where he is?"

"No."

"Jed would kill him if he found out."

"Would Aaron know where Jed is?" I asked.

"He'd sure know where to look," he said. "Jed and Aaron . . . and Orville . . . run together till three years ago. Don't expect Jed could go anyplace Aaron couldn't find him, if he wanted to."

I paused, waiting for him to tell me. I was pretty sure now he would. He got up and got himself another beer, drank some whiskey, and chased it with half a can of his Lucky Lager.

"You know where Covenant City is?" he asked.

"Southern Utah?"

"Just over into Arizona. It's on the map. Used to be called Smith Creek till it got raided in the early fifties."

"Is that where Aaron is?" I asked.

He nodded yes.

"How do I find him when I get there?"

"Go to the little store up by the school. Tell the guy you need to see Aunt Mary. She'll help you out, she'll take you to Aaron."

I stood up and thanked Orson, who was dabbing at his eyes with the handkerchief. "Hey, buddy," he said.

"Yeah?"

"You'll see that Aaron don't get hurt?"

"I'll see to it."

"And . . ."

"And?"

"I don't care if you kill Jed."

XI

Mona was sitting in the driver's seat, listening to a Bach gavotte on her tape deck when I climbed in beside her. She backed out and pointed us toward Salt Lake. It had started to rain a little, and the wipers were bopping back and forth.

"Get what you need?" she asked.

"I think so." I said.

"You're still not going to tell me who you're looking for."

"Nope."

Mona lit a cigarette, turned up Bach, and drove for a couple of miles. She had a furrowed brow. She turned Bach back down after she ground out her cigarette in the ashtray.

"Gabe?"

"Yeah?"

"You think Jedediah Kimball's still in town?"

"I don't know."

"You think he's the one who planted the bomb?"

"You're the one who's an expert on these matters," I said. "What do you think?"

"I don't know what to think. Too much feeling in the way right now. I can't believe it was the Algers. Not their style. And the Susan thing—killing a young girl seems extreme, even for crazy old Jedediah."

I was confused. "You mean you think there'd be more reason for Susan Whitesides's family to kill her than someone else?"

"Probably not," she said. "Still, when you mentioned it last night, it got me thinking. I did dig up rumors while I was poking around, rumors about blood atonement killings of unfaithful wives. Often the families were involved in that."

"Seems farfetched," I said.

"I guess so. Maybe I've just got the dead girl on the brain. I came awfully close to joining her, wherever she is."

"We both did, sweetheart."

We drove a while more in silence. The rain was coming down harder now, and it was very cozy in the car with Bach and Mona. She seemed to drive slower as we approached the city. She was getting nervous.

"Gabe."

"Hmmm?"

"Anything else you have to do in town? Tonight? Right now?"

"It's too late to call anybody for a date," I said. "I understand the Mormons go to bed early."

"I don't want to drive into the city just yet. Want to come with me?"

"I sure don't have anything better to do. Good company. Good music. Only thing we lack is some good booze."

"What time is it?"

"Eleven-thirty," I said, looking at my watch.

"I know a place," she said and squealed the Toyota into a left turn onto a side road. Soon we found ourselves on a bright four-lane highway heading west away from the city. A couple more miles and Mona pulled into the parking lot of a little bar. "What do you like?" she asked, as she stepped down to the gravel.

"Any good bourbon." I handed her a twenty, which she took.

"Be right back." She disappeared into the front door of the bar, which used to be a white frame house that looked like it was built in some postwar development and moved out here later. Most bars in Utah are very tacky. Bach was finished, so I turned off the tape deck and fiddled with the FM until I found Ray Price and Willie Nelson singing "Faded Love." My mood was shifting from classical to country. Mona came out carrying a brown bag with two pint bottles in it and handed it to me as she started the engine. She had gotten Jack Daniel's for me and a pint of sloe gin for herself. We kept driving west.

"What the hell is that?" she asked me.

"Where?"

"On the radio?"

"Oh. That's Willie Nelson and Ray Price. Shitkickers."

"My God. You turned to that on purpose?"

"Yeah. I have lousy taste in music. Especially when I'm with a good-looking broad."

"Jesus. I didn't really believe civilized people listened to that."

"I've never been accused of being civilized. It's my Utah roots," I said.

"Hell, nobody out here listens to that except people like Orson Kimball."

"Maybe you have to get to the point," I said, "where you think the important things in life are real basic. Booze. Loneliness. Men. Women. Pain."

"Jesus." She shook her head, but she didn't change the station. "You are something else, Gabe Utley."

The rain was dying down and Mona turned the wipers to slow and turned off the main highway. We were soon bouncing along an unpaved road a hundred yards south of the Great Salt Lake. By the time we stopped at the end of what had become a sandy trail, the rain had died to a few sprinkles whirled around in erratic gusts of wind coming off the lake. It was a wonderful, wild night. A full moon had begun arguing with the fast-moving black clouds overhead. The lake was lapping against the shore.

Mona grabbed my hand and led me down a perilous path among huge pieces of broken concrete to the lakeshore.

The briny smell was exhilarating. We sat on a rock, un-screwed our respective bottles, and sat staring out across the lake with its on-and-off shimmers in the moonlight. Mona pulled a little, uneven white cylinder out of her handbag, looked slyly over at me, and said, "You mind?"

Without waiting for an answer, she lit up, inhaled deeply, and passed the funny cigarette to me. I pondered for a mo-ment whether there was any good reason to stay clear-headed. I couldn't think of any, so I joined her.

"This used to be a resort—Black Rock," she said, indicat-ing a fifty-foot high outcropping behind us. I looked back at the big dark rock. "They've turned the goddamn lake into a sewer." She took another toke and chased it with some of her syrupy gin.

We were quiet for a few minutes.

"Gabe?"

I looked at her but couldn't see much. The cloud had won for the moment.

"Gabe, do you have a wife?"

"I used to. One day she informed me she was divorcing me and was taking our daughters away to Darien, Connecti-cut. She'd met a lawyer who liked jazz and stayed home eve-nings."

"Long ago?"

"Six months."

"My God."

"We'd been together fifteen years."

Mona didn't say anything.

"Actually," I went on, "I think it was Waylon Jennings."

"Who?"

"Waylon Jennings, another shitkicker."

"Sounds like a friend of Orson Kimball," she said.

"The last thing Kip said to me was that she couldn't take any more Waylon Jennings."

"That why you're out here?"

"Partly," I admitted.

"Of course, you were mostly to blame," she said, without varying her tone.

"I beg your pardon."

"You were to blame. You may not know that, but you were."

"You into blame?" I asked.

She smiled. The moonlight was on her now. Her smile was warm but shrewd. I wanted to drop this topic fast. The best way I thought would be to turn the question back on her.

"And you?"

"I knew you were going to do that."

"Didn't you want me to?"

"Sure, I did," she grinned. I liked the way she grinned.

"Well?"

Mona took a worthy haul of gin and said, "Mine was a Mormon bishop. I was his second wife. Didn't marry until I was thirty. After we'd been married a year, he all of a sudden got curious about what I'd done with my free time before I met him. He'd sort of begun to figure out that I hadn't learned all that from reading *The Joy of Sex* on the night table."

"He hadn't bothered to ask beforehand?"

"He hadn't even kissed me beforehand, figured I'd been saving myself for him." She drank from her bottle. "His first wife had died after a terrible bout with cancer. I figured out—not nearly soon enough—that she'd really been an extension of his mother. She even looked like his mother. She'd allowed him to make the transition from mom to wife without a hitch. She hadn't liked sex at all."

"And he didn't either? Like sex, I mean."

"Oh God," she laughed. "Oh God, no. He found out he loved it. I think that's why it took him a year to find me out, he was having too good a time. Finally he got to feeling guilty about it, started asking questions. I gave truthful answers, and it was all over. He didn't touch me again."

"You stay around long?" I asked.

"Two years. I figured at first he'd get over it. Then one day he came home and told me he'd arranged for an annulment of our marriage and that I was to move out by Friday. So I did."

We were silent again. She lit a second joint. I declined this time. The Jack Daniel's was taking care of me just fine.

"Gabe?"

"Yeah."

"I don't want to go back to my place."

"I wouldn't let you go back to your place," I said.

Mona leaned over and kissed me. A warm lingering kiss.

XII

The hard jangle of the telephone woke me out of a pleasant and very sound sleep. After the second ring I opened my eyes, after the third I noticed that Mona wasn't by my side, and after the fourth I picked up the receiver. It was Linda Peterson.

"Oh, Gabe. I'm glad you there."

I managed a "Hello, Linda" through the sticky morning barriers in my mouth.

"Gabe, I'm scared."

"I haven't gotten very far, I'm afraid. A few leads."

"I haven't slept all night, Gabe."

I was pulling a little further out of my sleepy daze. Linda sounded close to hysteria. "I do have one good reference. And I'm working as fast as I can. If you're that scared, Linda, I'd suggest it's time to call in the police. I can keep working on it, but it would give us all more of a chance."

"It's not that. I know you're working as hard as you can on finding Jennifer."

"Well, what is it then?" I asked.

"It's David. I'm very worried about him."

"Look, Linda, I talked to him yesterday. He's got a lot of things on his mind. Tell him to take two aspirins and plenty of liquid and get a lot of bed rest."

Linda started to cry. I felt very proud of myself and tried to dig out.

"I'm sorry to be so grumpy, Linda. It's just that I'm not sure what I can do about David. He was hard pressed yesterday to remember who I was."

Linda gathered her nerves together and uttered her next line without a whimper. "David tried to kill himself this morning."

That stopped me cold for a moment. Then I said, "Is he all right now?"

"I . . . I . . . think so. But he just sits there. Won't say anything."

"How did he go about it?" I said.

"I thought he'd gone to the office like he always does. But a few minutes after he left, I realized I heard the car engine running and went out to the garage to check. He'd run a hose from the exhaust into the car and closed the windows. I pulled him out and got him to fresh air as fast as I could."

"How does he seem?"

"He's breathing all right. He couldn't have been out there long. But he just sits and stares. Won't talk. Won't move . . . I've tried everything, Gabe. I can't get through to him. Please . . . you've got to help him."

"Have you called anyone? Family, friends, a doctor?"

"I'm afraid, Gabe. I know he couldn't stand to have anybody see him like this."

"I'll be right there, Linda. Don't let him out of your sight."

Fifteen minutes later I was ringing the Petersons' melodic doorbell. Linda greeted me in a bathrobe. Her hair was tied back with a scarf. She hadn't had time or inclination to make herself presentable. She embraced me, hard, as if I was the last friend she had. I was beginning to suspect I was.

"Oh, Gabe, I'm so glad you came. You must think me a hysterical fool. But so much is happening, Jennifer's gone, and David has never acted like this."

"Where is he?" I asked.

"In his study."

I followed her there. David was sitting slumped in his plush chair in front of the biggest roll-top desk I had ever seen. He was staring out the window sightlessly at the sunny, hazy day. With all its expensive electronic equipment—television, stereo, Betamax, a bank of computer terminals—the place felt a little like the control room for the Salt Lake Valley.

Linda tried to get him to pay attention to me. "David, Gabe's here." No luck. He didn't stir; not a muscle in his face moved to acknowledge my presence. I pulled up a chair beside him and tried next.

"David, will you talk to me?" I paused, giving him plenty of time to respond. When he didn't I tried again. "David, Linda is very worried about you. Won't you say something? How about a hello, or 'Get me a glass of milk,' or 'Where the hell's my paper?' Anything."

Still he said nothing. I didn't know whether to be annoyed, which was my initial reaction—his silence had an edge of pouting in it—or to be compassionate. There was real despair behind his glassy eyes. I decided I'd better do something, so I tried a direct approach.

"David, if you don't talk to me or Linda within the next minute, I'm going to call the police and report this." Linda moved toward me, frightened, but I signaled her not to worry. I wasn't planning to call the police, not yet. When he still refused to answer, I walked around him and picked up the telephone on his desk.

In an enormous burst of energy, David grabbed the base of the phone and ripped out the cord, shoving me back into the wall as he whirled around. He then lunged at Linda, uncoiling a powerful backhand against the side of her head that sent her crashing to the floor. I'd told her not to worry, indeed.

Next David charged across the room and crashed his foot through the face of his twenty-seven-inch Sony television set. Glass exploded everywhere. I tackled him just as he started for the big plate-glass window. I feared he would throw himself against it and end up splattered on his driveway in a garden of glass.

Still he continued to release the furious force that was driving him, pounding his fists and head repeatedly into the floor.

Linda, now bleeding profusely from her mouth and nose and from a bruise along her cheek, rushed quickly to help David. But he lashed out at her again with a right cross, just missing her this time. I pulled her away and shoved her to the other side of the room. He would have to take out his aggressions on me. I was better prepared than Linda.

When his fist came flying out at me, I grabbed it and twisted his arm behind his back. Then I pushed his face into the rug and planted myself firmly on his rump. It was like being on a bucking horse.

Finally the pain and the sense of sheer physical helplessness seemed to be calming him down. He was still making awful, tormented sounds, but they too had begun to subside. After a few minutes the tension left his body and he lay in a lump under me. I let go of his arm, tentatively. No resistance—he was all burned out. I moved off his behind but stayed down on the floor with him, speaking across the bloody white rug. "Now will you talk to us, David, or do I have to send for Trapper John to give you an injection?"

He just lay there breathing heavily, staring at me as if he was sure I was going to hurt him. I sat up slowly, and David began to stir. I helped him to his feet and over to the couch. Linda was plastered against the wall on the opposite side of the room, terrified. I helped him down then sat beside him. I didn't relax much, for there was still a lot of equipment in the room to be destroyed, and two live bodies.

"Now suppose you tell me what the hell is going on, David? Linda said you tried to kill yourself."

David looked at his hands, which had to be pretty sore. Linda, very wary now, sidled over to the couch and sat down on the other side of David. After a minute she took one of his hands in hers. He stared blankly at the wall across from us. Finally, he spoke. "Oh God, Linda, I'm sorry. I don't know what got into me."

Linda squeezed his hand and started to cry.

"I think you'd better talk about it, David," I said.

"I didn't mean for you to get involved in this, Gabe. I'm sorry." I believed he was sorry. In fact, he seemed sorry for even more than he was admitting. "I'll be all right. You can go now."

"I'm not going, David, not until I'm sure you're all right." And not until I was sure Linda was all right.

"I don't know what got hold of me . . . I'm fine now . . . You don't have to stay." He was getting better; his color was returning to normal, except for the blood on his forehead. But I felt he was too eager to get rid of me, and I didn't trust that he wouldn't turn on Linda again.

"People who try to kill themselves have something of a problem, David."

"I've been under a lot of pressure lately. You can understand."

"Your work?" I said.

"I guess so . . . that's really all there is for me . . . besides my family," and he squeezed his wife's hand. Linda gave me a little nod as if she felt everything would be all right. I got up figuring she ought to know, but still not convinced. I turned back toward them when I got to the door. "You sure you don't want to talk about what's troubling you, David?"

He mustered up his most-likely-to-succeed smile for me

and said, "We Mormons just have to work out our problems among ourselves."

"Maybe," I said. "But if Mormons are causing the problems, maybe you need someone else to talk to."

Linda gave me another it'll-be-all-right look and I turned to go out the door. I'd check back later in the day.

Then David Peterson did an extraordinary thing. He addressed me as a real human being.

"Gabe."

"Yeah?"

"Did you ever do something you hated yourself for?"

"We all do things we don't like to think we'd do, David. Sure I have. Lots of times."

"Something you really despised yourself for?"

"I try not to think that much about it. A little healthy self-doubt is fine. But self-loathing is highly unproductive."

"Did you ever do something for someone else that caused yourself and others pain?"

"My God, who doesn't? It's part of making choices in a diabolical world."

"You know, Gabe, I've never done that before, never, ever worried about it. All my choices have been right. Never a misstep. At least that's what people always told me. Did you ever think you listened too much to other people?"

"Mostly with me I don't listen enough."

David laughed. I hadn't heard him laugh in twenty years. "I guess this whole scene's been a bit melodramatic."

"I trust you don't do this often," I said, picking up on his more optimistic mood. "I mean, try to kill yourself."

"Oh, goodness, no . . . and you won't have to worry about it again." He seemed to believe it. I was beginning to, a little. Linda looked as if she believed it implicitly.

I probably should have left the house right then and gone about my business, but I wanted to see if David in his new, softer mood might have some help for me. "Before I go David, do you mind if I ask you a question?"

He nodded that he didn't mind.

"I've got to go out of town for a couple of days. It would be helpful if you could tell me why you think Jennifer ran away, or was taken away, or anything you know about Susan Whitesides."

David looked up at me. He appeared old and defeated. "I'm sorry, Gabe. I can't help you. I can't help Jennifer. I can't even help myself."

I let it drop. "Well, good-bye, David. I'll be on my way. You still going to try to catch the plane for Mexico today?"

"I'm not going."

"I can understand that."

"I mean, Elder Jensen has decided not to send me. He's sending someone else." He said this with a trace of bitterness in his voice. I decided not to pursue the matter, said good-bye, and walked out to the front hall.

Linda caught me before I was out the door. "Gabe." She took hold of my arm. "Thank you for coming."

"I see why you called," I said. "He's not in good shape. Don't you think you'd better get him to see someone? A family doctor?"

"He won't. I couldn't drag him to see anyone."

"Well, keep watch on him, Linda, he's not a well man."

She reached up and kissed me before I left. She still rattled old and persistent memory cages inside me. I kissed her back.

XIII

I stopped at a place called Ruth's downtown, bought a *Tribune,* and slid into a booth. I ordered two eggs over easy, bacon, coffee, and a big glass of grapefruit juice, the latter to chase away the vestiges of the Jack Daniel's from last night. After I made my list for the day, I immersed myself in the paper, trying to clear David and Linda from my mind. Not much in sports, no movies I wanted to see, nothing new in either the Lawrence Alger or Susan Whitesides killings. I complimented Ruth on her hash browns, paid my bill, and walked over to the hotel to check for messages. I hadn't taken time before I went to the Petersons.

There was something for me at the desk. A sealed plain white envelope with *Gabriel Utley* written neatly on the front. The note inside was in the same handwriting. The message was not as tidy as the script.

Mr. Gabriel Utley,
Our hope is that you will open your eyes before your blood is spilt upon the ground that the smoke thereof might ascend to heaven as an offering for your sins. Next time the bomb will go off and innocent people may perish with you. There will be no second warning. Forsake your evil mission.

A friend in the Covenant

My God! The bomb was meant for me as well as Mona. It was definitely time to get out of town. Before I did, however, I wanted to see her. And I wanted to check in with Lieutenant Olander.

When I approached him, Dale Olander was at his desk, talking on the phone and writing notes on a yellow pad. He didn't look especially happy to see me and didn't even ask me to sit down. I did anyway.

When he hung up the phone, he took his time finishing his notes, had a drink from a can of Tab, and rolled his chair over to a filing cabinet to tuck away the folder. Not in any hurry to talk, he obviously wanted to make it clear that he controlled the rhythms in this office. Finally he clasped his well-manicured hands together and set them on the desk. He addressed me as if he had never seen me before. "Yes, may I help you?"

Nothing to do but fill him in. "My name is Utley—rhymes

with ugly—and we met out front yesterday. You don't remember that and you just may be in the wrong business. Aren't cops supposed to be good observers?"

He eyed me sourly and took a final gulp from his Tab can. "I'm a busy man, Utley. And as I recall you're rather good at imposing yourself on people. Now why don't you tell me what you came for; I've got someplace to go."

I handed him my morning mail. "This came for me today." He read it over.

"Seems you've bought yourself a pack of trouble." His eyes narrowed. "Seems you almost got a very good friend of mine killed."

"You got Mona's present."

"Yes I did." He cocked his head at me. "So what are you here for, police protection?"

"I'll pass that. Thanks anyway, Dale."

"I wasn't offering, Utley. But I will confess to being more than a little disturbed by what might happen to Mona if she insists on keeping company with you."

"I guess you'll just have to let Mona worry about that," I said, realizing that I was going to be worried enough for all three of us.

Dale got very antagonistic all of a sudden, as if he was ready to throw me out. "Now suppose you tell me what you came for!"

"Look, Olander, I know you're not taken by me. We'd probably break up fast if we were engaged. But we've both got jobs to do and I think we can help each other out." I noticed I was talking very rapidly. "What I need from you is any help you can give me on the Susan Whitesides murder."

The lieutenant calmed down and looked at me shrewdly. "And what do you do for me?"

I leaned forward, my elbow on Olander's desk. "Mona tells me you're good at what you do." A little flattery never hurts. "She also tells me you know things you can't act on, that you can't really get to Jed Kimball. Maybe I can help you find Kimball."

"A maybe isn't really too helpful, Utley, especially from a tourist."

"A maybe's a good deal more than you've got now, right? Even from longstanding residents."

Olander opened his desk drawer and fumbled about for a stick of gum, which he unwrapped with labored ceremony. Then he fashioned the gum wrapper into another link in a long chain he produced from the drawer. "You know, Utley, that you're messing around in stuff that can get you and any number of innocent people killed?"

"I'm beginning to realize that," I said, as I took the note back from him.

"It's a kind of no-win situation. There are a lot of people up the street who don't want any waves, who'd be just as happy if Jed Kimball was never found, who figure these Fundamentalist types ought to be left alone to kill themselves off."

"And there are people right here in your department who feel the same way. Right?"

He gave me a little smile. "I didn't say a word. We're all committed to bringing criminals to justice here."

"And there might also be people up the street in up to their behinds," I said.

"You've learned a lot in two days."

"I used to live here," I said.

Olander put his nicely crafted little chain into the drawer and leaned back in his chair. "All right, Utley, let's say we stay in touch. No promises either way."

"Before I go," I reminded him, "I'd like to know anything about Susan Whitesides that might be helpful."

"Like what?"

"Like anything you haven't given out to the papers," I said.

"I hope there's a payoff here, Utley. I feel like a darn fool. But I guess you do have a kind of freedom I don't. Maybe you can find something."

"I'm trying very hard, Dale."

"At least you're very trying," he said, pleased with his little joke. "Ha-ha."

"Well, don't keep me in suspense," I said.

"There is something I haven't let out."

"Such as?"

"Such as a little inconsistency in the autopsy report."

He was having a hell of a time bringing himself to tell me anything. It was sticking in his throat. "Come on, Dale, I'm very discreet and a great guy to boot. Mona said so."

He went on, ignoring that I'd said anything. "Susan Whitesides's throat hadn't been cut until several hours after she died."

That's weird, I thought. "How was she killed, then?"

"Strangled. Strangled by someone who overdid it significantly."

"Some kind of maniac?"

"Perhaps. I don't know. But it is peculiar, especially if it's a cult slaying. Those people are very particular about seeing that blood is shed."

"Any clues as to who might have done it?"

"Nope. I have to confess that we're at a stalemate." He paused. I waited. "There is one thing I learned yesterday from a source who keeps me somewhat in touch with the Fundamentalist subculture."

"What's that?" I said.

"Susan Whitesides was married recently . . . in one of the cult ceremonies.

"To whom?"

"Don't know. But my source seems to think it was a big item."

"Someone important in the movement?"

"Probably. After all, she was Lawrence Alger's grand-daughter."

"And he didn't even give a clue who it was?"

"Well, he does have a guess. He thinks it might be Amos D. Jensen's son, Rulon."

XIV

I rented a small Chrysler LeBaron from an agency in the middle of town, left it there, and walked the block over to the *Deseret News* office. There was a soft mid-morning coffee-break hum in the city room. Copy for the afternoon paper had had to be in a few minutes before, and Mona was sitting cheerlessly at her desk, chin in hand, staring at the wall across the room. She didn't notice my approach.

"Hi, Mona," I said softly. She jumped like a startled rabbit. Her hands fluttered in all directions. They were just reaching toward a copy sheet under my nose when I saw the headline: DAUGHTER OF MORMON OFFICIAL MISSING MORE THAN A WEEK.

I picked up the sheet before she could expropriate it and read the copy while Mona turned various shades of red and registered various gradations of emotion between anger and embarrassment.

She had targeted who it was I was looking for, but a cursory reading told me she didn't know anything else. Her sources were all unidentified. "This going to appear in the afternoon paper?"

"No."

"No? Then why'd you write it?"

"They wouldn't print it."

"Somebody has some sense. Come on, let's get out of here," I said as I folded the copy into my pocket. I grabbed her arm a little unceremoniously.

She shouted much too loudly, "Let go of me, you son of a bitch!"

That was nice talk for the city room of the Mormon newspaper. All eyes were on us. She had to come with me now.

"How about a cup of coffee?" I said when we got onto the sidewalk.

"How about a drink, you goddamn bully?" she said as she headed west at a strong marathon pace.

She didn't say a word until we were restively ensconced in a dark booth in the Green Cockatoo. She showed her membership card and ordered a double vodka martini. I got a ginger ale. I had a lot of driving to do later today.

"Why in hell were you going to print that?" I asked. I was, if anything, angrier by now.

"I'm a reporter, Gabe," she shot back. "I sniff out stories and I print them."

"You don't ever worry what your stories might do to people?"

"I'm a reporter because I care what happens to people. It matters to me that people know the truth. I don't much like a managed press, no matter who manages it." Righteous ire was flaming out of her like a gas log.

"And it didn't occur to you that that story might fuck up what I'm trying to do? That it might hurt people?"

She looked right into my eyes. Her eyes were black darts. "I didn't get this from you, Gabe."

"How did you get it?"

"David Peterson confirmed it."

"Jesus." I called over the waitress and ordered a double bourbon on the rocks before I slumped down in my seat. Terrific—the dumb bastard couldn't kill himself one way, so he would do it another. Linda should have locked him up and kept him on strong sedatives. I accepted a Benson and Hedges from Mona.

"This morning?" I said.

"About an hour ago."

"You called him?"

"Yes."

"And he answered the phone?"

"Yes."

Where the hell was Linda, I wondered. Mona answered my thought.

"He wasn't on the phone long. Someone wrestled it out of his hands. His wife probably. He sounded very strange."

"And you believed him?" I said.

"Why not, it's his daughter."

I drank half my whiskey, trying to calm myself, trying to keep myself from strangling Mona. But then I thought of another question. "How did you get the idea to call David Peterson?"

Mona looked embarrassed. She didn't say anything.

"You owe it to me to tell, Mona."

"I'm a good reporter. I figured it out."

"Just like that? A revelation?"

"Kind of," she said, sheepishly.

"Mona, this is getting silly now. How did you find out?"

Mona smiled at me. "Did anybody ever tell you you talk in your sleep?"

"Christ." I decided not to kill her—at least, not right there. Instead I dragged up the image of the planted bomb to the front of my consciousness. It didn't come easily, but I persisted and finally was able to feel all right about her survival. I pulled out the note. "You remember the bomb yesterday?"

"How could I forget the bomb yesterday."

"Here," I said, and I handed her the paper. She had a real revelation this time.

"My God, Gabe."

"Good thing I'm getting out of town. My friends will be safer."

She placed her hand on mine. "Am I still your friend?"

We sat dumbly for a few minutes, each working through

our own thoughts. Mona ordered another martini. I finished my whiskey. I broke the silence.

"Mona."

"Hmmmm?"

"Will you do me a favor?"

Her eyes narrowed. "What?"

"Will you sit on this Jennifer Peterson thing?"

"I don't have much of a choice, do I?"

"You could leak it somewhere else. The *Tribune* would print it. Or the *Denver Post*."

"Maybe," she said. "Maybe it would get me another job."

"Another job?"

"Yeah. I think I'm not long for this one. I got, shall we say, a strong warning this morning."

"The article?"

"That," she said, "and my personal life-style. The editor's not too happy about the way I spend my leisure time."

"They know about things like that?"

"Bet your ass they know about things like that. Mostly they haven't troubled me, but couple an occasional post-work tipple with some aggressive journalism pointed in the wrong direction and one's job security can become very tenuous. Still, they've been very good to me. And I have my mother to think about."

"Thanks," I said.

"Gabe."

"Yeah?"

"I loved last night."

"So did I, except for my nocturnal monologue."

"I hope you won't hold it against me," she said.

"I'd better not," I answered. "Somebody ought to be supportive of the dumb risks you take."

"Gabe."

"Yes?"

"Will you take me with you?"

"Where?"

"Wherever you're going today."

"Nope. No sense both of us getting blown up."

"Okay," she said.

"But you can meet me in a day or so," I said. "How about Kanab?"

"When?" she asked.

"Tomorrow at six o'clock all right?"

"How about Perry's Lodge? The dining room," she said.

"Fine. We've got a date . . . And Mona—"

"Hmmmm?"

"Help me remember to buy a gag for when I sleep with reporters."

XV

I picked up my things, checked out of the hotel, and carried my bags the three and a half blocks to pick up my car. I didn't feel so much a foreigner in the city now. In fact, I felt so much a part of things that eyes were watching me from every conceivable hidden place. In a place you know well, you know that no person, no door, no bright sunny façade is without its malevolent secrets—dangers. I guess it is the contrast between the apparent surface and the dark recesses—the tension, the interpenetration—that makes up the whole.

Also, when you start to feel your way into—or back into—a place, you start to get intuitions about things, about your responsibilities to people you care about. As I drove out the narrow drive from the car rental onto State Street, I knew I should stop at the address given me by Jack Vigo for Jerry Romero. It wouldn't take long, so I turned a couple of corners and drove the few blocks to the front of a red brick apartment building that would soon have to make up its mind whether it would continue to decay or to join the ob-

sessive urban renewal going on all around it. Jerry Calabrese Romero lived in 107 on the ground floor.

Almost before I knocked, I was met at the door by Jack
Vigo, clad only in a pair of cut-off jeans and looking very
troubled. "Utley?" he said, as though he'd been waiting for
me. "Thank God you're here—It's Jerry."

"Where is he?" I asked.

Without answering, Jack led me to a back bedroom where
Jerry lay on a bed staring out a window at tree leaves and
blue sky. His face was a mess, cut and bruised. His nose had
been broken and he had cotton stuffed up the nostrils. He
was breathing through his mouth. As we came into the
room, he turned toward us and set his one open eye upon
me.

"Gabe?"

I sat on the edge of the bed. "My God, Jerry, what happened to you?"

"Whatever it was, Sam Spade, I think it was your fault."

"My fault?"

"That's what a very big guy with a roll of quarters in his
fist told me last night."

Jack Vigo, seeing I was more than a little perplexed, tried
to fill me in as Jerry popped something into his mouth from
one of many bottles on the nightstand. "Jerry was supposed
to pick me up after the play. We were going to a party.
When he didn't show, I waited a half hour or so then figured he probably had found a friend—or maybe his fantasy
about Gail had come true—and I headed off to the cast
party."

"When did you see him?" I asked.

"A friend got me from the party and told me Jerry was
hurt. He'd found his way to the apartment, but he wouldn't
go to a hospital and wouldn't even let me call a doctor."

I feared that whatever it was Jerry had taken would rock
him to sleep, so I asked if he knew who did this to him.
"Was it someone you know?"

He continued to stare at the tree for almost a minute, but he wasn't nodding off so I let him stare. Finally he turned back to me. "Three big guys. The one with the quarters and another who had a big mean knife—the kind you skin deer with—worked me over. A third dude, very tall, with gray hair, a blue pin-stripe suit, said he was going to let Number Two skin me next time I failed to mind my own business."

"Why'd he think you haven't been minding your own business?" I said.

"They said to stay away from you."

"Can't even talk to old friends in this town?"

"I guess someone thinks you've got your nose in bad shit, Gabe."

"And you don't have any idea who thinks that?"

"I know a lot of people in this town, Gabe."

"And I imagine you know a lot of secrets about those people, don't you, Jerry."

"I imagine I do."

Jack put his hand on my shoulder as Jerry was beginning to drift off to sleep. He wasn't going to play anymore. He hurt, he had learned something of a lesson he'd thought he already knew, and he wasn't in any mood to chat. "C'mon, Utley. He'd better sleep. Going to take him a few days to get over this one."

I got up and followed Jack into the living room, accepting as I did an offer of a cup of coffee. He brought the coffee in two hand-thrown cups of exquisite design and sat down opposite me.

"Cream?"

"Black's fine."

Jack was silent, staring at me as he sipped his coffee. His eyes were sharp now, shrewd. None of the artsy-fartsy prancing routine. His voice was measured when he spoke.

"Almost everybody in this town likes Jerry. He stays out of political tangles, if you know what I mean."

I nodded.

"The only time he gets in trouble is when he gets generous, tries to help old friends."

I didn't like the way this conversation was heading. "All right, Jack, I feel terrible about what happened to Jerry. But tell me this, why do you suppose whoever these guys are decided to pick on Jerry? Why didn't they just come to me directly? I haven't exactly been hard to find."

Jack was fast on his feet. "Almost everybody in town knows you're fucking around in some very sensitive matters, Utley. And certain of those bodies are obviously scared shitless."

"Come off it, lad. Smart folks don't do dumb things like you're suggesting. They're not going to hit some poor schmuck who just happens to be standing on a streetcorner, not if he isn't in up to his ass."

Jack slammed down his coffee cup. His eyes were like knives. "Don't try to lay this on Jerry, fucker. This is your fault. Jerry is a very vulnerable guy and you know that. Those thugs were talking to *you*, Cowboy. And there isn't a better way in the world to pass on a warning than through Jerry. Jerry's not going to the police. Jerry's got too much to lose. The police don't really like what Jerry does. So after he passes along the message, Jerry will just curl up in his room until he quits hurting, then next week he'll look you up and take you out for a drink and tell you you're the best friend he ever had . . . Well, I'm just not buying it, Utley." He fumbled for a cigarette, lit it finally on the third match, and sat looking at his coffee cup.

I stared at my hands for a long time. They looked bloody. I answered quietly—no more self-righteous outbursts— "I've known Jerry for twenty-five years, Jack. I knew him when he was stealing Chesterfields from the corner grocery store. I consider him one of my best friends. And I intend to find out who did this to him."

Jack inhaled deeply and gave me a look that didn't exactly say I was forgiven but did acknowledge that I hadn't hired a mercenary to beat up his friend. "I've been with Jerry three years," he said. "He can't seem to stay out of trouble."

"You don't have any idea who might have done this?"

"If I did, I'd have the cops in by now."

I stood up and went to the door. Jack just sat where he was. "Take care of Jerry," I said. "But I don't suppose I have to tell you that."

"No, I don't suppose you do."

"Tell him I'll be back in a few days."

"Swell! We'll have a party."

I slipped quietly out the door and got into my car.

XVI

I didn't really enjoy the drive through central Utah; I felt too much like a cricket trying to escape a flock of sea gulls. I kept telling myself that all I was doing was trying to find a sixteen-year-old runaway girl. It sounded simple when I said it out loud. Why wasn't it simple?

I turned on the radio and when the D.J. was announcing a song by Waylon Jennings, I felt I had my first good sign in days. That was the good news. The bad news was that the song was called "I've Always Been Crazy." I didn't need to be reminded.

I had a late lunch in a little town named Beaver, in a mom-and-pop café in the lobby of what was once the local hotel. Now there were only motels down by the interstate highway. I was served by a young woman—twentyish—who, because I was the only customer in the place, paused to chat after she brought me my coffee.

"You from up north?" she asked.

"I just came from Salt Lake. I live in New York."

"Golly, I never met anybody from New York. Just seen 'em on TV."

"I used to live in Utah," I said. "I was born over in Salina."

"That ain't far. Just over the mountain."

"Seems a long time ago," I said. "You ever get to Salt Lake?"

"Once I did. We went up to Conference." She assumed I'd know what she meant—the semiannual gathering of the Mormon faithful in and around the Tabernacle, to hear instruction from the Church leaders—and I did. "I loved it. So many people. Nice buildings. People dress real nice."

"Why don't you go up and stay a while? You might like the city."

She looked down and fiddled with her apron. "Can't. Jack—that's my husband—don't want to leave. No place to hunt up there, he says," and she gave a little snort of a laugh. But her eyes were sad as they looked back up at me. "Got two little girls. Guess we'll just stay here. Gettin' to be a lot of tourists through. Jack wants to start a restaurant out by the highway. Thinks we could make a bundle."

"Does Jack run this place?" I asked.

"No, my dad does. Jack has a farm. But he's tryin' to sell it. No money in it. And the work's hard."

I finished my coffee and left a $5 tip, quite aware that it would do nothing for the wistful sense of loss in her eyes. Something had passed her by.

As I drove on I thought about Brigham Young's dream of many hardy settlements grown to small cities along the Wasatch front, self-contained agrarian communities sustaining a happy and self-sufficient people. Mormons were urbanizing, becoming just like the rest of the world, at least on the surface.

I continued south in the fading afternoon and stayed the night in a little motel in Cedar City. The next morning I moved on through scattered Mormon villages nestled under great sandstone cliffs, through a landscape that seemed too big, too awesome, for any human dream. After the little

town of Hurricane, I climbed a twisting road up an escarp-
ment to an expanse of land that seemed to go on forever.
And in that vast stretch, I drove mile after isolated mile on a
paved road that seemed an impertinence in this country.

Then I saw it—Covenant City, a town set down in the
middle of all this emptiness. The people who lived here did
so because they didn't want to be bothered. I was about to
bother them.

My first impression was that I was entering a pleasant little
town peopled by industrious farmers, but something about
it was strange. The farther in I drove, the more I felt that
I'd stepped back in time, back into a nineteenth-century
Mormon village with wide dirt streets, houses surrounded
by trees and gardens, children dressed as they might have
dressed a hundred years ago.

There were few vehicles about; I passed a truck loaded
with garden produce heading to some distant market. A familiar sight. Yet the houses were strange. Many of them
looked like jerry-rigged motels, very large and built from
almost any material readily and cheaply available—brick,
lumber, cinder block, tin, clapboard. They were obviously
meant to house very large families.

I didn't lose a strong sense that I was intruding. Even
though no one seemed to pay much attention, I felt eyes
upon me, unfriendly eyes. An all-seeing eye? It was not a
place a stranger would want to linger.

I felt more closely watched than ever as I pulled up to the
town's single store, a co-op, austere and whitewashed stucco
with tiny windows and a single wooden door. A hand-let-
tered sign set in the window announced the specials of the
week—stone-ground wheat, unrefined sugar, peaches from
the north.

Inside, it was like a small American grocery store from
the 1920s. It smelled that way. The food was good and basic
and marketed for people who cared about the food rather

than the packaging. Two young girls in long dresses giggled to each other as I walked in. And as I wandered up an aisle, like any typical shopper, I began to feel a little more at ease—until I looked at the man behind the counter.

At first glance I had seen a pleasant, relaxed, sandy-haired man of medium height, wearing a white butcher's apron. When I looked again, I saw a man poised for battle. His body was tense, his jaw firm, and his eyes bored through me like lasers. I turned my eyes quickly to the produce, avoiding his stare, and began performing an awkward little shopper's ballet. I picked out two beautiful peaches and a loaf of fresh wheat bread. Then I started toward the counter—might as well get it over with.

I noticed that the two girls were quickly exiting the front door, no longer giggling, and that a second man had appeared in a doorway leading to the back room. It was the young man from Mary Ann Whitesides's in Salt Lake, with the tractor hat that said STINSON SHEEP. He was whittling a stick with a knife only slightly shorter than my forearm, and he was whistling an old Mormon hymn. I continued on my way to the counter, digging in my wallet for money.

"Nice day," I said.

The counterman simply stared at me, without a word.

I laid out my money, which he accepted, and tried another approach. "I just got into town. I'm looking for someone, a friend."

Finally the man spoke. "Can't imagine you have friends here, mister. You might try on down the road. Saint George. Kanab. Probably do better there." He paused briefly to put my money in the drawer and draw out my change. He looked me directly in the eye as he put the money on the counter. "I'm afraid we don't have many visitors here."

Since I could plainly see he didn't want to talk about the weather, I got right to the point. "My name's Gabriel Isaac

Utley—"maybe the Old Testament names would help me out—"and I was told you could direct me to Aunt Mary."

A profound, frozen stillness came into the air. The whittling and whistling stopped, and the storekeeper locked into place. Nothing moved. No one breathed. I had touched a major nerve.

After what seemed like half the day and was in reality probably fifteen seconds, the shopkeeper responded, still eyeing me skeptically, "What do you want with Aunt Mary?"

"I'm looking for someone. I was told Aunt Mary could help me."

"Are you a reporter?" the man asked.

"No."

"We've had trouble with reporters lately."

"I'm not a reporter and I'm not looking for trouble."

"Who told you about Aunt Mary?" he asked.

"A friend."

"We help our friends. But we've learned the hard way, Mr. Utley, that we don't have many friends."

I noticed that the guy with the big knife was now standing directly behind me, motionless, waiting. I wasn't sure at that moment that I wouldn't have my throat cut and disappear forever into the Arizona desert.

"You have any weapons?" the counterman asked.

"No," I lied a little. I had my .38 tucked under the rear seat of the car.

"Search him, Brian." And the young man pushed me forward, with my hands on the counter, and felt about my person with considerable enthusiasm. I had an image that he had put the big knife in his teeth.

"Go with him to Aunt Mary's, Brian," he said to the young man with the knife. "See that he gets there safely."

Brian walked toward the door, putting his knife in its sheath. The two of us strolled an uneasy and silent few blocks down a little-traveled lane to a large assemblage of buildings that were mostly attached to each other. The dominant material appeared to be cinder block, about half painted white, the other half unpainted. Three short but ample cottonwood trees shaded the sandy front yard where half a dozen young children played. As soon as they saw us turning in at the gate, we became the center of their attention. They stepped back well out of our way and watched us closely.

Brian opened the door for me, and I was let into a small, plainly furnished parlor. Wooden benches that looked like church pews lined two of the walls. A new rocker of antique design was set against a third. There was nothing on the walls. The floor was bare pine. It felt like the waiting room of a nineteenth-century dentist.

I had just begun to wonder what would happen next when a young girl appeared in the interior doorway, a breathtakingly beautiful young girl about sixteen. I just stood dumbly staring at her. I felt like Dante struck by his first vision of Beatrice. Her eyes were what attracted me first. They were huge, deep black pools, surrounded by the thickest natural lashes I had ever seen. Those incredible eyes absolutely dominated her face. But her face framed those eyes in a remarkable manner. She had heavy, arched, unplucked eyebrows, and a beautifully shaped nose, small in contrast to her eyes. Her mouth was a thin, unproven line, tight in its sense of discipline, quivering from a tension between shyness and curiosity. Her strong jaw, soft in its youth, was molded for resolution. Her hair was dark brown and very long—probably it had never been cut—and was braided into a single strand that reached well past her waist. Her ankle-length cotton dress was plainly fashioned but brightly colored and designed to cover her maidenly charms like a special wrapping—sleeves tied at the wrists, collar tied at the neck with a green ribbon. I had never seen anything lovelier in my life.

Then she was gone, with a movement like a startled fawn. Where? Ascended to heaven for all I knew.

I stood silently for five minutes, allowing the girl's image to etch itself into my brain like a steel engraving, before a man entered the room, apparently primed to engineer phase two of the obstacle course toward Aunt Mary. He spoke with a cool precision.

"Brother Anderson sent you down here?"

"If Brother Anderson tends the store, yes."

"You wish to see Aunt Mary?"

"Yes."

The man was of medium height and build, with short blond hair, almost white, combed straight back. He had small wire-rimmed glasses that framed and magnified two penetrating blue eyes. His brown suit was right out of the 1950s, as were his white shirt and white tie. He held out his hand, which was very large and callused—used to hard work. I shook hands with him as he asked his next question.

"You have a particular mission in mind?"

"Yes. I'm trying to find a young woman."

"And you think we can help."

"I was told that, yes."

"By whom, may I ask?"

"You may, but I'm afraid I can't say. Gave my word."

"Very well," the man said, still sizing me up. "You realize we don't accommodate many visitors. Aunt Mary rarely sees anyone who is not one of our people."

"Will she see me?"

The man stood planted, searching me with his blue eyes. "We've had a great deal of trouble recently. You can understand our being careful."

"I can understand that," I said. "There's been a lot of violence up north."

"Yes, there has, and we wish to prevent it down here. We are not a violent people."

"I only want to find the girl," I said.

"And you don't think that looking for this girl might bring us violence?"

"I hope not," I sighed. "I sincerely hope not."

The man led me down a long, austere, freshly white-washed hall, empty except for closed doors every few feet. Then we stepped out a back door and into a large yard that was really an orchard of cherry, apricot, and apple trees. A hundred yards and we were before a small frame house, inconspicuous and tucked in well among the trees and in the shade of a large barn to the right. The man walked up the wooden steps and knocked on the door, which was opened quickly by an unseen hand. The man bid me enter first and followed me in, closing Brian outside. I was convinced later that my mouth must have been open in a kind of awe as I looked about the room. If I had felt upon entering the town that I was moving back in time, here there were no visible clues that the twentieth century ever existed.

My first impression was of all the fabric handiwork. Great colorful crocheted afghans draped the sofa and chairs; a beautiful oval braided rug covered the floor. Quilted drapes, again multicolored, hung from ceiling to floor, hiding the windows. It was a room decorated by a woman determined to fashion her environment in antique soft sculpture.

My eyes were next taken by the pictures on every spare inch of wall—photographs mainly. Surely there were pictures of recent vintage, but the impression was of legions of rugged and determined pioneers staring out from nineteenth-century daguerreotypes, generations of forebears enclosing and protecting the room. Dominating all the others were large portraits of Joseph Smith, Brigham Young, and John Taylor, the first three Prophets of the Mormon Church.

Settled in the middle of all this, next to a huge cast iron stove, was a woman in an ancient wheelchair. She was an austere and beautiful woman dressed in black, with her hair pulled severely into a bun. A brightly colored quilt covered her legs. Her eyes were huge dark wells whose look said that I hadn't any secrets she wasn't privy to. With a slight movement of her hand she invited me to sit on the sofa.

"You're Gabriel Utley," she said, with just the suggestion of a question.

"Yes, ma'am."

"I'm Mary Louise Taylor Smith."

I stammered on, feeling that I'd been let into the holy of holies. "I appreciate your seeing me, Mrs. Smith. I came because—"

"Mrs. Smith? Mrs. Smith? Are you so far from your origins, boy, that it's Mrs. Smith?" She eyed me coolly, her cheek in her hand, mischief in her eyes. "Mrs. Smith—sounds like you're addressing a schoolteacher. Do you have an apple for me?" And she leaned back her head and laughed, a careless schoolgirl laugh. I was amusing her. Then she wheeled toward me confidentially, a broad grin still on her face. "I knew your mother, Gabriel Utley. She was a good woman." She paused and stared at me, sizing me up, the smile fading. "We had our disagreements. She chose her way, I chose mine . . . but we were like sisters. Blood ties run deep and we're all brothers and sisters in the gospel."

Then she leaned back, folded her hands in her lap, and eyed me critically. "But I suspect it all means very little to you, doesn't it? You could call me Sister Smith or Mrs. Smith or Aunt Mary or Kiddo and it would all be the same. But suppose for a few minutes you call me Sister Smith, just to humor me."

I participated in the ensuing awkward pause, cleared my throat, and went on. "All right, Sister Smith." Why did the word *sister* stick in my mouth, like the first time I'd said *fuck*? "I came for help."

"I guess I know that, Brother Utley. I receive word. I'm

not completely in a cocoon here. I know of the awful things happening in Salt Lake City. I even know about your missing girl. Lawrence Alger is my cousin; Susan, my niece. It breaks my heart."

"And you know about Jennifer Peterson."

"Yes, I do . . . I know she's gone. I know you're looking for her," she said. "And what brings you down here?"

"I'm here because I'm told that Aaron Kimball can help me and that Aaron Kimball is in Covenant City."

"Seems you're told many things, Brother Utley."

"Am I wrong, Sister Smith?" I asked, returning a shadow of a smile, feeling a little comfortable even with the *sister*.

"No, you're not wrong. At least he was here. Aaron came to us a few months ago, terrified. Jedediah had killed Orville and had declared blood vengeance against him. We took in the poor man and his family—certainly at great peril to ourselves. It has been our policy to mind our own business, and we like to think we settle our own problems in a peaceable manner. We feel strongly the pull of traditions that go back to Joseph Smith, yet it is not always possible to remain pacifists in a violent world. We care too much for the gospel and its furtherance. We believe with absolute conviction that we carry forward the keys of God's Priesthood and that Jedediah Kimball's claims to prophecy are of the devil. We cannot condone his murders."

This fascinating woman appeared to be in a talkative mood. My mind flooded with questions. How many answers did she have? "Do you know who murdered your cousin, Lawrence Alger?"

She paused, considering, then answered me. "Yes, of course. It was Jedediah. He wants desperately for our people to follow him as the true Prophet, Seer, and Revelator. He has a marvelous vision of unifying all of the Latter-day Saints, all the movements. And it is a proper vision. Yet his conditions are abominable. The unity must come in the acknowledgment of him as its leader, and almost no one can tolerate that. He is an arrogant man, an evil man."

"Are your own people not willing to kill?" I said, thinking about all the knives and threats.

Mary Louise Taylor Smith's jaw clenched firmly; she leaned toward me, her eyes focusing hard. "Brother Utley, you have no clear idea. When you concern yourself with things that matter, really matter—with the Kingdom of God—the world becomes a violent place. When you trace the roots of anything important, people are willing to kill and people are willing to die. To die is nothing, not if you die in the service of eternal truths. When human life becomes the ultimate measuring stick, you see a people who have lost their God."

She paused again. The humor was gone from her face, and her incredible eyes were penetrating the inside of my head. I felt vulnerable, trivial. Yet my pale liberal instincts took over, and I persisted.

"I have reason to believe that Jennifer Peterson is with Jedediah Kimball. I want very much to find him. I think Aaron Kimball can lead me there."

Mary Smith leaned back and laughed again. She found humor in the strangest things, I thought. But at least she did find humor somewhere, which was more than I could say for any of her colleagues I'd met so far. "Brother Utley, if the Peterson girl is with Jedediah, it is precisely what she deserves. Jedediah collects young girls like they were cattle. And he has marvelous devices to attract them. If she is part of his harem, one of two things will happen. Either she'll figure him out and leave of her own volition, or she'll dull her senses and stay with him, like the common chattel she undoubtedly is."

I was annoyed that the woman was so callous about what I was sure was a very serious matter. I was a bit sharp in my reply. "I think Jennifer might have been kidnapped."

"Nonsense!" she stung back instantly. "That's not Jedediah's style. He can get attractive girls with a hog call. He'd hardly risk kidnapping a Mormon bigshot's daughter. He may be evil, but he's not a fool."

"And what about Susan Whitesides?" I asked.

Amusement flooded back into her face. She laughed. "You are tenacious in your mundane little search, Brother Utley; I will give you that. And if I had an answer I would give it to you."

"It couldn't have been one of your people? . . . It had something of the flavor of a ritual killing."

"We don't murder young women, Mr. Utley!"

"And you know nothing personally of Jennifer Peterson?"

"That's right."

"All right, I accept that. Will you take me to Aaron Kimball?"

"Yes, I'll tell you where he is. But you must remember that he's under our protection. He has our word, and our word is sacred."

"I don't want him hurt either."

Aunt Mary looked at me, fondly, I thought. "I believe you, Gabriel, I believe you. You have good blood in you."

"I don't think my search is trivial," I said.

"I hardly said your search was trivial, Brother Utley. I suspect no search is trivial, not if it is honestly engaged in. What is trivial is your life." She paused and wheeled her chair around to the draped door behind her, hung with carefully woven and beaded strands of silk. "Do you want to know what on this earth truly matters, Gabriel?"

I nodded that I did.

"Eliza, come on out here, will you?"

Out through the silks came the young girl who had first let us in. "Gabriel, this is what is important. This is what God has given us as a sign of his covenant. Innocence blooming with possibility. That is the sign. And I think you understand me. But there aren't many men worthy of Eliza.

God creates far more righteous women than men. That's why his natural order is the Covenant of Celestial Marriage—polygamy, if you will. That's why men like you aren't worthy of Eliza. You with your good blood could be. But you aren't."

I had nothing more to say. I simply gazed first on the smiling, knowing, and fulfilled face of the older woman and then on the beautiful, blushing, and unrealized face of the young girl. God was being kind to me today.

On the way out, I asked the man with the blue eyes who finally introduced himself as Kay Smith, one of Aunt Mary's sons, why I had been taken to this imperial woman for a decision. "Aren't women subservient to the Priesthood? Don't your men have many wives? Isn't even your mother one of many wives?"

Smith leaned against a tree and picked a lovely red Delicious apple. "Of course she's one of many wives. But you must understand, Mr. Utley, that what is important is the family network. The Kingdom of God is a vast, unbroken interweaving of generations of the faithful. Even you haven't been able to escape that in Aunt Mary's eyes." He smiled as he took a big bite out of the apple.

"And that's why she's special?" I asked, not quite convinced.

"Not entirely. It doesn't hurt that she is the granddaughter of John Taylor, the last of the Mormon presidents who honored the Priesthood, and she is the first wife of Wilford Smith, who started our branch of the church. Neither of those facts hurts her standing in the community . . . And, as you can well see, she's an extraordinary person."

XVII

It was well into the afternoon, and I had a strong urge to drive to the little house north of Saint George, where Aaron

Kimball was squirreled away. But I was torn, since I had promised Mona I would meet her at six this evening in Kanab. If I drove to Saint George, I would miss Mona. I had about decided that Aaron would keep until tomorrow and that Mona might not, when I stopped at the highway and noticed the big black car waiting two hundred yards up the road. It was a black Lincoln with very dark windows.

Whoever was inside the car helped confirm my decision to go to Kanab. I wasn't about to lead anybody to Aaron Kimball. I turned left and accelerated my Chrysler along the highway toward Kanab. Sure enough, the big black Lincoln turned around and glided along after me.

I kept looking back but had no way of knowing who or even how many were in the car. It kept a respectable distance. I tried to figure how to lose it, but there was only one road in the whole territory that wasn't made for off-road vehicles, and I wasn't about to test the little LeBaron in a waterless desert.

I had one reasonable chance to break free, just down the road, though it wasn't going to be easy. Pipe Springs National Monument was the only other inhabited area in the entire region. The old fort there had housed a Mormon settlement a century ago. It had been the scene of much violence, mainly from Indian attacks, and eventually had to be abandoned. The fort was still standing and preserved as a tourist attraction.

I followed an enormous Winnebago with Texas license plates onto the little road that led to the visitors' center. I parked between the Winnebago and a Dodge camper and reached under my backseat for my .38. Then I got out and went into the visitors' center to watch the malevolent black car turn into the parking lot.

A man got out and stationed himself behind my car. Terrific—I just might have set myself up. I began hoping the family of eight that tumbled out of the big R.V. and the half dozen or so other tourists wouldn't leave before I did. I didn't want to be alone here with these guys. Two other men got out and walked up the path to the center. I had never seen any of the three before, but I didn't like their looks. A tall man in a black suit sported mirror glasses. His partner had on a white shirt and tie, dark slacks, and black oxfords. They looked like the kind of FBI men who hung around the edges of the youth movement in the mid-1960s, before the Bureau got somewhat hip to disguises.

If I hadn't suspected that these folks felt real ill will toward me, I might have been able to enjoy myself. The two awkward "security" men in an awkward situation were trying to act nonchalant, trying to mix with chattering tourists who lived in big mobile houses. There were probably a dozen of the latter puttering around inside the center. Each time I glanced their way, the two men turned and attempted to find some display to look at.

I decided the only way I might find anything out was by trying the direct approach. As I walked toward them, they got terribly flustered. The tall one in the suit pointed out an ancient rifle to his companion. The two started up a little artificial conversation. They shifted from one foot to another. These guys were not used to mingling graciously at cocktail parties.

"Hi," I said, in a cheerful boy scout salute. "You guys been here before?"

They tried to ignore me and simply turned away. I took out a stale cigarette, tapped the tall guy with the mirror glasses on the shoulder, and asked, "Got a light?"

The other man, the one without the glasses, stepped back three or four feet, his hand moving automatically to his back pocket.

"I don't have a light," the man in the suit said stupidly.

I turned to the other, the one with his hand in his back pocket, a sweaty overweight man with a salt and pepper crewcut. "How about your friend here? Do you have a light?"

He was a bit more articulate than the first. "I don't smoke . . . bad for your health." There was real menace in his voice.

"Ah well, I suppose I'll have to wait until I get to Flag-staff," I said, as I slipped the cigarette back into my pocket. Then I stood simply smiling first at one, then the other, as if expecting them to pick up the conversational ball. I got nothing from them, so I carried on.

"You guys tourists?"

The guy in the shirt answered this one. "We're tourists like you're a tourist, Utley."

"Well, I've never been here before. I'm learning some things."

"Good," said the same man. "You need to learn a few things."

"Ah, really? Maybe it'd be helpful if you told me what."

"Like maybe how to mind your own business." His rep-artee wasn't very original. He'd seen too many cop shows on TV.

"Well, suppose you tell me who's trying to define just what my business is for me."

"Let's just say we're keeping an eye on you. Making sure you don't get into trouble. We're sort of protecting you."

"Protecting me. Protecting me from what?"

"We got worried when we were told you don't know the territory very well." He wasn't as dumb as he appeared at first and second glance. There was a shrewd bully under that ridiculous hair cut.

"That's interesting," I said, "and who told you I didn't know the territory?"

The man with the crewcut smiled. I got the feeling he smiled only when he had a situation firmly in control or was ready to do someone bodily harm. I suspected the latter, and my higher instincts told me not to push my luck.

I was doing my little shuck and jive in front of these two while racking my brain for a strategy to lose them. I didn't want them accompanying me to Kanab; I wanted Mona all to myself. And I certainly couldn't have them finding Aaron Kimball's whereabouts. Not quite beside the point, Jerry Romero's battered face kept hovering in my brain. They wouldn't try anything in front of all these tourists, but there was a lot of empty desert out there.

Then I looked out the window and saw a brightly painted, mud-spattered van pull into the parking lot. Decorated with a hand-painted picture of Willie Nelson singing his heart out in Monument Valley, the van looked interesting. It looked even more interesting when a young man with long shaggy hair flowing out from beneath a floppy leather Western hat tumbled out the driver's door. He had on faded designer jeans, scuffed and dusty Justin cowhide boots, a heavily embroidered denim vest, and a T-shirt with a picture of Willie Nelson on it. From the other side, out stepped his lady friend, very young and blond and braless in a white undershirt, cut-off jeans, and sandals. She wore an Indian headband. Both had big sunglasses.

They entered the visitors' center, where I was still standing and staring at my new friends, and headed straight for the restrooms. I decided I needed to go to the bathroom too.

"Well, 'bye, guys. Hope to see you around."

"You can count on that, smart ass," said Mr. Crewcut.

"Oh, and guys—"

"Yeah?"

"If you're supposed to be incognito, you ought to get different clothes. J. Edgar Hoover is dead and in heaven." And I bopped into the men's room.

In the very clean, institutional restroom, I started a conversation with the young man. Frank was his name, Frank Pittman—road bum, country music freak, sometime drug dealer, and escaped rich boy from Indianapolis. He said his girl friend's name was Debbie. Some up-to-the-minute talk about Willie Nelson's latest movie persuaded Frank that I was all right. His natural sense of adventure and a $100 bill persuaded him that helping me out might be a kicky thing to do.

After we had exchanged clothes (I kept the .38), I walked to the door, hoping I was not wrong about the range and depth of Mr. Crewcut's and Mr. Mirror Glasses' perceptions. I hoped it was not just a cliche in my tired brain that all folks dressed like Frank Pittman looked alike to those guys. They eyed me as I pulled down the hat and came out the door of the john, but looked away casually, getting back to whatever photo display they were pretending to examine. So far so good.

The next test was Debbie, with the sun-bleached blond hair and the marvelous breasts, who was peering into a glass case containing hundred-year-old cooking implements. She didn't notice me until I put my arm around her and whispered into her ear that she shouldn't be surprised, praying she wouldn't scream and kick and demand to know what I'd done with Frank. As it turned out, I had nothing to worry about. Debbie merely blinked through glazed, bloodshot eyes—a druggy film clogging any instant reaction. She looked vaguely surprised but responded amiably as I led her toward the main door.

We were halfway to the van when she finally looked up at me and asked, "Hey, who're you, man?"

"I'm a friend of Frank's," I whispered from behind my big Foster Grants, "and we're playing a little trick on some pals of mine."

"Hey, far out." Did people still really say *far out?*

The other Salt Lake Mafia types seemed hardly to notice us as we strolled to the van and got in. We had no trouble backing out, driving out the little road, and tooling away very rapidly toward Kanab.

I figured we didn't have a lot of time. My friends weren't going to leave me in the men's room all day. Even fifteen minutes in a public facility would seem excessive to most people. So I calculated we could at most be well out of sight before Mutt and Jeff burst into the john to find out what the hell I was doing.

"You from around here?"

I had almost forgotten about Debbie, who was lounging casually in the seat next to me. She certainly didn't appear to be concerned that I was driving ninety miles an hour in her boy friend's Dodge van, with knuckles white as snowballs gripping the wheel. I didn't have a chance to answer before she tried again.

"You a friend of Frank's?" she asked, languidly.

"Sort of," I said. "We met in the men's room."

"Really?" There was a touch of surprise in her voice. "'Course, Frank's kind of like that, you know. Makes friends real easy. I met him at an Asleep at the Wheel concert a couple of weeks ago, out in Colorado . . . We decided to go away together. He's a great guy, real laid back."

I figured that if we could get to Fredonia, a little town a few miles south of Kanab, we could hide the van and I could call Mona. If I—we—could get that far, there'd be a pretty good chance of leaving the Keystone Cops in the dust. If our luck was really good, maybe we could get all the way to Kanab.

"Is Frank gonna meet us later?"

"Yes. He'll pick you up in Kanab later today."

"Wow. This is kinda exciting . . . We're goin' to the Grand Canyon, ya know."

"No, I didn't know." But then she didn't really mean it as a question. "You'll get there tomorrow. It's nice at sunrise," I said.

"Yeah, I bet it is. We're gonna get into some great grass and just watch the canyon all day." She dug around in her shoulder bag. "Hey, you want a joint?"

I thanked her but begged off for the present. She lit up and took a deep drag of very strong marijuana into her lungs. My God, her lungs—I found myself noticing again that she had great breasts. Terrific—driving ninety miles an hour down a desert highway, trying to get the hell away from four goons in a big black car, and I start staring at a teenager's breasts. How would Aunt Mary feel about that? Now, why did that cross my mind?

But if Aunt Mary hadn't noticed, Debbie had. "Hey, you like what ya see? Frank says I have real nice tits." She stuck out her chest as if she were displaying a row of war ribbons. "And I kinda like you. I can see why Frank likes you. You got a real nice face. And I kinda like older guys."

Older guys—Jesus, I could be her father, chronologically, at least. Attitudinally I felt as if I was back in the Stone Age or maybe the nineteenth century. For some reason Eliza, the beautiful shy girl at Aunt Mary's, came to mind. Her image was engraved vivid as life.

"You wanna fuck maybe later on?" Debbie said, wrenching me away from Eliza. Was I turning her on? Not likely, not all by myself. It probably had more to do with high speed, youth, and good grass than with me and my tense, aging, half-cared-for body.

"I mean, Frank doesn't mind. We have a real free relationship. Frank's free from all those hang-ups about sex. And he's been great for me. We've had terrific times."

I found myself asking myself how free Frank really was. Free enough to allow his current chick to screw around under his nose? But I found myself thinking that he just might not mind, that he really could be as liberated as Debbie seemed to think he was. Then I found myself wondering why I was thinking about any of this at all. Why wasn't my mind on Mona in Kanab? Maybe it really was. I felt hornier when I thought of Mona than when I looked at Debbie.

In spite of these mad erotic sidetracks, I was watching the rearview mirror very carefully. There was nothing in sight. We were halfway to Fredonia and I was still free of the Mongol horde.

I felt a little nudge against my arm. "Hey, you don't want to talk?"

"I've got a lot on my mind, Debbie."

"I wasn't just shittin' ya. About wanting to fuck."

"I know you weren't."

"Frank says it's a very special gift you have to give."

"And I appreciate the offer. It's a very appealing gift. But I've got a lady waiting for me in Kanab. We're kind of a thing." Somehow I felt like a crotchety adult taking a nice toy away from a very loving child. It didn't help when I looked over and saw that Debbie was crying, the tears rolling in rivers down her face. I held her hand the rest of the way into Fredonia.

Still seeing no sign of the big car, I turned north out of Fredonia and headed for Kanab, about seven miles away. I might as well go for it. Debbie took out a Virginia Slim and lit up. She seemed stoical about my rejection. Life's too short to linger. She'd even started to worry about Frank.

"You sure he'll be all right?"

"Frank?"

"Yeah."

"He'll be fine. I tied him up in the men's room."

"You tied him up!"

"Yes. That way my friends won't think he was in on this with me. They'll treat him better."

"I see." But she really didn't.

We pulled into Kanab about a quarter past seven. I parked the van around back of a seedy little gas station, where it would be impossible to see from the road, and walked Debbie along a back street to Perry's Lodge. I didn't see Mona's Toyota. She was either smart or not there yet. We crossed the main highway and entered the lobby of the attractive white frame building, which had housed and fed many a Hollywood star in the past forty years. The walls were lined with autographed pictures of the likes of John

Wayne, Ward Bond, and Harry Carey, Jr. But we had no time to dawdle there.

With Debbie in tow, I walked straight to the dining room and spotted Mona sitting at a corner table, working on a bottle of chablis. She just stared while Debbie and I walked over and sat across from her. Her eyes were very big.

"You undergoing a mid-life crisis or have you joined the band?" she said, staring at my Willie Nelson T-shirt.

"Hi, Mona. Debbie, this is Mona, the lady I was telling you about."

"Pleased to meet ya." Debbie extended her little hand. Her eyebrows arched very high, Mona shook it and said, half politely and half ironically, "Debbie?"

"Yeah. I'm with Frank."

"Frank?"

"Yes, Frank," I said. "It's a long story, Mona. Debbie and Frank were a great help in making sure I got here—alone."

"I can see you're alone." Amusement shone in Mona's still-puzzled eyes. "But don't tell Debbie that."

Debbie giggled a little She was having a great time meeting Mona and gazing about the classy dining room, grooving on all that dope. "Hey, this is a real great place, I mean, real elegant. Did all them movie stars really eat here?"

"Yeah," Mona said, "Susan Hayward probably sat at this very table."

"Who's Susan Hayward?"

But enough banter. I took Mona's hand. "Look, at least three guys in a big black Lincoln are on my tail—mirror glasses, the whole bit. Debbie's boy friend switched clothes with me and let me take his van. You'll love it, nicely painted with shitkicker singers all over it. Debbie and I have been doing about a hundred and forty miles an hour since Pipe Springs, praying they wouldn't find Frank in the john and do a hundred and fifty after us. So far I think we're ahead, but we've got to move fast. Where's your car?"

"My God," Mona said, "all in one breath. I'm impressed.

But it sounds rehearsed. You sure you and Debbie here haven't joined a polygamous cult dedicated to the worship of Willie Nelson and big breasts." And she looked at a bewildered Debbie. "I think I see a little hay in your hair, dear."

"Hay? I haven't been near no hay."

"Just fooling, dear," said Mona, as she took Debbie's hand patronizingly. I'll be damned, the woman was jealous. I was charmed for an instant, then fear took over.

"Look, lovely woman, I'm not kidding about the big guys in Robert Hall suits. Debbie, I told Frank you'd be in the lobby, that you'd wait for him there. You can look at the pictures. He'll be in a white Chrysler LeBaron and he'll leave that here. You two can walk to your van, and you can be at the Grand Canyon by sunup tomorrow." With that I left Debbie twenty dollars, grabbed Mona by the hand, and was out the back door. "Where are you parked?"

"Don't I even get a kiss?"

Certainly she did. I kissed her hard, and for a moment longing and lust replaced fear—but only for a moment. Then Mona led me to the red Land Cruiser sequestered on a quiet residential street a couple of blocks away. She was smart.

We were five miles north of town before I stopped watching out the back window. There had been no sign of the black car. Perhaps we were all right. I took Mona's hand; she returned the pressure. "You got here," I said.

"Guess I did."

"No trouble? No guys in black cars following you?"

"Not so far as I know, Gabe. But then I was a little crafty."

"What do you mean?"

"I was frightened. I didn't want to stay alone last night. All the threats are getting to me, I guess."

"I can understand that," I said. "So what did you do?"

"I spent the night with my sister in Park City."

"So you don't think anybody followed you down?"

"I don't think so, but then I'm not sure what I'd be looking for."

"Well, if my tails were any indication, they're not subtle. I guess we must just assume we're alone and get on with it. Do you mind driving me a place or two?"

She turned and grinned her smug reporter's grin at me. "Not if it might lead me to a story. I'll take expenses."

"It might lead you to a story. On the other hand, it might bag you a lot of grief. I'd say it's about a tossup."

"Why not?" she said. "I'm a gambler. Besides, the odds have gotten pretty rotten in Salt Lake."

"Okay, we're on."

"You got a deal. Where to first?"

"I'm going to take you there one step at a time," I said. "You'll be safer if I don't tell you anything."

"Safer?" She was dubious.

"Yeah. Less chance of having your lovely fingernails pulled slowly out with a pair of rusty pliers."

"Jesus." She winced. "You've got to be kidding."

I smiled. "Maybe. But whoever's in this plays rough. And where we're headed, I don't think things will get any easier."

It was almost dark, and I figured the best thing to do would be to drive a while and find a place well off the road to camp out. We could, I suppose, drive on to Saint George and shake Aaron Kimball out of bed at 2:00 A.M.. But why bother his sleep? If I was going to bother anyone's sleep, it would be Mona's.

XVIII

Eleven miles off the road we set up a little temporary camp at a place called Pink Coral Sand Dunes State Park. I knew

I'd be picking sand out of my ears for a week. But it was secluded and hardly a place the Mormon Mafia—or whatever Mafia—would be likely to look.

I gathered wood and built a juniper fire while Mona set up camp. "I only have one sleeping bag," she smiled in the firelight.

"I can take that." I smiled back and went out for another load of wood.

"I'm afraid it'll have to be canned stuff," Mona said when I returned. "Pork and beans and tomatoes. I wasn't exactly expecting to rough it. My fantasy was more in the line of a couple of exquisite steaks and a big bottle of good wine at Perry's."

"I know. I think our fantasies matched. But life is full of surprises."

Mona looked long and very warmly at me. "It certainly is." I had to lean over and kiss her for that. God, she tasted good.

After the beans and tomatoes, we lounged back against the rolled-up sleeping bag—I was disappointed to discover it was a double—and drank our coffee.

"I called Jerry before I left this morning," she said. "He told me what happened."

"How is he?"

"Feeling better. Bewildered, like a big friendly dog who can't figure why he should have had the shit beat out of him."

"Do you have any sense who it was?" I asked.

"Nope. My best guess is that some member of the Kimball clan took offense at his pointing you to Brother Orson." Mona went to the fire and flicked the coals about with a stick. "But then I'm not trusting my best guesses right now. A lot of strange things happening. There was a big press conference yesterday afternoon."

"Who called it?"

"The Mormon Church. Amos D. Jensen himself presided.

Here, let me get you a paper." She got into the car and pulled out a folded newspaper. "Here. On the front page."

I saw it was the *Tribune*. She grinned at me. "They scooped us. Morning paper. Usually the Church is careful to time announcements for the *Deseret News*."

"Must have been in a hurry," I said, and read the story in the light of Mona's Coleman lantern.

Amos Jensen had apparently been in top form. "The killings have to stop," he said, "and if all the Fundamentalist cults have to be destroyed to achieve it, then so be it. We cannot tolerate violence. God will not be mocked!"

"Sounds like he was pretty worked up," I commented to Mona.

"You should have been there," she said. "He was purple when he said that. Never seen him so agitated. Not in public."

"You think that'll drive the cults underground?"

"Hard to tell," she said. "They don't like publicity. They're still on the other side of the law."

"It'd be interesting to see if the law would hold up in court anymore," I said. "I wonder what a test case on the practice of polygamy on religious grounds would yield before the Supreme Court these days?"

"A lot of powerful Mormons don't want to find out," Mona said.

I looked at the accompanying photo before I put the paper away. There he was, impressive white hair firmly set in place, a look of rage on his face. Amos D. Jensen, defender of the family, of traditional moral values—inimical to what I planned to do with Mona in about fifteen minutes.

"He's a scary man, Jensen," Mona said, leaning over my shoulder.

"All true believers are scary. Especially ones with a lot of power."

"Gabe." Mona was ready to change the subject, and I certainly didn't mind. I folded the paper and tossed it on the fire.

"Yeah?" I answered.

"I got jealous when you came into Perry's with Debbie," Mona said as she spread out the sleeping bag.

"She's got nice tits. She told me so herself."

"They're a lot younger and firmer than mine."

"Maybe . . . but the price isn't high enough."

"What?"

"They're a gift too freely given."

"Maybe I'm a gift too freely given, as you say."

"That's the age-old question, Mona, maybe life's central question. How difficult must such a gift be to come by to make it worth anything?" And my helpless mind registered the image of the young girl in Covenant City. "The Mormons, the Catholics, and the Puritans all have a nifty little secret."

"They do?" Mona was fussing with the picture of Willie Nelson on my chest. "Tell me about it."

"Yes, they do. They know—the Catholics, anyway, and any Mormons and Puritans lucky enough to figure it out— they know that the harder it is to get, the better it is, eventually. It's a secret poor Frank and poor Debbie will never be able to learn."

"You're not making much sense," Mona said dreamily, beginning to fuss with my—or rather, Frank's—jeans.

"Probably it doesn't make sense," I said. "The risk is, if it's too hard to get, you'll never get it and never know how good it is. I rather think that a lot of those old polygamists with a dozen wives never really figured it out, never really got it. Never had any fun at it."

"I imagine some did, though, Gabe. Don't you think some did?" Somehow I was out of Frank's T-shirt.

"I'd like to think so," I said, moving definitely out of any mood for further discourse. "I'd like to think that at least occasionally one of those old boys had a good roll in the hay." My boots had been pulled off. My pants were on their way.

"I still get a little pissed when I think of Debbie's tits," Mona said, as she unbuttoned her own shirt. "I think it's unfair some poor drugged-out creature should be so pretty and have tits like those." She paused and frowned over at me. "You sure you weren't turned on by her tits?"

"I didn't say I wasn't turned on. I just paused and thought about what they were attached to . . ."

"You like what mine are attached to?"

I was through talking. I simply helped Mona take her clothes the rest of the way off and crawled into the sleeping bag with her.

XIX

We stopped in Saint George to gas up—my God, that little Toyota ate a lot of fuel—and to buy me some clothes. I was tired of wearing Frank Pittman's unwashed Willie Nelson T-shirt. A charming Mormon town, once dominated by sturdy old pioneer buildings (the solid red sandstone Tabernacle and the elegant white Temple), St. George had been over-run by tourists and by wealthy Californians escaping their self-made squalor. Great expensive houses, architecturally from another world, rimmed the sandstone and lava mesas dominating the landscape. I wanted to linger here as short a time as possible. We ate breakfast at a place called Dick's on the main drag and were heading north before eleven. We didn't have to drive far to be back in rural southern Utah, with the great rock splendor of Snow Canyon to our left, the verdant loveliness of the Pine Valley Mountains to our right, and miles of empty and arid desert ahead of us.

While Mona drove, still not sure where, I studied the

rough map Kay Smith had drawn for me, looking for two volcanic cones within a few hundred yards of each other. It was a place called Rattlesnake Valley. But landmarks in unknown territory are frequently difficult to discern, so we ended up lost and frustrated and in the empty parking lot of a little combination store and service station up the main road. I showed the young woman behind the counter my crude map and described as best I could what we were looking for.

"Rattlesnake Valley? Ain't never heard of it. And I lived here all my life."

"Do you know about the two volcanic peaks?"

"There are a lot of old volcanoes around here, mister. My boy friend likes to try one just down the road on his motorcycle. Never made it up yet, though." Mona stood off to the side, looking at dusty post cards, exuding amusement at my plight.

"Well, how about the old house? An old pioneer house, rough sandstone, two stories. Way out away from everything." I was trying any kind of handle.

"Oh Lord, that could be any place. A lot of pioneers used to live around here." She wasn't unhelpful, just not very interested in my problem. And why should she be? She was eighteen, pretty, and plump, and she had a boy friend with a motorcycle.

"Well, is there anyone else around I could talk to? Who runs the place?"

"Oh, that's my dad. He's out back, trying to get the truck started."

I headed out the door and around back. Mona decided to follow. Why not? Might be an even better show out here. As I turned the corner of the little brick store, which doubled as a residence, probably for the girl and her family, I heard Dad before I saw him.

"God-damn-son-of-bitch-motherfucker!" I knew how he

felt. He was flat on his back under an old Chevy truck doing something in the region of the oilpan.

"Excuse me, sir."

Nothing.

"Mister!"

Still nothing.

"Hey, buddy!"

"What?!" He shouted very loudly.

And out he crawled, grease and oil and dirt all over his face, shirt, overalls, and work boots. "What the hell you want?" He got up, futilely brushing himself off.

"I'm looking for a place," I said.

"Well, this sure as hell ain't it."

"I know that. Do you know where we can find Rattlesnake Valley?"

"Rattlesnake Valley? Used to be a place. My granddad called it that. Nobody's called it that in years."

"He called *what* that?" Why was I still shouting? The wind wasn't that bad. The man didn't act hard of hearing.

"You needn't shout. I ain't deaf."

"Sorry."

Mona chuckled in the background.

"Rattlesnake Valley." And he paused, thinking. Then he pointed down the road, the direction we had come from. "Down south, about five miles, there's a dirt road, hard to find, runs between two volcanoes."

I showed him my map and he helpfully traced our route from where we were now. His grimy fingerprints practically obliterated everything on the paper. But I thought I had a reading. "Thank you," I said. "Appreciate your help."

"Glad to oblige," he smiled, indicating two front teeth missing.

I took Mona by the arm and was headed back to the car when the man called us back. "Folks!"

"Yes?" We turned around.

"Be careful." It sounded ominous.

"I appreciate the warning, but why?"

"Nobody goes out that way anymore."

"They don't?"

"Nobody that don't want trouble." His stare was hard and warning.

"Why, is the road dangerous?"

"The whole place is dangerous. A couple men was killed out there last year. Found their bodies. Naked. Their throats slit. Never did find out who done it. In fact, never did find out who the men were. And"—his tone got even more portentous—"they's been kids gone up in there and never come back . . . three or four in the last couple of years."

I thanked the man again, but he had one more warning before we got away. "You know what's behind all this, don't ya?"

"I'm afraid I don't," I said, increasingly skeptical.

"It's the Gadianton robbers." He paused as if I ought to know what he was talking about. I did vaguely. Mona squeezed my arm. He saw I wasn't sure. "Wicked men. Ghosts. From *Book of Mormon* times. They haunt this whole country. They particularly like all the polygamists, feel they're kindred spirits. Heard tell that Jed Kimball's one of them."

That startled me. "Jed Kimball? How is he mixed up in this?"

"He knows the place. He knows every place around down here. He's got real powers. You don't want to mess with him."

I felt a chill up my spine, in spite of myself. By the tension in her hand, I could tell that Mona was affected. Whatever place we were headed for certainly had the locals spooked. Once the chill evaporated from my spine and Mona quit clutching my arm, I began to think rationally that creating an aura of mystery, of terror, would be just what people would do who didn't want strangers about.

Still, the Jedediah Kimball comment was strange, and it stuck in my mind.

XX

No wonder we hadn't spotted the road. An enormous stand of sagebrush obscured it from the south, and the volcanoes were much more clearly in evidence from the north. We turned and started down a dusty rabbit track of a road, heading east, passing the first lava cone a mile off the highway and the second soon after.

We turned left at a fork in the road and motored down a slight incline. We were driving as slowly as we could, but we were stirring up a cloud of dust that could be seen, I was sure, as far as St. George. It was very dry out here, the vegetation mostly sage- and rabbitbrush. No signs of human habitation—not yet.

After four or five more miles we came to a shallow hollow with a stream and a little desert marsh at the bottom. The road was a narrow dugway cut into the side of the embankment. I was glad we had Mona's four-wheeler. The Chrysler wouldn't have made it. We stopped by the stream and got out to water up and brush off the dust.

This was an eerie place. Every insect in the territory seemed to have congregated here—flies of every possible description and sound, bees, dragonflies, mosquitoes. There were croaking frogs at our feet, but otherwise it was dead silence, as though the world had returned to the little creatures. Mona and I were aliens as had been the cow whose carcass lay in the water, mostly rotted and eaten by the maggots. We didn't linger long.

It was about noon when we arrived at the house. The Mormon pioneers tried everything. Here in the middle of a hostile, sandy desert stood a little two-story stone house surrounded by poplars and cottonwoods. The trees were parched and scraggly now, but obviously once tall and leafy. There was evidence that the front yard had once been a lawn and that the whole place had been surrounded by an orchard. Now the only crop appeared to be the rusted hulks of vintage cars. The old house, still stately in its wilderness setting, if dilapidated and in need of repairs, presided over an automobile graveyard.

A scruffy, underfed mongrel dog first sensed our presence and ran barking and snarling to the gate, yellow teeth bared. There was no other sign of life beyond a couple of mangy goats grazing—on what?—by the side of the house. Mona charmed the dog rather quickly, and I unlooped the wire from the cedar post and pushed aside the barbed wire fence enough so we could step through. We walked slowly up the rutted driveway toward the house and got about halfway when a shot rang out. We stopped in our tracks. The dog whimpered and skulked, tail between its legs, back to the house. I was hoping we weren't to be the next two found dead in the desert. I wasn't sure I'd like being found naked.

Nothing more happened. Probably nothing would have happened had we simply turned around and gone back the way we'd come. But I stepped forward another step. Another shot was fired, this time kicking up dust four feet to my right. Mona didn't move. I decided to try conversation.

"Hello!" I couldn't quite figure out what ought to come next, so I waited. No answering hello, but no answering gunshot, either.

"We're not here to harm you!" It was an inane remark, but what the hell do you say to an unseen gunman? Apparently it didn't convince him, for there was still no response. There was nothing to do but be direct, I thought.

"I'm looking for Aaron Kimball!" A third shot answered, this time a foot to my right. "I have a message from Aunt Mary!" Why not? It seemed to open doors in Covenant City.

There was no shot this time. I tentatively moved forward a couple of steps, signaling Mona to stay put. Nothing happened.

"Will you talk to me?" Still no shot. It seemed we were making some progress. Negotiations could begin any time.

Suddenly a large woman in a long, faded calico dress stepped out the front door. She may well have been the ugliest woman I had ever seen, with a huge pockmarked face and a big shapeless nose, framed by long scraggly hair. Her eyes were tiny black dots in her red face. She carried an equally ugly shotgun, which she was aiming at me. It was not the gun, however, that had been doing the shooting. I assumed that one was still primed and aimed at us from some hidden recess.

I repeated myself. "I want to talk with Aaron Kimball. Aunt Mary Smith sent me here. I mean you no harm."

Finally the woman spoke. "You don't look like someone Aunt Mary'd send here. You look city—you and that lady there."

"I am from the city. I'm down here trying to find someone. Aaron's brother Orson sent me to Aunt Mary. Said she'd tell me where Aaron was."

A hand slid out the door to the shoulder of the woman. The shotgun lowered and a man stepped out, carrying a rifle that was probably the one firing earlier. He was very large, especially his stomach, which was covered by a huge pair of overalls. A faded flannel long-sleeved shirt and well-worn work boots completed his outfit. His entire head was shaved clean, but from his ears down he wore a full beard. He and the woman together, with their guns, looked like a pair of crazy nesters from a Hollywood movie. The man stepped forward a couple of paces and started to speak.

"H-h-how do you know O-O-O-Orson?" The man had a terrible stammer.

"I talked to him in Salt Lake."

"Wh-wh-wh-why would he t-t-t-tell you wh-wh-wh-wh-where to find m-m-m-m-me?"

Conversation was not going to be easy. "Could we come in? We're both thirsty. Had a hard time finding you today."

There was a pause while the man thought it over. He seemed to think at about the same rate he spoke. "A-a-a-ll right. C-c-c-c-come on in." The man and the woman waited outside while we walked the rest of the way to the front door, then they followed us into the living room.

My first impression was the smell. The place stunk heavily of many old meals cooked in rancid grease, of human sweat, and of stale urine, as if there were overflowing chamberpots stowed in every room. My second impression was visual. There was clutter everywhere—clothes strewn about, boxes stacked randomly, and toys, cheap plastic toys, handmade wooden toys. There were a few old magazines scattered about, mostly *Reader's Digest,* and some books, a Bible, a very old *Book of Mormon,* and a couple of others that looked as if they came from some religious publishing house. I could hardly see the ragged and sagging old sofa for the litter, or the three-legged coffee table propped up by a tower of mismatched bricks. Three old random kitchen chairs provided extra seating. On the walls was faded wallpaper with a couple of awful magazine pictures of Jesus taped to the paper. The area was dominated by an enormous painted desert scene done on black velvet.

Then people started appearing in the room. A dozen children crept into view, ranging in age from barely old enough to walk to maybe fifteen, all dirty, poorly dressed—those who were dressed at all—and smelly. They were all hungry looking. And the women—besides the one who had first greeted us there were two others who stood together and looked to be twins. One was holding a baby. Then it occurred to me that one of the children—a girl maybe thirteen—was also holding a baby, to her breast. She was nursing it.

"S-s-s-s-s-set down," Aaron Kimball said, indicating two of the kitchen chairs for Mona and me. "S-s-s-s-s-Sarah. G-g-g-g-g-get these folks a d-d-d-drink." One of the twins, the one without the baby, left the room. As I sat, the man crossed to me, holding out his hand. "I-I-I-I-I-I-I'm Aaron K-K-imball."

"I'm Gabe Utley," I said shaking his hand. "This is Mona McKinley."

"P-p-p-pleased to m-m-meet you." He sat on the sofa. The rest of the women and children stood as they were, a very sad and crowded tableau. "Th-th-th-th-these here are m-m-m-m-my wives and children." At least four must have been his wives, including the thirteen-year-old, I thought. I also thought how remarkably quiet all the children had been when we first arrived, children schooled in fear probably, trained to be dead silent when ordered to. There was evidence of that now as they stood like statues staring at us. There were no sounds from them, only an occasional whimper from the babe in arms who could not have been more than three weeks old.

"Wh-wh-wh-why did you c-c-come?"

"I'm trying to find someone, a young girl. I have reason to believe she's with your brother Jedediah."

The man started to quiver—with a combination of rage and fear?—at the mention of his brother's name. I decided I should tell my story fast. Two-way conversation would be slow going with Aaron. "A friend of mine told me where I could find Orson, so I went to him."

"And h-h-h-h-h-he talked?"

"He certainly didn't want to," I said. "He only talked when he was sure I meant you no harm. He sent me to Aunt Mary, in Covenant City."

"Sh-sh-sh-she's been g-g-good to u-u-u-us."

"What I came to see you about, Aaron, is where I might find your brother."

"Wh-why would y-y-you think I-I-I-I-I'd know?"

"Orson said you ran with him every place . . . until a couple of years ago. He said you'd know where he might hide out."

"I-I-I-I-I-I don't i-i-im-im-im-imagine there's many p-p-places he could g-go I-I-I-I-I-I couldn't find h-h-h-h-h-him."

"Where do you think he might be now? Where would he go when every policeman in the state is after him?"

Aaron started to laugh. Sarah took that opportunity to bring Mona and me our drinks. I received a greasy brown plastic glass from her hand, drank half the contents very fast, and almost coughed it right back out. It was warm, sweet Kool-Aid. Mona didn't manage to suppress her cough, but lady that she was, she thanked Sarah and continued sipping.

Aaron had finished his laugh by now and had eased himself up to the edge of the sofa. He was warming to his subject. "J-J-J-J-Jed's at his b-best when the F-F-F-Feds are after him. A pack of bl-bl-bl-bloodhounds couldn't s-s-sniff him out."

Then a look of sadness drew down his face, like a slow curtain, as I suspected he was remembering he wasn't with Jed anymore, not evading the Feds himself. Rather, now he was evading Jed.

"But he couldn't fool you, huh?" I said.

"N-no. H-h-h-h-he couldn't fool m-m-me. I-I-I-I could find him."

"Will you tell me where I could find him?"

But Aaron had sunk back into the sofa, his head in his hands, obviously very upset. The big woman who had greeted us stepped forward. I was afraid we were going to be thrown out, though she had leaned the shotgun against the wall. "Aaron's goin' through hard times. Ain't been the same since he split with Jed. They was always close. Now he mopes all the time. Don't do nothin'."

"Is it true that Jedediah's after Aaron?" I asked the woman.

She squinted and looked hard at me, as if she didn't trust me. But I doubted she trusted anybody. "That's right," she answered after a minute. "Been after him for over three months."

"Why?" I said, noticing that Mona hadn't opened her mouth since we arrived. Her big reporter's eyes were alert, however. For an instant I felt very protective of these people, a little resentful that Mona was here, intruding into their lives. It was all right, however, for me to be here intruding into their lives—sure it was. I felt terrible for some reason. The woman, Aaron's number one wife, it seemed, obviously felt I'd overstepped my bounds in asking why.

"This is family. You ain't family."

"I'm sorry," I mumbled, feeling sorry. "It's none of my business."

"Well, just what is your business, mister?" the woman asked. "Just why'd you come out here bother'n us?"

I explained to her about Jennifer Peterson, about my belief that she was with Jedediah Kimball, and about my mission to retrieve her. The woman remained immobile, as did everyone in the room, I noticed. The kids were still standing like statues. The first to move was Aaron, who brushed back his bald head, wiped his eyes—he had been crying— and adjusted his big frame back up to the edge of the sofa.

"Y-y-you think J-J-J-J-J-J-Jed stole the g-girl away?"

I said that I thought it was a good possibility.

"B-b-b-b-b-b-bastard's got no right to all the w-w-w-w-w-w-w-w-women."

"I beg your pardon?" I said, as if I was in an English drawing room. Mona shot me a sly grin.

"You know wh-why we split up?"

"No, I don't."

"H-h-h-h-h-he took one of my w-w-w-wives . . . Th-the p-p-p-p-pretty one." She wouldn't have to be dazzling, I thought—and hated myself for thinking it—as I looked about the room. "I-I-I-I-I-I tried to k-k-k-kill him," Aaron concluded, his eyes ablaze with excitement and hatred.

Mona couldn't resist. "You tried to kill him?"

She shouldn't have done that. The big woman slapped her across the face, hard, and when she turned her head back around, she was bleeding from the lip.

"Shouldn't butt in," the big woman said. Mona tensed, ready to attack the woman, then thought better of it and leaned back in her chair, her fingers to her mouth, tasting the salty blood, feeling for damage. Women didn't talk out of turn in this household. Aaron went on.

"B-but I-I-I-I-I was dumb. Thought the w-w-w-w-woman would h-h-help. But sh-sh-sh-sh-she told h-h-h-h-him I was c-coming. H-h-h-h-he was ready."

"What did he do?" I asked a little dumbly, getting caught up in the family feud, feeling more than a little voyeuristic. I wished Aaron could tell the story faster. As if she had read my mind, the big woman, wife number one, carried on. Perhaps she too was impatient with her husband's stammer.

"Jed held a shotgun on Aaron. Said 'cause he was his brother he was gonna give him a few hours start. Said 'cause he figured maybe Aaron had a right to be a little mad, him takin' the pretty one and all, he'd give him a fightin' chance. So he fired a barrel into the sky and said he wouldn't fire the next one for three hours. But said Aaron better be gone 'cause the next barrel was for him. Didn't want no challenges to his leadership of the Church. Said if a man was gonna be a Prophet, he had to have claim to the women. Aaron had no right to keep a woman the Prophet wanted. And Jed wanted Allison."

Aaron Kimball was sitting on the edge of the sofa wringing his hands, his face red with frustration and rage. In a flash he was on his feet, grabbing anything he could get his hands on, throwing it at the wall, at bodies, at whatever or whoever happened to be in the way. The people in the crowded little room scattered like a covey of birds as the man of the house threw boxes, plastic dishes, and books around the room. I stood helplessly against the wall as Aaron, in his final act of destruction, picked up the chair I had been sitting on and began smashing it against the fireplace in steady rhythm into a flurry of splinters. By the time two of his wives wrestled him to the ground, the chair had been reduced to an eight-inch-long sliver that he continued to bash against the floor.

When Aaron quieted down, the first wife motioned for Sarah to leave and gave Mona a look that said, "Get out of the room or I'll clobber you again." To my surprise, Mona went. There were only the three of us left, all sitting on the floor. The woman turned to me.

"You've upset him real bad." I started to mumble an apology, but she went on. "Never mind. He's real upset by his brother. Afraid he'll show up any day and kill him."

"I don't really want to get mixed up in family business," I said, crouching beside the two big and sad Mormon Fundamentalists. "But I need to find Jed. It won't do Aaron any harm, and it might help bring Jed to justice."

I knew as I said it that it was the wrong thing to say. Aaron looked at me, calmer now, but with fire in his eyes. "Th-th-th-this is family. W-w-w-w-we work out our own p-p-problems. I-I-I-I-I don't want no p-p-police in on this. J-J-J-J-Jed don't deserve th-that." I sat amazed at the incredible loyalty, feeling again that I was messing about in emotional bondings that went deeper than I or anyone had a right to probe. But I had my job to do.

"Will you help me find Jed?"

"W-w-w-w-will you promise you won't turn him over to the p-p-police?"

I paused and looked at the filthy rug on the floor, thinking about my promise to Dale Olander, weighing which pledge I thought more important. Then I looked Aaron in the eye. "I promise," I said. "I won't turn him in. I only want to find the girl."

Aaron grinned at me. "Y-y-y-you b-better be careful. J-J-Jed don't like having p-people mess with his w-w-w-w-w-w-w-w-women." He was treating it as a joke, as if I was going to be in the same kind of little jam he was in.

I was afraid I already was.

Aaron's first wife hefted him gently and lovingly back up to the sofa. Sarah and her sister, the baby now deposited somewhere, rushed in to pick up the worst of the litter and the children began reappearing. They seemed unconcerned, as if this was a common occurrence. Probably it was. The young wife with the baby moved around behind the sofa, behind Aaron. The baby was still nursing. The mother had her thumb in her mouth. Mona stood leaning in the doorway to what I assumed was the kitchen. One of the children had her arms wrapped around her leg. Mona had a gentle hand on the child's head.

Aaron looked up at his wife. "M-m-m-mama. W-would you get some p-p-paper and a p-pencil?" Then he stood up. "Wh-wh-wh-why don't we go out b-b-back and I-I-I-I-I-I'll show you where I-I-I think J-J-J-J-J-Jed's holed up." I followed him back through the door into the kitchen, touching Mona's cheek as I walked by. She smiled wanly. The big woman followed after and went to a drawer and pulled out a stub of a pencil and a paper napkin that looked as if it had been used and folded up. Aaron sat at an old chrome and Formica table and drew me a map that led to a remote canyon in the wilderness of south central Utah. Then he turned over the napkin and drew another map, of another remote canyon. Two possibilities.

"Th-th-th-this is where J-J-Jed hangs out when h-he's in real t-t-trouble." I checked the napkin mentally against the detailed map I had been using and figured I knew how to proceed to both canyons, then I tucked the greasy paper in my shirt pocket and snapped shut the flap.

"Thanks, Aaron. I know this isn't easy." It was hard to find words that didn't sound phony.

In a gesture of mixed desperation and intimacy—I don't imagine he'd had much traffic with adult males in the past weeks—he grasped my hand over the table. "R-r-r-r-remember. I-I-I don't want you turning J-J-Jed over to the p-p-police."

"I won't, Aaron. I give my word. No police."

Then he leaned in closer to me, his eyes hot and moist. A long silent stammer preceded the words he eventually spoke. "Y-y-y-y-you can k-k-kill him if y-you like!" I had leave of two brothers to kill Jed. Involuntarily my hand moved away from Aaron's. Then his face lit up with a big grin, as if he'd played a joke on me. "Y-y-you don't have to, though. I-I-I-I'd really l-l-l-like to take care of that m-m-my-myself." And the grin got even wider.

The family was moving on into the kitchen now, filling up this little room. I figured it was time to go. I had what I came for. Mona was still holding the naked little girl in the doorway, but her attention was back in the living room. She started when I asked if she was ready to leave. She turned her head to me, and her eyes were red and teary as she nodded. I felt she was afraid to open her mouth for fear she'd cry. Her eyes returned immediately to where they'd been before. I walked into the living room, heading for the front door, curious as to what was affecting her so.

Standing in the middle of the room, clutching her child, was the young wife, her eyes glued to Mona, tears streaming down her face. I looked at her more closely. It was possible she was no more than twelve, her dress was torn and filthy, her hair matted and stringy, her bare feet covered with scabs. She had a big cold sore at the edge of her mouth.

Mona reached down and kissed the child at her feet and

followed along after me, smiling at the young mother as she crossed the room, smiling and weeping with her.

XXI

I had my hand on the door latch, ready to open it, when the first shot rang out.

All in an instant, the front window shattered and the young mother, a look of shock on her teary face, opened her arms and let the baby pitch in an arc to the floor. The side of her face exploded in a mass of hair and brains and blood.

Mona lunged for the baby, too late to prevent it from falling. I crouched and ran to the kitchen where, with military precision, Aaron's oldest wife was ushering the children down a ladder under a trapdoor into a dark cellar. Aaron was reaching for rifles and shotguns mounted on a crude wooden rack on the wall, handing them to his wives. A shot crashed through a window to the kitchen, and Sarah's sister grasped her chest. She slid to the linoleum, gasping against the cupboards. By this time the children had been dispatched to the cellar, the trap closed and a piece of linoleum placed over it, and the big woman was charging into the living room. She picked up her shotgun and crouched by the front door.

Aaron slipped under the window through which the second shot had come, while Sarah tended her sister. I pulled out my .38 and went back into the living room. Mona was trying to comfort the screaming baby whose mother lay dead on the floor. I crawled to the front window, trying to see what the hell was going on out there.

All was silent for the moment, a terrifying and eerie desert stillness. Mona had quieted the baby. All I could hear were the flies buzzing and the slight rustle of leaves on the trees through the now-open window.

Then the shooting started again. Not two isolated shots this time, but rather a barrage from every direction, round after round, shattering windows, zinging off stone, ripping wooden door frames and window jambs. I could hear Aaron or somebody firing back. Aaron's wife, flat on her stomach, was shooting through the screen door. I fired a couple of random rounds from my .38, but I couldn't see anybody out there.

Then came another minute of stillness, after which I heard the murmur of voices outside. There were some intermittent shouts, someone barking orders. I couldn't make out anything coherent beyond "Get over there" or "Come 'round here." Then came another brief lull, after which a clear and rugged voice pierced the bright early afternoon stillness.

"Aaron!" A pause. "Aaron Kimball!" Another pause. "You in there, Aaron!"

Aaron didn't respond.

"You answer me, Aaron! You answer me or I'll kill your whole family!"

I whispered in a hoarse tone across the room to Mrs. Kimball. "Is that Jed out there?"

She didn't take her eyes off the barrel of her shotgun but answered simply, "I reckon."

I looked over at Mona who was holding the child close, staring at the sprawling, lifeless figure of its mother. "You all right?"

She nodded, but she looked as though she dare not move much for fear she'd vomit.

The voice pierced the air again. "I got a dozen men with me, Aaron. You don't come out in one minute, we'll come in and kill everybody in the house. I'm going to start counting. Now, I ain't going past sixty. One. Two. Three . . ." And he kept on in a methodical, cruel way. ". . . Thirteen.

Fourteen . . ." On twenty-seven, Aaron came into the living room, rifle dangling at his side, a beaten look on his face. His woman stood up slowly and sadly, but with no effort to restrain him. There came a dreadful air of resignation in the room.

"You going out there, Aaron?" I asked simply.

"Reckon I have to. Got my family to think about." I noticed he didn't stutter once.

"Is it Jed?"

"Yup. Guess he found me. Didn't really figure he wouldn't. Pretty hard to hide from J-J-Jed."

". . . Fifty-one. Fifty-two. Fifty-three . . ."

"I-I-I-m comin' out, Jed! Hold yer h-horses!"

The counting stopped. Out the window I saw a big man in new Wrangler jeans and a red-and-black checked flannel shirt step out from behind the trunk of an enormous, old, gnarled cottonwood tree. He walked forward across the yard and stood, waiting for Aaron. Two men stepped into the open behind him, ten yards back. The man in the red-and-black shirt had a double-barreled shotgun in his hands.

Aaron knelt down and touched the lifeless head of his young wife, then walked to the door, giving the big woman, his first wife I was still surmising, a momentary glance. She remained impassive, stoical as a seasoned soldier. Then he walked out the door.

The two brothers stood twenty feet from each other in the front yard; Aaron hadn't even carried out his rifle. I noticed Jedediah's face for the first time. He was clearly the most striking of the brothers, probably six-feet-four, with a strong rugged face, not unhandsome. His hair was long, almost to his shoulders, and he had a week's growth of beard. His mouth was a firm, determined line, and he had the coldest blue eyes I had ever seen. I had trouble recognizing the sullen unkempt kid I knew and remembered from high school. I wondered if I had changed as much. It was Jed who spoke first.

"You got that reporter woman in there with you?"

"She ain't n-n-n-no p-p-part of this, Jed."

"Well, what's she doing here?"

"That how you f-f-found me?"

"Been following that pretty red wagon since Kanab. The lady asked questions in the wrong place."

"Y-y-y-y-you'd've found m-me anyways."

"Maybe. But I appreciate the favor." Then Jedediah Kimball raised his voice. "Hey lady! . . . lady! If you're in there. And I know you are. You listen to me. You been causing me and my people a lot of grief lately."

I looked over at Mona, who had set down the baby and was alert as a cat. Her eyes were big and she was trembling, less from fear, I felt, than from an anxious desire to spring out the door and interview the one and only Jedediah Kimball. He was not an easy man for a reporter to get to. Kimball went on.

"Don't care much for what you write. You're messing around in things that aren't none of your business." There was a strange quality to the way Jedediah Kimball put sentences together, as if he was trying to sound educated but wasn't. "Some of my people want to swear out a blood oath against you. I've been telling them it isn't worth the bother. I told them you could learn your lesson. Told them it wouldn't do any good killing a reporter. It would just go to prove what people already think about us. And one thing you can count on about us is that we mind our own business. We keep family matters in the family!"

Mona couldn't resist. She had to face her antagonist. She got up and walked to the front door, opened the screen, and stepped out onto the stoop of a porch. I noticed as I looked over that Sarah was standing sadly in the doorway to the kitchen, blood staining the entire front of her dress. It seemed that her sister needed no more attention.

"Well, I'll be damned. Here she is in her flesh and blood." Jed Kimball seemed surprised that the lady had the guts to face him. "You are brave for a woman. But then I kind of like that." The son of a bitch was flirting. I had a visceral sense that he really did think he had a proprietary right to every woman he took a fancy to. And I was a little stung with jealousy.

"Let me just give you a warning though, honey. I just might start listening to my followers if I read any more of those articles. I'd say it'd be real dangerous to print any-thing else." And a big grin broke across his face. "Besides, you're a real attractive woman and God's kingdom needs all of those it can get . . . If you was more inclined toward my beliefs, I think you'd be a real asset to the Kingdom." He paused and eyed Mona from head to foot. "We could use someone who can write good." And he grinned broadly again. The man was fascinating. There was an edge of self-mockery in his demeanor. He was toying with Mona.

Then all of a sudden his mood changed. It was as though a dark cloud had suddenly rolled in. He moved back a step, raised his shotgun, and said, "Now get back in the house, lady. What's gonna happen ain't none of your business. If you stay, I'd just as soon kill you as make love to you. So get on inside!"

I was crouched beside the window, helpless with anger and frustration, itching to shoot the man dead. But I hadn't any idea how many there were out there. From the shooting it sounded like a whole division. And I hadn't any doubt that if I shot Jed, everybody in the house—women, chil-dren, Mona, and I—would all be dead within fifteen min-utes. In spite of that awareness, I felt like a classic coward, realizing I could do nothing but hope Mona would have the good sense to do as she was told. She did. There was a limit to her journalistic bravado. She walked back into the house.

Next Jed Kimball turned his attention to my window. "You in there. You with the little toy gun. You, the lady's boy friend. You want to live, you want all these other folks to live, you'll do as I say."

I didn't say anything.

"Here's what you do," he continued. "First, throw out the .38." He paused and I obeyed him. "Now go around the house and gather all the weapons you can find. Bring them out the front door and take them over to Brother Heber there . . . Heber's the man in the green shirt."

I resisted one final impulse to kill him and save the world a lot of further trouble, then did as I was told. I gathered up the guns, took them out the door, and set them at the feet of Brother Heber, a big glowering lug of a young man—a boy, really—with short hair and dumb eyes.

"Now, come on over here. I want to look at you," Kimball ordered. I walked over and stood five feet from him, making a little triangle with Aaron.

"What's your business here?"

It was an impersonal question. He hadn't recognized me. I debated whether to tell him my business or not, and decided against it. Jed Kimball obviously took his women very seriously. He wouldn't like that I was planning to steal one of his wives.

"I'm with the lady," I said.

"You wasn't with the lady till yesterday."

"No, I met her in Kanab. We had a date."

"Why were you in Kanab?"

"Looking up an old friend. Seeing the sights. It's been years since I've been in southern Utah."

He didn't believe me, but he seemed satisfied for the present. "I got a hunch I ought to kill you. But I guess I got no reason, except maybe the company you keep. Just you be careful. I don't want to see you poking around in our business anymore. I can't imagine my brother here and their family are the sort of people you pay social calls on."

I didn't respond; all I did was look over Aaron's way. He wasn't saying anything. He, of course, could have exploded my story, gotten me killed on the spot. But he was silent. He just stood there, apparently drained of will or emotion.

"Now get back in the house with your lady. She's probably missing you . . . maybe she's missing you." He looked me up and down. "Can't imagine, though, why she'd be missing you. You're kind of a sorry son of a bitch." He threw his big head back and laughed. I turned and walked to the door, feeling stung to the depths of my manhood. I sure as hell wasn't prepared to play in Jedediah Kimball's masculine arena.

Mona's face was impassive as I went in. She appeared unimpressed by the display of macho oneupmanship just displayed outside. I was grateful for that. It worried me that I was caught up in it, reduced by it. I returned to my window, wondering what Jed Kimball would do now. Would the two brothers reconcile? Call off their little feud? I hadn't long to wait for my answer.

Jedediah Kimball hoisted his shotgun back to its original position, looked hard into his brother Aaron's eyes, and blew him halfway across the yard. The sound of the gunshot was deafening. For a few seconds Jed stood there, looking as hard as a granite statue, staring at his brother twitching and dying on the ground. Then he turned and walked away, back toward the road. One of his companions followed along, making sure he took the guns with him, including my .38. Four other men emerged from around the side of the house. Heber backed away, with a rifle aimed in our direction. None of us moved until the seven men in whatever vehicle they had arrived in were a heavy cloud of dust a hundred yards down the road.

My immediate impulse was to chase after them, though the gesture seemed more and more futile the closer I got to Mona's Toyota. I needn't have worried about a choice. When I arrived at the four-wheeler, I saw that our visitors had slashed all four tires, and under the open hood, the distributor cap had been stolen away. We weren't going to drive this vehicle out of here, not now.

I walked deliberately back to the stone house, afraid of

the scene that waited. Aaron Kimball's first wife was kneeling over his body, keening like an Irish peasant woman. Inside, Sarah was covering the body of the young wife, shooing away flies. The sister in the kitchen had already been covered with a soiled tablecloth. The children were evidently still down in the cellar. Mona stood slumped against the living room wall, holding the baby that had begun whimpering again.

"They're gone," I said weakly.

Mona didn't respond. She simply hugged the baby closer to her breast.

"They took care of your car, slashed the tires. It'll have to be towed."

Mona nodded that she understood and pressed her cheek against the baby's.

"Doesn't look like there's a car that'll run on the entire place." This was a hard conversation to carry on. "I'll ask the woman."

"Gabe." Mona talked through the tears streaming down her face. "Gabe."

"Yeah."

"They found this place because of me."

"You heard Aaron, didn't you? He knew Jed would find him."

"But why did it have to be me?"

"I guess that's a risk we take, messing about in other people's lives, Mona." I didn't feel much conviction.

I went outside and asked if there were any working cars. There weren't. I also asked Aaron's wife her name. Adrene Snow Kimball. I thanked Adrene, went and got Mona, who handed the baby to Sarah, and moved toward the gate. Mona and I started walking down the dusty road, silent and buried in our own particular broodings.

The man at the service station agreed to drive us to St. George, for an outrageous fee. We were too tired to argue. But he refused to touch the wounded Toyota. "Won't go in there, not for nothin'. Maybe some garage in Saint George'll come up and get it. Folks that don't know no better."

We checked in at a motel, showered, dusted off our clothes, and headed down to the restaurant. I picked up a *Deseret News* on the way in. I saw it on the bottom of the first page: PROMINENT MORMON OFFICIAL DIES OF HEART ATTACK.

It was David Peterson.

XXII

I was on Linda Peterson's doorstep by ten o'clock the next morning. I don't know what I expected—maybe for her to come to the door in a ragged dressing gown, with a half-empty gin bottle dangling from her hand—but I was surprised. She was well groomed and well dressed, alert as a tiger, with no liquor on her breath. She hugged me hard as soon as she opened the door.

"I'm so glad to see you, Gabe."

"I came as soon as I saw the paper. I was in Saint George."

She asked me in. There were a lot of people milling around, family I assumed, with appropriately sad faces. Linda took me by the hand and led me through the people to David's study and closed the door. When we were alone, she embraced me again and kissed me on the mouth. It was a confident kiss.

"Please sit down. Let me get you something." Without allowing me to answer, she went out and came back shortly with a Lowenbrau in her hand. "Thought you might like this. I stocked it in for my brother. Guess I ought to be honoring David today, not doing such things, but I've got to begin sorting out what's important to me and what's not important."

She sat down beside me on the couch. "I didn't know how to reach you, Gabe. I was afraid you'd never come back."

"I've been down south, tracing leads," I said. "I think I'm close. At least I think I know where I can find Jed Kimball."

But Linda had other things on her mind right now, especially David's death. "You saw the story in the *Deseret News?*"

"Yes."

"Did it seem peculiar to you?"

"How do you mean?" I asked.

"Do you believe David died of a heart attack? Just like that?" Her eyes were searching my face for a reaction. She had a stubborn set to her jaw.

"He'd had a hell of a time these past few days, Linda. Such things can kill a man."

"But he'd gotten over the worst of it, Gabe. I know he had."

"Did he finally tell you what was bothering him?"

"Not exactly," she said. "He couldn't bring himself to do that. But he had made some kind of a resolution to see out whatever it was, to confront the problem directly."

"This all sounds very iffy, Linda. I can understand your not wanting to believe David would bring a heart attack on himself . . ." I paused. "Or that he would really go through with killing himself."

"It's a conversation we had at breakfast," she said, ignoring me, "before he went into the office yesterday. The day before he was blaming himself for getting into whatever mess he was in. David was always like that; he had a lot of guilt in him. I suppose that's why he wanted so desperately to succeed, to assuage the guilt. But at breakfast that morning he was different. I saw something in him I'd never seen before."

"A man with high blood pressure, perhaps?"

"No, Gabe, no. There was a determination in his face.

Before he left he said he wasn't going to sit still and take it. That he was going to do something about it."

"Whatever *it* was," I said, skeptically.

"I do know it had something to do with Amos Jensen."

"David's problem?"

Linda looked at me as if I'd asked an important question. It sounded stupid to me, but something was churning behind her eyes. She got up and paced the room for a minute, then came back and sat down by me. She was very serious.

"Gabe."

"Yeah?"

"David and I weren't happy."

"I figured that out. I remember what you were like happy."

"He'd hardly spoken to me for close to two years. I guess I hadn't connected that to what happened these past few days."

"And you're connecting it now?"

"I'd thought there might be another woman. David was so guilty around me, didn't look me in the eye for days at a time."

"But you don't think that now?"

"I don't know. But somehow it doesn't square with David. I couldn't believe he could live with himself if he committed adultery." Why did the word sound archaic?

"And it wouldn't do much for his advancement in the Church," I said.

"Amos Jensen called and told me yesterday," Linda said.

"You find that surprising?"

"I guess not. It's just the way he did it. His voice was strained, like he was taking it hard. Yet I didn't believe he cared, somehow." She shook her head as if she was trying to shake something loose. "Oh God! Forgive me, Gabe. I'm sure I'm just being stupid, feeling I failed David some way. I mean, we all get ourselves into psychological messes—

traps we can't get out of. And David had so few resources."
She gave me a sly smile. "And he wasn't a drinker." The
smile faded, but she kept looking.

"Will you hold me a minute, Gabe?"

I did. She clung hard. Then she leaned up and kissed me
with a closed-mouth adolescent's kiss that took me back
twenty years. She pulled away, still staring at me as if I was
all she had in the world. Jesus.

"Gabe." Her mind was working again, though her eyes
never left me. "Gabe. I want you to do something for me."

"Besides find your daughter?"

"Yes. Besides finding Jennifer . . . I want you to find out
how David died, why he had to die."

I breathed hard, looked in those eyes again. "You've already given me one task. I haven't finished that one yet."

"But you said you were close."

"Well, I didn't exactly mean simple and close. More like
damn dangerous, time consuming, and close. I'm going to
have to crawl around in the desert for a while, probably a
long while."

"Dangerous?"

"Yeah. I'm feeling a little like I've wandered into a Hollywood western. The problem is, John Wayne is the villain."

Linda looked at me. Puzzled. "It's still the same, isn't it?"

"What?"

"I never know when you're joking. I can never tell when
you mean what you say."

I looked back at her. "If you look right into my eyes,
you'll see an opaque screen pulled down between what I see
and how I feel about what I see. I saw a man and two
women shot down in cold blood yesterday. Shot down by
the man your daughter may be keeping house with. It's
going to take a long time for the image of those dead bodies
to settle to the bottom of my brain."

"Oh, Gabe. How awful."

"Jed Kimball's one mean son of a bitch, and if I make one

more move toward him I'll be right at the top of his list. But I'll get to him," I said, hoping a verbal commitment would make it easier.

"Maybe you won't have to go back," Linda said, with what seemed like real concern.

"How's that?"

"Don't you think maybe David's death will bring her home? I mean, the funeral and all."

"I wouldn't count on it, Linda. You wouldn't either if you'd seen Jed Kimball's eyes. I don't think he'll buy her a bus ticket north. He keeps his women very close."

"Are you thinking now she might have been kidnapped, Gabe?"

"I don't know, Linda. I just don't know. About the only thing I do know is that I seem to be stirring up an insane beehive."

"There is something else you know, Gabe."

"What's that?"

And she looked at me with those damn eyes. "That you're going to ask around about David's death." She took my sweaty hand. "You will do this for me, won't you?"

And here I was, suckered again. I was working very hard to think of Mona's marvelous eyes, to remember that Linda was, after all, a recent widow. It helped when I thought that maybe I owed this to David, sort of. After all, I'd been half in love with his wife for twenty years.

"How should I start?" I said, heaving a sigh. "Do you have anything concrete? Did David leave anything you know he thought was important?" I was thinking of those papers David was wearing out when I first visited him.

"He kept anything he really cared about in his briefcase."

"Do you have it?"

"No, I don't," she said, as if a light had just gone on. "It must be at his office."

"Is that where he died?"

"That's where Elder Jensen told me he died," she said, with more than an edge of cynicism.

"You're not giving that mellow-toned old prince anything on this are you?"

"Not until I find out what happened."

"Fair enough." There was a very tough lady emerging from the ashes of David's death. "I'll stop by David's office and pick up his briefcase." She went and got me the key to his office without my asking. "Why don't you go through his things here. I'll give you a call."

I phoned Mona and told her I'd be late for our luncheon, then went out and bought another .38—very easy out here in the West. Then I stopped by the rental agency to tell them where they could find their Chrysler and went to another agency and picked up a Jeep. From there I drove to the Church Office Building to retrieve David's briefcase.

I was sad somehow, as I walked up the hall to David Peterson's office, that his little dream had been snuffed out. But maybe it wasn't too late, not for someone with a strong sense of an afterlife. I guess my idea of heaven is that everybody will get exactly what they want. Of course, that's also my idea of hell.

It was lunch hour, and David's secretary was not at her accustomed post. It looked as if it was going to be easy. But things are never easy, are they? When I had let myself in, I saw immediately that I was not the first to feel the impulse to go through David's things. There, sitting in David's chair, busily thumbing through a stack of files, sat a distinguished white-haired man in a gray pin-stripe suit, with a pair of black-rimmed reading glasses perched on his nose. It was none other than Amos D. Jensen. Even up close he looked fifty.

He blinked up at me as he sensed my presence. It was not a benevolent blink. His hands swiftly closed the file he had open, as if he'd just taken it off the stove. There was an edge of desperation in his face as he turned toward me—at least, that's what I thought. His expression quickly changed into one of imperial annoyance.

"What are you doing in here?" he asked, like a king who'd just been caught on the chamberpot.

"Linda Peterson asked me to stop by and pick up David's briefcase."

"Really," he said, peering over his glasses, obviously finding it difficult to believe that Linda would send someone who looked like me to perform an intimate task for her. "Well, suppose you tell me first just who you are?"

"Utley. Gabe Utley. I'm an old friend of David's. Went to school with him and Linda." I had hardly begun speaking when Amos Jensen's eyes narrowed and he brought his hands together, joining the tips of his fingers just under his chin. A tight little smile, almost a smirk, creased his mouth.

"Gabe Utley." He chewed on my name as if it were a plump grape. "Gabriel Utley." I didn't like the way he repeated it. "I know the name. Been hearing about you."

"Favorable things, I hope."

"Not entirely, Mr. Utley—or shall I call you Brother Utley? It is Brother Utley, isn't it?"

"I guess it used to be," I said.

"You're far too modest, really you are, Brother Utley." I sure as hell felt uncomfortable about the way he kept repeating that. "You're still on the books, Brother Utley. I checked it out the other day."

"You did? I'm flattered." I wasn't really flattered. I was just nervous.

"Not at all. We like to keep track of our own." He was enjoying himself. Somehow I'd brightened up his day. "Even the wayward ones. Even the wayward Saints are precious to us."

Jesus, I wished he'd get off this. "I didn't come here to discuss the state of my membership in the Mormon Church," I said.

"Suppose you sit down, Brother Utley." I didn't want to, but I did. "Now let me get this straight. Linda sent you here to pick up her deceased husband's briefcase—the briefcase in which he kept all his important Church papers."

"That's right."

"You will forgive me for being a little unbelieving, Brother Utley. But you come barging into David Peterson's office with a key you might have stolen, for all I know, and ask me to hand over his briefcase. Gracious, that's a lot to swallow. What's even harder to swallow is the fact that you're a licensed private investigator who seems to have nothing but mischief in mind, and a certifiable heretic who hasn't had a kind word for the Mormon Church in over twenty years. My, but you're a naïve lad if you believe I'll give you anything but the end of my boot."

My stubborn streak was setting itself firmly in place. I leaned in toward Amos Jensen. "A woman has a right to her husband's things. I'm here to get them. You're welcome to call her."

Not one to be out-leaned, Amos Jensen leaned over the desk toward me. "David's Church affairs are none of his wife's business, Brother Utley. If you know anything at all—and it seems you've been able to pick up a few off-bits of information in the past couple of days—you know that I or one of the other Brethren was closer to David than he was to his wife. She's been mentally ill for years and she's been an alcoholic for a good deal longer than that." His face was not kind as he said this, not compassionate. "Now there's nothing I want more in this world than for Linda to be happy and for David's reputation to be preserved. I want his good name to be buried with him. And that's what you'll care about if you're really his friend."

I didn't like what Jensen was saying. I didn't like it at all. The old bastard was subtle in his threats. "Why should it even occur to me to worry about David's posthumous reputation? Why should Linda worry? All I want to do is pick up his briefcase, for God's sake." I was gettling a little exercised.

"I'm not going to let you have his briefcase, Utley." He'd shifted to the impersonal. I was grateful for that. "I'm not going to let you have his papers because I don't want Church business blabbed to the newspapers by a New York cynic."

"I'm not a reporter," I said, feeling very much on the losing side of this whole conversation.

"You've been having illicit sexual relations with a newspaper reporter, Brother Utley, and I would be irresponsible turning you loose with sensitive information that could damage the reputation of one of our finest young General Authorities. Now suppose you just walk out that door, buy Linda Peterson and that cheap whore you keep time with each a bottle of liquor, and go away and wallow in your decadence. You have no business here."

"Finding out about David Peterson's death is my business," I said very grimly, proud of myself that I didn't smash his handsome old face into David's expensive pen set.

Amos D. Jensen leaned over the desk again. "All right, Mr. Private Eye, Brother Gabriel Utley, friend of the Petersons. You want to know how David died? I'll tell you." He moved even closer, his minty seventy-year-old breath mingling with mine. He looked as though he was going to enjoy telling me what he was going to tell me. "Here's how he died. David Peterson died while he was huffing and puffing on top of a cheap whore in some sleazy fleabag hotel down on Second South Street. That's how he died. Now isn't that a hell of a way to go?" And he leaned back in his chair. The smirk still hadn't left his face. "Now, are you going to tell Linda that?"

I sat in silent disbelief—disbelief in the story, yes, but equal disbelief that Amos Jensen would have the balls to tell it. "You expect me to believe that?" I said incredulously.

He shrugged. "Makes no difference to me whether you

believe it or not. I gave up a long time ago trying to account for people's perversions, Brother Utley. Evil takes a lot of ugly forms."

"You and I both knew David Peterson pretty well, Elder Jensen. Now I can't imagine you thought David was the brightest guy you ever met. Yet you seemed to find him able enough to be useful to you. You did advance his career; Linda said you did. He wasn't a complete idiot. You also know that David cared about his reputation a lot. He had nervous fits about that. You can't make me believe he'd ever taken a cup of coffee in public . . . And now you're trying to tell me that this man, who wanted to be a Mormon Apostle more than anything in the world, would hustle on down to Second South in the sleaziest part of town and pick up a two-bit hooker in the middle of the morning. You sure as hell must be more of a kidder than you let on."

My analysis of the situation did not amuse Amos D. Jensen. "Mr. Utley, I didn't invite this conversation and I don't intend to carry it on any further." He stood up and spoke to someone who was now standing behind me. "Brother Lewis, I have finished with Mr. Utley. Will you escort him out of the building, please."

I turned and saw an old acquaintance, the man with the crewcut from Pipe Springs, framed in the doorway. He was nicely turned out today in a blue polyester suit. He was not smiling.

"Before you leave, Brother Utley, I will say this," Jensen said. "You must understand, and I'm sure you do, that David was not himself lately. He'd had some rude shocks. I'm sure his future looked pretty bleak to him . . . Maybe he just gave up." Jensen was even gentle as he said this, as if he'd been fond of David. I still wasn't buying it.

"Maybe he did," I said. "But you've laid out a hell of a farfetched story."

"There are witnesses, Mr. Utley, reliable witnesses."

I was angry enough to try one last thing on the tall, handsome, and pompous Mormon Apostle. "I can't believe you're not a shade worried that David is smart enough to come back from the grave and haunt you."

Amos Jensen said nothing to me in response. His composure and his authoritative eyes intact, he turned to his man, "Brother Lewis. You see this man here?"

Brother Lewis nodded that he did.

"Well, Brother Lewis, you may have noticed that this man walked into this building, came up the stairs, and barged right in on me without any apparent problem whatever. Now what do you make of that, Brother Lewis?"

Brother Lewis turned a very deep shade of crimson, did a shuffle with his feet, and mumbled something like, "I'm sorry, sir—Elder Jensen—it won't happen again."

"Now kindly escort him out of here. I don't want to see him again. Understood?"

Brother Lewis clearly understood, and he gripped my arm with his big knotty hand. All his frustration and hate seemed to have gone to his hand, and I thought for a second that he would snap my arm. But he wasn't set to do me physical violence now, not right here. That, I was sure, was for later.

On my way out of the building, I was surprised to see the gray-haired man in the blue pin-stripe suit walk rather confidently into the Church Office Building. He had on a gray flannel shirt this time. He didn't seem to notice my unceremonious exit down the front steps. Who the hell was he? I knew I'd better find out, for Jerry's sake, if for no other reason. But this was obviously not the time. I'd need a large foreign army to get back into that building just now.

#

Mona wasn't at her desk in the *Deseret News* city room, but Howard Peterson was sitting disconsolately at his, nibbling absently on a sandwich.

"Hi, Howard," I said as I slid into a chair next to him. "Sorry about David."

"Hello, Gabe. Thanks." He took a sip of Fresca. "Have you seen Linda?"

"Yeah. Seems to be holding up okay," I said. I felt a kind of intimacy with Howard at this moment. But then maybe I was creating it because I wanted some information . . . Was I really that calculating a son of a bitch?

"I think she'll be all right," Howard said. "She's tough. She'll be better off than David would've been . . . alone I mean."

"I suppose so," I said. He nibbled some more, drank some more soda. "Howard."

"Yeah?"

"What's the story you get on how David died?"

"Heart attack."

"Do you know where it happened?"

"In his office. At least that's the official story."

"Is there an unofficial story?" I asked.

"The church people have been rather vague. It's clear what we're told to print. But from what I hear, he was out on some sort of assignment and was found by a couple of Church security people."

"You have any idea where? Or what assignment?"

"Well, he'd told me the day before—I stopped up to visit him and Linda—that Elder Jensen was sending him out to Magna the next morning."

"Magna?" I said, a little startled. "Why Magna? What could possibly be out there that would interest either David or Amos Jensen?" For some reason I had a sick feeling in the pit of my stomach, but I dismissed my worry. After all, there had to be lots of things in Magna besides Orson Kimball's trailer.

"I'm sure I don't know," Howard said. "Seemed peculiar to me. But David's always been close to the vest about Church business."

I thanked Howard for the information and asked if he knew where Mona was. He said she'd gone down to the police station.

"Did you catch the broadcast Sunday?"

I felt about four inches tall. "I'm sorry, Howard. But I was out in the desert in southern Utah. Didn't have a radio."

He was glum, not about my not hearing the broadcast, but about his brother, I thought. And I couldn't blame him. It all smelled bad.

Mona was in heavy conversation with Dale Olander when I walked into his office and sat down as if I belonged there. Olander stared at me as if I'd lost my mind, as if nobody had better do that. "Got something you want, Utley?"

"Well, I've got something of a date with the lady here, and I'd like to talk to you."

"You're interrupting a private conversation, if you'd like to know. I'll see if I can fit you in sometime this afternoon."

"How about if we all go to a nice restaurant for lunch? There's a great place down in Sugarhouse—got an even bigger clown than the one over here." I don't know what was getting into me. Information overload, perhaps. But Dale Olander was not amused, and neither was Mona.

"Jesus, Gabe," she said. "What do you think you're doing? Dale and I were talking. I told you I'd see you later." She was addressing me as if I was a naughty three-year-old. In a way, I suppose I was. Probably I was a little jealous of Dale, short as he was.

Dale stood up, with a threatening look on his face. "Utley, if you don't get out of here, I'll throw you out. I'm tired of your insolence."

I stood up. Dale was better off sitting while doing battle with me. Of course, he did have the whole police department behind him. "Dale, I'm very tired. I had a long drive, and I've found out some pretty awful things about a friend of mine and I'd like you to help me."

"Goddamn it, you come storming in here like a street bully, invade my territory, insult me, and then expect me to help you out. You're a real asshole, Utley, you know that? You know that? My God, you're an asshole."

Mona was smiling. I sat back down, letting Dale have the advantage of height. I shot up an apologetic smile at him, as if he'd sort of won. And he had, sort of. "You're pretty when you're mad, Dale. And I bet you feel a lot better now. Right?"

Dale blustered a little, huffed and puffed, then sat back down. He opened his drawer, drew out a pack of gum, opened it, shoved two sticks in his mouth, and chewed them. "Goddamn! Goddamn, but you set me off, Utley."

"But I'm not really a bad guy, right?"

One corner of his mouth turned up. It was part of a smile. He did feel better. "Goddamn." But the steam had gone out of his cursing. "Now just what particular information might I offer you Mister Private Detective?" He spoke each syllable with distinct enunciation, halfway between sarcasm and patronization.

"Well, suppose we start with David Peterson," I said.

Olander's face clouded.

"The David Peterson who supposedly died of a heart attack yesterday morning."

"What do you mean, 'supposedly'?" he said, warily.

"I mean that I've been getting all kinds of contradictory messages about how he died. I thought maybe the police would set me straight."

"As far as I know he died of a heart attack, Utley."

"Do you know where?"

"In his office at Forty-seven East South Temple."

"Did any of your men investigate?" I asked.

"We don't make it a policy to investigate heart attacks. The Mormon security people could handle anything that needed to be handled. A doctor there in attendance filed the report."

"Have you asked for an autopsy?" I said.

"Now why the hell would we ask for an autopsy? You don't perform autopsies routinely on heart attack victims."

"Even if there's some reason to question the means of death?"

"Listen, Utley. I have no reason to doubt that David Peterson died of a heart attack. I have no evidence—not even any suggestion—otherwise. Now let's leave it at that, all right?"

"I understand he was taken to the L.D.S. Hospital," I said. "Any chance they'd have done an examination?"

"Damn it, but you're persistent. I can't imagine any reason why they'd think three thoughts about questioning the cause of death. The statement was released by a doctor from the hospital. I have no reason to doubt his report, or his colleagues'." Dale was breathing hard again. "Now I don't intend to say anything more about this. Understood, Utley?"

"Understood, Lieutenant." And I saluted and stood up. "Now, I'm serious. How about you two joining me for lunch? I'm paying." Dale was up and ready to go in an instant. He probably knew I wouldn't take him to the fast-food place with the mechanical clown. He was no fool, I was becoming surer.

Mona was silent all through our late lunch at a very good little place on South Main. She'd been mostly silent since Rattlesnake Valley. I left her to her isolated melancholy throughout lunch. I noticed she ate very little of the salad she ordered. Come to think of it, I didn't eat anything either.

Over dessert—cheesecake for him, coffee for me—Dale Olander startled me out of a brooding silence. "You were with Mona when Aaron Kimball was killed?"

I spilled my coffee into my lap. Olander smiled. He knew he had surprised me on that one. "How do you know that?" I said.

"Mona and I get on well because we help each other. Not like you, Utley, tight as an owl's ass about what you know."

"I help all I can, Dale."

"Sure you do, sure you do. And I'm the patron saint of stool pigeons." Dale was starting to loosen up with me. I was afraid I was beginning to like him. "You and Mona were both there, huh? Even before the Saint George police arrived."

"If Mona says we were, I guess we were, Dale." I was not pleased with Mona at this moment. Yet I couldn't exactly slug her, not with her curled up in the corner of the booth, close to tears.

"Is there going to be a full investigation?" I asked.

"Not if the Saint George police have anything to do with it." He paused. "Possibly not if I have anything to do with it. I've been getting some pressure today."

"Can I guess from where?" I said.

"You can guess, I suppose."

"Will you blink twice if I'm close?"

Olander smiled and shook his head. But he knew I knew.

XXIV

When I looked over at Mona again, I knew it was time to go. I paid the tab and walked with her to the Jeep.

"You don't look good," I said.

"I don't feel good."

"I'd better take you home. You all through at the paper?"

"Yeah. Filed my story this morning."

We were driving toward the Avenues when it occurred to me. "I don't even know where you live."

"You're heading there," Mona said.

"I know. But, I mean, I've never been there. Why should that seem funny?"

"I don't know," she said. "Maybe it's because we've been everywhere else."

Mona lived in the back part of an old house on one of the middle avenues, not far from the city center. The place looked small and solid and nondescript from the street where I parked the Jeep. But as we went around back and climbed a flight of wooden stairs, I saw that she had a lovely apartment. We entered through a terrace, full of plants and wicker porch furniture, that commanded a nice view of the city and the mountains. The inside was little more than an efficiency unit, but it was tastefully decorated in wood, heavy woven fabrics, and an exquisite braided rug that brought images of Aunt Mary's room to my mind. As soon as we entered, Mona plopped down on a big feathery couch and put her feet up.

"Gabe."

"Yeah."

"Would you get me a glass of wine and a couple of Tylenol."

I did and grabbed myself a beer as I did so. In fact, I grabbed two beers and sat in a chair across a coffee table from her. We sat silently, each staring at our own particular spot on the rug. My spot kept turning into Jed Kimball's eyes. It was going to take more alcohol than was available to either of us. I was on my fourth beer when Mona finally spoke.

"It won't go away."

"I know."

"It was so coldblooded."

"You won't buy that it was just family business?"

"She was just a child. Hardly out of a training bra."

"It's a bitch," I said, "messing about in people's lives."

Mona went on, "I was so goddamned idealistic when I

started out. I was going to show this society to itself, show the Mormons what they were really like."

"Now you're worried that you've failed?" I said.

"No. Not that . . . Maybe more worried that I've succeeded too well. And that it's a kind of arrogance to presume you know what people ought to know about themselves. When you do that, you can open up ugly things in their lives."

"That's bad?"

"What's bad is when people get hurt."

"Like Aaron Kimball."

"And like Aaron Kimball's family. What are they going to do?"

"You think they'll be a hell of a lot worse off? You can't believe that, Mona. You looked around that place. And it wasn't only poverty, it was fear, the constant terror at every sound. At least they won't have that anymore."

She finished her third glass. I poured her a fourth. "I guess you're right. At least about that. But it'll be a long time before that picture leaves me . . . the picture of that girl . . ."

"I know. But that's the risk you take, messing about in people's lives. Me too. I mess about in people's lives, and my motives are hardly noble. I don't think I ever was idealistic."

"Why do you do it?"

"I don't know. It's a way to make a living."

She smiled at me, and I thought I saw a sparkle come back to her eyes—a good sign. "A way of making a living, my ass. I saw your face when you looked at Jed Kimball. You know you really see yourself as a crusader."

I laughed. "Sure. I want to bring cowardice back in vogue. Fuck heroics. Let a few innocent people get hurt, watch three or four people die in a day. All for a cause, to make the world safe for us chickens."

"It really bothered you that Jed got the better of you out in the bullring, didn't it?"

Why didn't this goddamned woman go back to being depressed? Maybe I kind of liked her tucked safely away in the corner. "Yeah, I stood there trying to deal with the almost inescapable fact that he has a bigger cock than I do."

That silenced her, except for three minutes of hysterical laughter. I was succeeding beautifully in cheering her up.

"Maybe I can go on a crusade for substandard pricks. A minority whose time has come . . . You can write the book."

She was laughing so hard she spilled her wine all over the couch. I wiped it up and poured her another glass. Maybe I could get her too drunk to talk. But when she stopped laughing, she was still going on about crusaders. "If you're not some kind of perverse crusader, why do you do it? I mean, there are a lot of ways you could make a better living."

"Like what?" I said, realizing I was handing her the rope with which to hang me. She was not gentle with my masculine sensibilities.

"Such as . . ." She dragged it out. She was getting drunk. "Such as a juggler. Such as a truck driver—plenty of your kind of music there. Such as the Prophet of a new religion. I mean there are all sorts of possibilities." She was giggling so hard she couldn't light her cigarette.

Finally, I couldn't help myself, and I was laughing right along with her, feeling freer than my higher instincts told me I ought to feel.

"Know what my ambition was when I was a kid?" I said.

"No, what? Tell me. I think the key is right here. The key to your whole personality. The real reason you do what you do. The primal model."

"That's a heck of a buildup," I said.

"Well, come on. Don't keep me waiting."

"All right, you asked for it . . . A rodeo clown. I wanted to be a rodeo clown."

There wasn't much she could say to that. She didn't try. She just kept giggling. She had two cigarettes lit now, one in each hand. I laughed with her. But then she faked me out. She put out one of her Benson and Hedges and stopped laughing, all in an instant. And she got very serious and stared right into my eyes. "Why do you think you wanted to be a rodeo clown?"

"Why?" I racked my brain. I had hoped this would all disintegrate into hysterical irrelevant merriment—to cheer Mona up—and maybe, I admit, some tittery sex. All the signs had pointed that way. I tried to laugh again, but she was dead serious. I would have to give a fucking answer.

"Well, let me try to figure it out." I paused, musing over possible ripostes. Then I settled in and told her why: "They travel a lot. And they help cowboys. And they get to hide behind makeup and funny clothes. And they always have enormous angry bulls coming at them. And—and here's the capper—they get to curl up and hide in barrels."

Mona leaned across the coffee table and kissed me. "And they also get laughed at a lot, don't they?" Then she fluffed up a sofa pillow, lay down on the couch, and immediately went to sleep.

Now what the hell was that all about? But I didn't dwell on it. I simply sat drinking Mona's beer, smoking her cigarettes, and watching her sleep. I liked to watch her sleep.

But I hadn't very long to enjoy myself. The phone wrenched Mona out of her sound and well-deserved rest. I was very angry right then at whoever it was. But I couldn't stay mad long. It was Jerry Romero.

"Gabe," Mona said, holding the phone close to her. "Jerry's trying to reach you. Are you here?"

"Afraid I am. So much for that barrel." And I took the phone.

"How are you, Jerry?"

"Ambulatory, old friend. Not quite bouncing on a trampoline, but ambulatory. Bastards knew what they were doing."

"I'm sorry, Jerry. I didn't realize how rough these jokers play."

"Well, as you know, I never was great in close. I was best at running—I always could run like a gazelle. You were always so beautiful you could just stand and wilt them."

"Sure. That was me. That isn't even a good bullshit line. Are you up and out enough to see your truly beloved?"

"Ahhhhhhh, Gabe. Ahhhh, Gabie. I'm up, but I'm not lovely enough. Not yet. But you know what?"

"No, what."

"She came 'round. She actually came 'round. Came 'round bringing goodies."

"Flowers for the sickroom?" I said.

"Yes. How'd you guess. Flowers for the sickroom. Flowers for the nose. I've been sniffing for two straight days. Dear old Mom never serviced me like that . . . 'Course, Mom would never let me fuck her either. Come to think of it, neither will Gail. The world's a terrible place, Gabe. Full of horrible monsters, dragons . . ."

"And clowns, Jerry. Clowns all over the place."

"That sounds like a hell of a lot better vision of the world than mine."

"You choose your fantasies," I said. "Can't always choose your women."

"My God. I'll write that down! Gail will like that. I'll win her by poetry. She has to be sure I can't win her by force. Not yet. Not at the present. But I've taken heart."

"You have?"

"Yes, I have. I now have you. Loyal and a little in debt to me."

"In debt to you I am, Jerry. Check some dead men for loyal."

And Jerry's tone turned suddenly serious. "That's kind of what I called about, Gabe. You remember Orson Kimball?"

A wave of nausea surged through me. I was afraid I knew what was coming. All of a sudden there weren't other things in Magna. "I could hardly forget Orson Kimball," I said. "Why? Is something wrong?"

"Some of Jack's friends called a half hour ago. Some friends who kind of watch out for Orson. He didn't show up where he was supposed to be last night. Very unusual. They got worried, went to his trailer. He wouldn't answer there either."

"He couldn't just be away for a couple of days?" I asked.

"Afraid not. Orson has his paths, well-worn paths. Never deviates. They think something's wrong."

"All right," I said. "I'll go on out to Magna, check things out."

"Jack would appreciate it, Gabe. Orson's friends would like that."

"Jerry."

"Yeah?"

"I'm sorry I got you mixed up in this, you and your friends."

"What are friends for, asshole? You've been my best friend over twenty years. What the hell's it all about if you don't help your friends?" He paused a few seconds. "Gabe. Do you mind taking me with you?"

"You sure?"

"Yeah. I sort of feel implicated. You don't mind?"

"God, no. It's a ride I don't want to take alone."

I picked up Jerry fifteen minutes later and we were on our way west, toward the fifteen-hundred-foot smelter stack out in Magna. It was built that high to give some vegetation on the mountain nearby a fighting chance. Power companies are all environmental good will. It was twilight when we pulled into the Shady Pines Trailer Court. Why weren't there any pine trees? The place looked much worse in the daylight.

I knocked on the door to the trailer, but there was no response. I tried the door. It was locked. Ragged kids were making noise all around the court. There was no sound around the Kimball trailer. I looked at Jerry. "Guess we better break in?"

"I guess if you want to get in and you have no key, that's what you do. Unless you want to call the police." Jerry grinned at me.

"Yeah, that's what we ought to do. Well, here goes . . ."

I picked the lock with a nail file and a credit card. When I opened the door, the room did not smell good.

Orson Kimball was stretched out on his back. There was blood everywhere—pooled on the floor, spattering the walls, all over his clothes—more blood than I'd have thought possible. There was evidence of some horrible struggle. Orson's magazines, his pathetic little collection of erotica, had been hurled all around the trailer, not just the careless strewing about I had seen before but a willful and frantic act of destruction. Topping it all off, a particularly revolting full-color publication called *Young Hard Cock* was plastered onto the front of Orson's bib overalls, secured in place by a butcher knife that had been driven with great force through the magazine and into the dead man's chest. I noticed last that Orson Kimball's throat had been cut from ear to ear.

Jerry went to the sink and vomited. I stood brushing flies away, feeling sick at heart. If Mona felt bad about Aaron, I felt worse about Orson. I was stumbling about in this unknown territory, exposing a lot of innocent folks to some uncontrollable demon. You want to find someone, Demon? Just wait a few minutes and old Gabe will lead you right there. I was sorry I'd ever come out here. It was clear I ought to get back to home ground where I knew what the fuck I was doing.

"I guess we'd better call the police," I said.

"Jesus, Gabe. Who could have done this?" I don't think I'd ever seen Jerry so upset. If anyone exuded a sense that he'd seen it all, it was Jerry. Yet he was white with fear and nausea.

"I wish I knew, Jerry . . . Someone awfully sick—and scared."

"You think it was Jed Kimball?" Jerry said.

"Maybe."

Dale Olander and his men took statements from Jerry and me. He didn't even ask what the hell I was doing out here. Mona had arrived, much recovered, sniffing around, asking questions, bright as a squirrel under an acorn tree. I was the one who was brooding this time.

Jerry and Mona and I were about to finish up and leave when I saw the inconspicuous figure of Arvin Smith IV sidle around the edges of the scene and go up to Dale Olander. I left Mona and Jerry and walked over where Dale and Arvin were talking.

"Hi, Arvin."

"Hello, Gabe. Seems you do find your way around."

Dale held off the ambulance men from taking the body while Arvin went into the trailer. He spent about five minutes looking around. I didn't know whether he found anything.

"A terrible business," he said as he came outside again, brushing past the men with the stretcher. "Damned loony."

I lit a cigarette. I was feeling a little queasy. "Want to get a drink somewhere?" I asked Arvin.

"Why not? I wouldn't mind sitting down. It's not pretty in there."

I walked over to where Mona was scribbling in her notebook, with Jerry standing beside her looking green. "I'm going off to get a drink with Arvin," I said. "Could you catch a ride with Mona, Jerry?"

Mona answered for Jerry, who looked close to throwing up again. "Don't worry Gabe. I came with Dale. Jerry can ride back in with us."

"Thanks," I said.

I offered my good-byes to the lieutenant, who told me to stay in touch and not to go anywhere without telling him. I almost told him he was making me feel needed. I was actually becoming fond of the officious bastard.

The streets of Magna after dark matched my mood perfectly. It was a dirty, dilapidated town, with a smell of coal dust in the air, the other side of the world from the antiseptic white building where I'd chatted with Arvin Smith before.

"Where do you want to go?" Arvin asked.

"There's a little bar over there," I said, pointing to a place called Ray's on the other side of the street. "Or would you prefer a soda fountain?"

Arvin laughed. "You're the boss tonight. Besides, I don't imagine I'd know many folks out here."

"Well, if you wouldn't mind . . . I could use something to drink just now."

We parked and walked across the street to Ray's, which was tucked in between an abandoned shoe shop and a dry goods store that looked like it would soon be abandoned. Ray's had a neon Coors sign in the center of a dirty window. The rest of the window was covered with very old stained-glass contact paper. Inside, an ancient Brunswick pool table lay empty under a plastic Olympia beer lampshade. There was a shuffleboard bowling machine to our right, very old and still only a dime to play. Back farther was the bar, with an assortment of old men who looked to be retired miners and smelter workers. A retirement bar? Could be worse fates, I thought. No one acknowledged our presence. Arvin and I both appreciated that.

We slipped into a dark back booth and I ordered a beer. Arvin ordered a Coke.

"Any idea who took care of Orson Kimball, Arvin?"

"Nope," he said, as he popped in a jellybean.

"Not even any guesses?"

"Nope." Arvin didn't feel talkative. Now he was the brooder. He seemed troubled, so I changed the subject.

"I met Amos D. Jensen today," I said.

"I know."

"Not much you don't know."

"Not about things like that." He sipped his Coke. "He wasn't charmed by you."

"Why should he be? I don't pay my tithing."

"I imagine that's part of it," he said. "The other part is that he's scared of you."

"I doubt he has much to be scared of. I'm a very mild guy. A little catholic for him, perhaps."

"And a little nosy," Arvin said.

"I was just inquiring about an old friend."

"David Peterson," Arvin said, chewing on a piece of ice.

"Yeah. He seemed awfully interested in David's files this morning. That's where I met him."

"Oh? That I didn't know."

"What do you mean you didn't know. One of your goons was there. Or don't they tell you everything."

I thought Arvin looked a little taken aback. I was sure it wasn't something he experienced very often, being taken aback. "What do you mean, one of my goons?"

"Big guy, a lot of stomach. Crewcut. Looks like he enjoys intimidating old ladies."

"Abe Lewis," he said.

"Yeah, Lewis. That's what Jensen called him. I met the same guy in northern Arizona, he and those others in a big black Lincoln. They were tailing me, remember?"

Arvin Smith grinned his crooked grin at me. He seemed to have recovered. "Those weren't my goons, Utley. My goons tail you and you won't know it." He was back on safe ground, the gray eye dominating the brown one.

"Well, who the hell's goons are they?"

He simply shrugged, as if he didn't have a clue.

"And another thing," I said, getting more exercised than I ought to be. "There's another guy I keep seeing places. I just saw him this afternoon going into the Church Office Building."

Arvin looked puzzled. "What guy? What does he look like?"

"Hard sucker to miss," I said. "Six feet six with wavy gray hair, and he seems to be glued inside a blue pin-striped suit."

Arvin's eyes narrowed. Something registered. For a moment he was upset, then he replanted his bureaucratic glaze and changed the subject.

"Find out anything down south?" he asked.

I knew there was no point of pursuing the other matter. "Found out it's awfully sandy."

"And a little dangerous?" he smiled, popping in a red jellybean.

"Maybe."

"You find who you're looking for?"

"Not yet."

"Not even any leads?"

Why were the tables turned? Why was I answering the questions? I couldn't seem to control anything—some investigator.

"I'll let you know when I tie it up," I said.

"You do that. And soon, I hope. You sure are thrashing the water everywhere you go."

"There's a lot of water out there to be thrashed."

I finished off my second beer. Arvin was only midway through his first Coke. "Can't help it if you people solve your problems out here by killing each other."

Arvin was not amused. "You people? That covers a great deal of ground, Utley." He was getting agitated again, as if he'd lost the reins, and I think he was out of jellybeans. Maybe that was the problem.

Someone stuck in a nickel—yes a nickel jukebox—and played "The Wild Side of Life," by Waylon and Jessie. I felt better.

"What about David Peterson?" I said, continuing where I'd left off some time ago.

"What *about* David Peterson?" I was fascinated that Arvin spent more time chewing the ice than drinking the Coke. Won't that break your teeth?

"He didn't die of a heart attack," I said, going on the offensive.

"He didn't?" He sucked another cube into his mouth. "I only know what I read in the papers."

"Like hell you only know what you read in the papers, descendant of Porter Rockwell that you are. Try this . . ." I was gulping my third 3.2 Coors. "Howard Peterson stopped by his brother's the night before last. I guess he was worried about him. He had good reason to be worried. Seems if someone else hadn't gotten to him first, he would have killed himself pretty soon . . . Anyway, Howard said David told him Amos Jensen was sending him out to Magna the next morning. That would be yesterday morning. The morning he died."

"David hasn't been in control of himself for several days. Want to believe the ravings of a madman?"

"I'm having a hell of a time sorting out who's mad from who isn't mad out here."

Arvin smiled his I'm-in-control smile at me. "There are a lot of things to see and do out here in Magna."

"That's just what I tried to tell myself earlier today when I talked to Howard."

"Spend a weekend here and you'll find out. I'll get you a room at the Red Dog Hotel down the street. Under ten bucks. And nickel jukeboxes to boot."

"You're not going to talk about David Peterson," I said.

"There's nothing to talk about, Utley . . . David Peterson's dead. His reputation is intact. His fans still love him. And his wife will be able to marry some nice doctor and live happily ever after, secure in her husband's honor and integrity." He looked sharply at me. "Now why not just leave it at that. I wouldn't think you'd want any more bodies on your conscience."

There was nothing more to be said. He was a stone wall. I got up and paid the bartender and we walked out into the cloudy night. "Mind giving me a ride back to my Jeep?"

"Not at all. Wouldn't even mind giving you a ride to the airport and buying you a ticket to New York City. On Uncle. But I don't suppose you'd do that."

"Nope. Don't suppose I would."

XXVI

I drove slowly back into the city, trying to figure out just how Orson Kimball's murder fit in with everything else. I couldn't at first imagine Jed, hunted as he was, coming to Salt Lake and risking being seen to kill his other brother. But then the next minute I could imagine it very well. Maybe I wouldn't be able to if I hadn't seen his eyes. Mainly, on the drive back I just felt terrible, as if Arvin was right, as if I was whipping up too many waves. Too many trusting people were getting drowned.

But it was fruitless right now to dwell on it. I stopped at a liquor store in the center of town and bought two bottles of very nice wine and a fifth of George Dickel whiskey, then set off back up the hill to Mona's apartment—my barrel for the night.

I tried to think nothing of it when I saw the plain blue police car out front. You can tell by the EX license plates. I took my liquid offerings in hand and climbed the steps to

Mona's terrace. The blinds were drawn. Forging ahead, I refused to believe my sensors. A mature, sophisticated lady surely would not prefer a short, humorless cop to me. And, my God, hadn't I led her to four murders in two days? I was a reporter's dream.

But I was hardly convinced as I knocked—twice, feeling really dumb that I just didn't leave quietly. But surely she wouldn't . . .

Mona in a dressing gown peered out through a gap in the door. "Yes?"

"Mona?"

"Gabe!"

"I brought goodies," I said, as I held the wine bottles aloft like trophies.

"You can't come in, Gabe."

There was a long pause on my part. Now I was the complete clown. Finally I blurted out something like, "Okay . . . I'll call you tomorrow."

"That's fine. I'll be at work early. Maybe we can do lunch."

"I'll leave the wine," I said, a little petulantly, my wounded pride oozing all over the terrace.

"Sorry, Gabe."

"No problem. I've got my work." And I set the wine down by the sliding door, negotiated the steps, ambled nonchalantly out to my car, drove downtown, and checked into the Holiday Inn.

I had an awful hangover the next morning when I phoned Linda Peterson a little after eleven. She had found something in David's safe and wanted to talk. We agreed to meet for lunch at the top of the Hilton, which was just across the street from the Holiday Inn. Dressed appropriately in black, she looked gorgeous when I met her in a lobby. But the perfume wasn't funereal, nor was her smile. She gave me a little affectionate peck on the cheek.

Linda had fresh shrimp and oysters and a thick clam chowder. I had three large glasses of grapefruit juice and five cups of coffee.

"You found something?" I said.

"Mostly it was just stocks and legal papers and three or four hundred dollars cash. But there was also this." And she pulled a manila envelope from her purse and handed it to me. It had Linda's name on the front, and it was marked Personal, underlined.

I undid the clasp—Linda had already cut through the strapping tape that had sealed it—reached in, and pulled out a small sheet of David's personalized notepaper that had a cryptic message written in tight, agitated longhand:

Linda, I'm leaving this with you in case anything happens to me. As you can tell, in the wrong hands it could be explosive. You're all I have left. I'm sorry. David.

"This is all?" I said. "There had to be something else in the envelope."

"I know. I went all through the safe and everywhere David might have kept anything important. This is all I found."

"Did you cut through the tape?" I asked.

"No. It was that way when I found it."

"Would anyone else know how to get into the safe?"

"Not that I know of . . . except . . ."

"Except?"

"Except maybe Jennifer."

I didn't call Mona before I left for southern Utah. I suppose I wanted to be complete in my misery. My humor was not improved by the big black Lincoln that was practically tailgating me. I felt as though I were leading a parade south in search of Jedediah Kimball.

It was four in the afternoon before I felt like breakfast. I stopped at a little hamburger stand in Gunnison, Utah, and ordered a fish sandwich and onion rings. An enormous Pepsi-Cola helped wash what was left of my hangover away in a flood of sugar and bubbles. Brother Lewis and his dour band ate bag lunches on up the road. They stuck close by. They were not about to lose me this time. I would definitely have to try a different strategy. I was sure they wouldn't fall for any Willie Nelson van swap nonsense. But I had a couple of thoughts about that and decided, for the present, to ignore them.

Not many people were stirring when I arrived in Kanab, well after dark. I checked in at a shabby little local motel. I had a cash flow problem. Linda didn't have any money just now, and I had been doling out too many $20 bribes. My followers stayed at a less shabby Best Western across the street. They would not, I was sure, all sleep at once. But they seemed more interested in where I would lead them than in breaking my neck, so after a fresh trout dinner at Perry's, I went to bed and slept very well until 5:00 A.M.

I decided first to check the more convenient of Aaron Kimball's two desert addresses for his brother—an old Mormon settlement, now abandoned, that was tucked away up one of the canyons east of Kanab. It was called Lucifer's Bend. According to Aaron, this was where most of the Jed Kimball commune made their home. There was some possibility that Jed would be there. This place was reachable by vehicle. The second place, the one Aaron was surer of, was trickier. I would have to think about horses or a very long hike. In neither case did I want Amos D. Jensen's thugs trundling along after me.

I had picked up what I needed for the journey in a sporting goods store in Richfield the day before. Brother Lewis had looked at guns while I had made my purchases. If he'd had half the brains he really needed for his job, he'd have been over by me, buying camping gear. Guns will only serve if you can keep up with your antagonist.

The black Lincoln was a quarter of a mile back as I drove out of Kanab into the rising sun. It stayed close when I turned left onto a dirt road and proceeded up a canyon. It was still in sight when I turned right onto a Jeep trail about seven miles up the canyon. Then it must have dawned on the goons that while they had a big heavy Lincoln with a low center and highway tires, I had a four-wheel drive vehicle with big rugged tires, and there was no way they were going to follow far.

They lasted until the first stream crossing, where I left them spinning wheels and puffing and grunting, trying to push the car out of a foot of red Utah mud. Even with a proper vehicle, they would never follow me through the crisscrossing ranch trails in this rough country. They were taken care of, I felt, for the time being. Amos Jensen needed to hire some better guys. Of course, maybe they were good for what he most needed them.

A few more stream crossings and a couple of impossible rabbit tracks later, I stopped and ate my on-the-trail lunch, mainly beef jerky. At first it felt good to be alone. The goons were hopelessly behind. I was my own man. Here I was in the middle of the southern Utah desert, alone, armed with a little toy gun, encouraging ideas in myself that I could track down a homicidal desert rat and steal one of his women. I chewed harder on my jerky and took out a picture Linda had given me of Jennifer in a prom dress. And I reminded myself that it was the girl, not the homicidal maniac, who I was after. It was her image I must keep firm. Of course, the only way to find her was to find him.

And there were other little matters that stung me on. I had made a couple of shabbily kept promises to two of Jed's brothers. I had naïvely told them I wouldn't create any problems, that I would just quietly and gracefully waltz my way to Jennifer Peterson, leaving everything and everyone else untouched. So far the dance had been a singularly graceless stomp, with dead bodies in its wake.

And one more thing stung me, deeper than I would like to believe—Jed had roiled my lurking macho demons, somehow engaged me in the great primal struggle for the women. I had something to redeem. When you get past a certain age it's probably best to stop playing with adolescents—of either sex. I didn't like the part of me that was going in after Jed as if I were heading onto the football field—to impress the cheerleaders.

But I assured myself once again that I was surely an adult and climbed back into the Jeep and chugged forward.

After several miles of uninhabited plateau country, I began my descent down a precipitous dugway into another canyon. I could see that this wasn't going to be easy, even for my Jeep. A shallow stream, in this country called a river, snaked its way from side to side between the high sandstone cliffs that enclosed the canyon. I drove fast through the stream, watching out for quicksand, and stopped frequently to remove boulders from the trail. Yard by yard, I made it down the stream toward the old Mormon settlement.

About mid-afternoon, the canyon started to widen and I knew I was close. I parked the Jeep on solid ground and began to walk on in. After about half a mile, I came upon a cluster of buildings set on a little bluff between the stream and the cliff. Most were small pioneer cabins wrought from red sandstone. There were probably about fifteen of them. But while it seemed at first sight that the whole complex was long abandoned, little signs revealed that temporary patchwork had been undertaken. I could see a few wooden roofs made from new lumber, Celotex siding patching up a building here and there, even a little shack put together out of tin roofing material. Lucifer's Bend wasn't much, but it could house a few dozen people.

I approached the first building in the hot afternoon sun. Everything was still. I went inside, and found rough bunk beds built three high against two walls. The little building would sleep six. There were a few plastic dishes stored in an old fruit crate set in the corner. But there was no sign of any current inhabitants.

As I approached a second, larger structure, I noticed a Ford Bronco parked down the hill by the stream, obscured by a clump of willows. Somebody must be around. Instinctively I pulled out my .38.

Whoever it was, was not in the two-room house I entered next. There were only a few lizards and a lot of flies. People had left this place hurriedly and quite recently, within a couple of days. There was still food on the table, some beef jerky and an open can of pork and beans. There was even some reading material set on a shelf above a big old brass double bed in the second room. Besides the standard Mormon books—*Book of Mormon, Doctrine and Covenants*—were some badly printed tracts. They had been written by Jedediah Kimball. At least I was in the right place, if apparently a little late. Maybe not a little late. I thought I heard voices.

I edged down the hill toward the Bronco. I'd find out who it belonged to. Just as I touched the door handle, with my .38 still out, a man in a white shirt stepped out from behind the tin shed and barked an order. He was holding a .44 automatic.

"Just hold it right there!"

Since the sun was in my eyes, it took me a second to see the man clearly. I breathed a little easier—at first. It was Dale Olander.

"Utley?"

"That's right. You want to point that thing somewhere else, Dale?"

"You just out camping?" Dale asked, obviously not pleased I was there.

"Same as you," I said. "Heard about this little spot from a travel agent. He promised it wasn't crowded. Seems he was wrong."

Dale let down the barrel, deciding I didn't need killing.

"You've got a bad agent, Utley. You don't get sound advice."

"Apparently it's cheap advice," I said. "I thought he was a bit more exclusive about who he talked to."

Then a feminine voice from just up the hill helped clarify the situation. "Hello, Gabe."

It was Mona.

"Hello, Mona," I said, without looking at her.

"Welcome to Kimballville," she said.

"Looks like we're all a little late. Maybe they weren't prepared for tourists."

"You're just bitchy because we got here before you did."

"I confess I did think I'd escaped most of the perils of the city. No such luck, I guess." Damned if I'd make it easy for her.

"You're not pretty when you pout, Gabe."

"It's the old clothes," I said. "They turn everything gray."

Dale felt the need to break in here. "Aw, c'mon, Gabe. Seems we're all in this together."

"I'm not much for groups, Dale, I will confess that." Dale was appropriately stung and Mona was getting angry.

"What were we to do, Gabe, sit and wait for your call? Other people care about getting this Kimball mess cleared up. You may see yourself as the Lone Ranger, but others of us have been working on this a hell of a long time. And we care. I care. I'd rather have my nightmares down here doing something than sitting drinking in my room."

"How did you find out about this place, Mona? Pick my pocket?"

"That's a shitty thing to say, Gabe."

I knew instantly it was a shitty thing to say.

"I've got half a brain, Gabe Utley, in spite of what you think. You wouldn't tell me a damn thing. So I put it all together myself."

"Including this place?"

"Yes, including this place. This is my story, you know.

And I do know some things all on my own, without picking your pocket. I have my sources, sources it's taken me a lot of years to build up. Jed was seen in Kanab yesterday buying a case of Baby Ruth bars. Sounds like your teenybopper has a sweet tooth."

"So you bring down an army and scare the whole lot of them away," I said.

"I guess we're just not as tough as you, Gabe."

"Or as stupid."

Mona glared at me. "Now he's going to sulk, Dale."

I talked to Dale. "Isn't this a little out of your jurisdiction, pal?"

"Just along for the ride, Utley. Kind of a vacation, helping out the lady with her story."

"Is she going to share her Pulitzer with you, or are you just getting used?"

With that I accomplished what I thought I wanted. I had made Mona furious. She stabbed back. "Don't talk to me about using people. We can compare track records on that one."

Enough had been said, and Dale broke us apart. We all declared a truce, settled into a little camp beside the stream, and pooled our resources for dinner. "We" were Dale, Mona, me, and a big plainclothes policeman who had had a rifle trained on me from across the stream during my entire visit. They had better food than I did, steaks and fresh corn and Idaho potatoes. I recognized the two bottles of wine in the cooler.

I became satisfied early in the conversation that they didn't know about Jed Kimball's other hideout. And I didn't tell them. During the meal, I tried to forget how hurt I'd been by Mona. I refused to drink the wine.

Finally, having had enough of the silent treatment, Mona grabbed me by the hand and led me up the hill. Jack and Jill. Dale and his buddy stayed calmly by the fire, roasting marshmallows.

Mona and I sat on a rock with a good view of the canyon, including the settlement, the river, the Bronco, and a marvelous moon just creeping up over the edge of the steep sandstone cliff. She refused to let go of my hand. She drank her wine from a Styrofoam cup. I drank my water from a tin cup.

"You're not really angry with me are you?" Mona said, matter-of-factly.

I couldn't answer properly, so I didn't say anything.

Mona waited long enough to get a little peeved, then tried again. "You're acting like you're seventeen."

I felt seventeen.

"You have to understand that I've carried this story with me for two years, Gabe. It's been a nasty monkey on my back. When I don't have nightmares I have real live telephone threats. And since what happened at Aaron Kimball's, it's been stabbing at the inside of my head. I can't conjure an image without Jed Kimball superimposing himself over it."

"You knew I'd promised Aaron I wouldn't go to the police," I said.

"*I* didn't promise Aaron anything."

"No, I guess you didn't."

"Jesus, Gabe, Jed Kimball is a bloodthirsty killer. We both watched him shoot a man—his own brother—in cold blood, without a hesitation. You can't tell me you think a man like that should go loose. I mean, think of the girl, the girl with the baby . . . I sure as hell have been."

I still didn't say much. I'd ceased to be troubled by the fact they were here. Right now, I was more troubled by something else. Mona knew what it was.

"What you really don't like, Gabe, is that I went to Dale, isn't it?"

I smiled an aw-shucks-it-isn't-really-that-bad smile and said, "Maybe. I guess I just got the signals crossed."

"How long you been here, Gabe, in Utah?" Mona said.

I tried to tot it up and found it difficult. It seemed like a year. But I knew Mona's point. "Not much more than a week, you mean, right?"

"Right. Now what do you expect? To rush in, sweep a virgin maiden off her feet, put her in her proper place, and live happily ever after, summoning her for favors of various kinds whenever you feel like it? Well, I've been through the virgin maiden bit."

"That wasn't exactly my image of it all," I said.

"No, I suppose it wasn't. And I guess I don't really believe it was. But I've struggled hard, Gabe, out here in this macho society. Sometimes I feel at the mercy of every chauvinistic right-wing patriarchal male in the state of Utah. I get tired of it. I guess I just don't want it from you. Dale's been good to me. He's been there when I've needed him."

"What do you want from me?" I said.

She took a long time answering this. She drank some more wine, threw some more stones. "I don't know." Another sip of wine—she killed the cup this time. "Maybe the point is that if you have to ask, there is no point in my telling you."

"That an invitation to stay away?" I said.

Mona smiled and started chewing on her cup. She answered, mocking me, "No, it's not an invitation to stay away." She took out a cigarette, lit it, and took a deep drag. "Not unless you want it to be."

"Dale won't mind?"

"There you go again."

"It doesn't seem to be a stupid question, ultimately," I said.

"Maybe not ultimately. But Dale hasn't any idea of running my life. He gives me the space I need. He doesn't make demands. I like that . . . Besides, he's got a wife."

"Okay," I said. "No more about Dale."

Mona brought my captive fingers to her lips. "And you will stop by?"

I took the cigarette from her and took a drag myself. But I didn't say anything.

XXVII

The next morning I lingered in Lucifer's Bend for a couple of hours after Dale and Mona rode back up the canyon. There was not much of interest. It seems Jed Kimball and his people were used to moving around and taking everything important with them. I did read through a couple of tracts to try to get some sense of how the man's mind worked.

The first was a rather standard call to repentance—the-world-is-deep-in-sin-and-Jesus-is-coming-soon-and-you'd-better-watch-out sort of thing. I found the other pamphlet, titled "The Lord's Anointed," more interesting and revealing. In it Jed staked his claim as Joseph Smith's successor. He traced his line of authority through the Mormon Priesthood back to Smith and Smith's claim to have been ordained by Peter, James, and John, Christ's original apostles. He argued that the official Mormon Church had abdicated its claim to authority by giving up The Principle—I assumed he referred to the Law of Celestial Marriage, polygamy. But the claim of ordination was only half the story for Jedediah Kimball. He described a vision from Joseph Smith charging him with the mission to unite all of the Fundamentalist sects into one powerful unit that would challenge the authority of the new "Whore of Babylon," the official Mormon Church.

Jed's sense of prophethood didn't make me feel any easier about tracking him down in his den. But I had come this far and I had my own particular demons chasing me.

I inched my way back up Lucifer's canyon, up the narrow dugway, and onto the plateau. I found my way, with the help of a geological survey map, to the little town of Cannonville and made it by early afternoon to Escalante. I ordered a late breakfast of eggs, bacon, hash browns, and coffee at what looked to be the only restaurant in town, and sat pondering yet again what I was about to do.

My Jeep wasn't going to help me much on this journey. I'd need a good horse and a great deal of desert savvy just to get where I was going. The Escalante wilderness has been known to eat people alive, but I had been there before. In fact, I had spent three weeks there in my late teens, living off the land, with no horse, no food, no water; just a piece of rope, a hunting knife, some flint and steel and whatever survival wits I could muster. It turned out to be a moment of truth for me. I had found out a couple of things about myself. I realized I could accomplish about anything I set my mind to, and I knew that whatever I set my mind to I would prefer to do alone. I had definite misanthropic tendencies. I guess it took my wife fifteen years to find that out. So, on one level, I was looking forward to descending into the wilderness. I'm at home in the desert. On the other level, I knew there were scorpions down there, particularly one human scorpion. I hoped my desert lizard instincts were a match for his.

I finished breakfast feeling even kind of charged by the challenge ahead, paid my bill, and asked the waitress who I might see about renting a horse. She directed me to a ranch just north of town.

"You sure you want to go down in that territory alone?" the burly rancher asked, with a twinkle in his eye. I had hoped the old Utah farmboy would come through more forcefully than the New York street hiker. Apparently it hadn't. "That's awful dangerous country out there, the Escalante wilderness. Don't know if I'd feel real good about your taking one of my prize horses out there without someone to guide you."

The rancher was a tall, sun-browned Escalante native

who'd worn cowboy boots and Levis when John Wayne was still doing B Westerns in satin suits. He obviously loved the country and loved to put on outsiders.

"Afraid I need to go down there alone," I said.

He grinned broadly, tilted back his Stetson, and answered, "Well, son, outside of snakes, scorpions, horseflies, lizards, cougars, and wolves, I don't suppose you'd need to worry. Not in the daytime. It's night I'd worry about."

"Night?" I said, hoping if I played along, he might give me a big, strong safe horse that knew the territory.

"Yeah, night. That's when it gets real bad down there. There's animals nobody ever seen comes out at night." And he got in close, making sure I didn't miss this. "And there's stories . . ."

"Stories?"

"Yup, stories. Stories about night creatures. My people—going way back—tell that's where the spirits of the wicked go when they die. They kinda congregate down there . . . Lots of folks go in and they never come out."

I was indeed worried that I might go in and never come out. I didn't tell him why. I didn't tell him either that I'd gotten my survival merit badge as a boy scout in that maze of rock and sand and water and crawling creatures.

It ended up that he was satisfied that he'd scared me sufficiently and that I was satisfied I had a good horse. He began to get suspicious that I'd seen horses other than in Central Park when I inspected three potential mounts. I seemed to know what I was doing. I was a little surprised myself. It had been a long time.

I chose a big sorrel mare who looked to be about four years old and sturdy enough to take several days in the wilderness, where ample feed might be a problem. I also rented a small horse trailer and a hook-on hitch for my Jeep from the rancher. I even dickered him down considerably from his original price. If those New York boys don't know shit about wilderness, they do know how to get a good price.

I thanked him, gave myself a week, and was off back down to the grocery store in Escalante to stock up on freeze-dried food.

When I turned onto the bumpy dirt road that led south into one of the last real wilderness areas in the United States, Amos Jensen's boys were gone. I felt very alone. Mona and Dale were on their way back to Salt Lake City. I was on my own now, tracking down a man who would probably shoot me on sight. I was on my way to try to take away one of his women—a pretty young one he'd hardly had time to enjoy.

The Escalante wilderness is still wilderness because human beings, even in this age of environment-changing technology, would have a hard time making it yield to their nefarious purposes. It is a vast maze of tortured slickrock surface cut through every which way by deep sandstone canyons. There is a pattern, however, to the labyrinth, and it's a pattern determined by the flow of water. The thousands of canyons and crevices have all been carved by water finding its way to the Escalante River, which finds its own way to the Colorado River, now bunched up in a stagnant pool at the mouth of the main Escalante canyon. The only way into the canyon wilderness is to follow the water tracks, and there was no way a motorized vehicle could get where I was going in search of Jed Kimball.

I turned off the main bumpy dirt road, originally made by intrepid Mormon settlers, onto a dusty trail that took me down three or four miles to the head of a shallow, dry canyon. I stepped out into an arid world of sand lizards, gnats, and endless slickrock vistas and packed up my horse. As I started down to the bottom of the little hollow, I began to feel familiar sensations—the horse under me, the empty desert around me. I felt strangely like I was on home ground.

The hollow got progressively deeper and evolved into a canyon, though it was still dry and sandy at the bottom. I'd made sure I had plenty of water and salt pills. The only groundwater was in occasional potholes in the rock, swarming with enormous tadpoles and various insect life forms. The potholes were not appetizing unless you had been a long time without water. The sandstone walls were probably two hundred feet high when we encountered our first signs of fresh water, seeping into little springs from the walls of the canyon—not enough to flow yet, but enough to satisfy my thirsty horse. I was getting very fond of my horse, whose name I'd been told was Canyon Connie. She was sure-footed and seemed to know the territory, and she was lively enough to keep me alert. She had already tried three or four times to brush me off her back against a convenient boulder or cottonwood tree.

I decided to make camp about twilight on a sand promontory under a great overhanging amphitheater. The canyon bed was a steady running stream by now, and the sandstone walls must have been five hundred feet high. There was some grass for Connie to feed on and enough wood for a nice fire. I brushed a dead scorpion out of my way and spread out my sleeping bag. I cooked up some freeze-dried stew, made some instant coffee, and leaned back against a log to experience the death of the fire and the conquering of my space by the still canyon darkness. I had carried along a little flask of Old Granddad just for the occasion. It was a clear starry night. I was actually having a good time, finding I rather preferred these sheer canyon walls to those of New York, even doing what I was doing. I fell asleep watching canyon swallows and bats fight it out for the air space.

I was off again at dawn after a quick cup of Grape Nuts and coffee. The canyon got increasingly tricky as I worked my way through narrow passages slick with rapidly rushing water, then down and around great piles of boulders. It was clear that this little stream couldn't have done all the work of carving this amazing, snakelike canyon. There was evidence all around that every day down here was not sunny and bright and the stream small and amiable. I knew from my experience with this country that periodically great floods of water and mud and trees and boulders came rushing down the canyon, scouring it, deepening it. Scenes of great natural violence played themselves out. Humans venturing into these passages must be wary.

At mid-afternoon I came to the main river. It was at present a placid stream not more than a foot or two deep, but there was probably quicksand. I lunched on some dried fruit and cheese and crackers while I got my bearings. The side canyon I was looking for figured to be down about ten miles. Aaron Kimball had told me I had to be watchful because it was easy to miss. That's why it was a good hideout.

The going was a little faster in this wider main canyon, but I still had to be careful. The river meandered where it wished, and I felt I was in water more than I was on sandy dry ground. I was careful also because I was getting nearer Jedediah Kimball's hideout.

I camped out again by the river and had freeze-dried chili for dinner. Canyon Connie was holding up well and appreciated the oats I had for her this evening. I left the Old Granddad alone tonight. I wanted to sleep lightly.

The entrance to Maiden Canyon was indeed difficult to find. I went a mile beyond it, even with my napkin out and matched against my geological map. As it turned out, I spent the entire morning trying to locate it. Finally I concentrated on a talus of rocks probably twenty feet high, topped by a stand of willows. It was only from a certain vantage point that the crevice in the cliff was apparent. I tied Canyon Connie to a clump of tamarisk, climbed my way up the tumbled rocks to the willows, and stepped into a narrow passageway that couldn't have been more than three feet wide. It was probably six hundred feet high.

I had a big lunch of beef jerky, cheese, sourdough bread, and a generous portion of dried apricots, then made sure Connie was secure and my gear stowed away. After that I climbed back up to the entrance to Maiden Canyon and walked seriously into the narrow opening. There sure as hell wouldn't be much of an escape route if I needed it. What I was doing was really mad. But I put that out of my mind and plunged ahead.

The trail was the floor of the canyon, which was a three-inch-deep flowing stream. I had entered a very strange world, dark and cool and damp. There were places where the little gorge widened to six or seven feet, and I had a little dry rock to stand on. There were also places where I had to press sideways to pass through. At one point I had to crawl on my hands and knees through water two feet deep to escape a twist of sandstone where the passage above was no more than six inches across.

After a mile of this, the canyon became steeper and wider. I could occasionally see the sky and didn't feel quite so much as if I were in a great stone vise. Another mile, and I saw a stand of greenery ahead, willows and maidenfern. Beyond that the canyon opened out significantly. The cliffs were probably no more than four or five hundred feet high, and there were trees and little clusters of grass alongside the stream, which was slow-moving, almost meandering.

I could see the sky clearly now, though the sun had gone from the canyon, even at 4:30 in the afternoon. I rested, checked my .38, and drank from a deep spring dripping from the face of the cliff. Then I moved on, cautiously up the now easily manageable but still winding canyon. I was looking to my left now for Indian ruins set high in the cliff. According to Aaron, it would be in those ruins that I would find his brother, Jedediah Kimball. I was hoping mightily that I would also find Jennifer Peterson. Maybe I would be extraordinarily fortunate and find Jennifer Peterson and not Jed Kimball. Fat chance.

Another mile, and I saw the first sign of Indian cliff dwellings in an enormous arching amphitheater on the left side of the canyon. The rough stone dwellings, probably seven hundred years old, were set in the cliff; it looked as if I would need a long rope ladder to scale the fifty feet up the sheer canyon wall to the well-preserved ruins. The ruins themselves were a ghostly presence in the purple twilight, architectural monuments to a long-dead people. I could see no signs of current life.

That image, of the deserted Anazasi dwellings, was the last thing I remembered before I awoke in pitch blackness, over a day later. And it took another day and a half to fully remember the details of the trip leading there. Something had crashed hard into my head and sent me into oblivion.

XXVIII

During the hour or so it took me to crawl back to consciousness, my perceptions were a blend of terrifying nightmares, murmurs of voices, and throbbing pains in my head. Children's laughter seemed to dominate. Later I became aware of the dull ache in my stomach and the dry swollen ball in my mouth. Even almost fully conscious, I could detect no light. Either it was very dark or I had gone blind. I moved about, with great difficulty at first, and found I was in a very small sealed room. There was rough stonework on four sides and below me, adobe and logs above. A firmly secured wooden door, if you could call it a door, was in one of the walls. It was more like a plug, not more than two feet by two feet. The ceiling could not have been separated from the floor by more than four feet. The room was almost square.

The nightmares, the worst of them anyway, went away. The throbbing ebbed. But the voices grew louder. The other two sensations, which I recognized as hunger and thirst, also got louder. Where the hell was I and who belonged to those voices? I wished I could hear them well enough to make sense of what they were saying. I opted not to become violent or even to pound on the wooden door or window or whatever it was. I was beginning to remember how I had gotten into this fix.

I tried for a half hour or so to dislodge the wooden door. No luck. Next I tested the ceiling. It was hard and secure. Then the walls—even worse. I was trapped in this little cell, only vaguely aware of where I was, more than vaguely aware that I was in a lot of trouble. And I was damned thirsty.

After what seemed like hours, someone started making noises beyond the door, a little gray light appeared around the edges, then the wooden plug was removed. A dark figure appeared, framed in the gray light. I stayed crouched against the far wall, fearful of the figure. I reached for my pistol. It was gone.

A pair of hands set something onto the floor of my little room, then quickly disappeared. The wooden plug was set back in place and secured with a sound thump, and whoever had come in was gone. I felt over toward whatever it was that was left and found a tin cup full of water and a tin plate full of food, pork and beans and venison jerky. I sipped the water slowly then ate the food and felt better, though I found myself wishing whoever it was had slipped in a bottle of extra-strength Anacin.

I sat for what felt like several more hours, trying to figure a way out of this fix before the door plug was removed again and before I drowned in my own waste. They were better at bringing things in than at taking things away. My cell was starting to smell very bad. Again the hands reached in to remove the cup and plate. The light framing the dark form was brighter, yellower, this time. I could see the form was a woman. The hands put in a fresh cup and plate.

"Who are you?" I said. My voice came out as barely a whisper.

The woman said nothing, but she lingered a moment before replacing the door. It was corned beef hash this time, some canned tomatoes, and a Baby Ruth bar. Whoever it was was trying to feed me well—even a little surprise now and then. I was grateful that someone cared even that much.

The third visit yielded only faint light behind the woman. Apparently it was dark outside. The cup and plate were taken away, and fresh supplies substituted.

"Will you talk with me?" I said. My voice raspy and out of control from all the silence.

No response. But she didn't move to close the door.

Then she said, "I shouldn't. He wouldn't like it."

That voice. My God, had I gone mad in this four-by-four cell? I recognized the voice, yet I didn't recognize it. I had to keep the conversation going. "Who wouldn't like it?" I sounded like a croaking adolescent.

"My husband," she said. I really was going crazy. Perverse memories were flooding into my brain, visions of an old 1956 Studebaker. Whose voice was it?

"Well, can I talk with him? Your husband?"

"He'll talk to you when he's ready."

We both paused for a few moments, waiting. The woman didn't move. I thought she wanted to linger. Then it hit me, and I felt better that I could tie the voice and the old Studebaker in my brain. At least something was working. It was Linda Peterson's voice. Further memories of the backseat of my old Studebaker. But enough of that. I got back to the present and acted on my educated hunch.

"Jennifer?" I said quietly.

Her shadow started a little, I thought, but didn't reply. It stayed in place, however, making no move to close me up again.

"You're Jennifer, aren't you?"

Another long silence, but I knew I had found Linda's daughter. After a very long time she spoke to me in a strained whisper. "Who are you?"

"My name is Gabe Utley. I'm a friend of your mother's."

Her tone got a little nasty. "Why did you come here?"

"Your mother's worried about you. She asked me to try to find you."

Her tone shifted from nasty to callous. "Was she sober when she asked you?"

I didn't answer that one. She went right on. "I bet my dad doesn't know you're after me."

"You don't know about your father?" I said.

"What about him?"

"He's dead." I couldn't think of a subtler way of putting it. I was not in subtle surroundings.

She uttered a gasp and her shoulders started to shake.

"You didn't know," I said. "I'm sorry."

"How did it happen?"

"A heart attack, most likely," I said.

"Who found him?"

"Why do you ask that?"

"Did Amos Jensen find him?"

I was more than a little surprised. "Amos Jensen called your mother with the news. I don't know who found him."

"I knew it. I was afraid that old bastard would get him," she said.

"Why do you say that, Jennifer?"

"You really don't know, do you? You really don't know."

"No," I said. "I guess I really don't know."

She paused. "Jed's been getting a real bum rap, you know. They think he killed Susan. But they're wrong."

"Maybe," I said. "But I was over at his brother Aaron's when Jed came to call. Did he tell you about that?"

"He said Aaron had been getting dangerous lately, that he wanted to be Prophet. Jed had to do something."

"You know Jed killed Aaron," I said.

Jennifer grew defiant. "I don't know why I wanted to feed you. You say terrible things."

"What?"

"I made Jed let me take care of you."

"You made him?" I asked incredulously.

"He thinks I'm terrific. I'm his favorite, you know. He gives me anything I want."

"Did he tell you he killed his brother?"

"Jed told me there was trouble, that he had to shoot Aaron."

"Did he also tell you he killed two of Aaron's wives?"

Silence.

"One of them couldn't have been more than thirteen," I went on. "Practically blew her head off."

I waited a while longer. Still no response.

"Aren't you a little afraid that the same thing could happen to you?"

"Boy, you really are a dumb motherfucker. Jed knows how to take care of his women!"

"He's had a lot of experience, sweetheart."

"I suppose next you'll tell me he's old enough to be my father."

"Well, it had crossed my mind. He's my age and I used to date your mother."

"You are a naïve son of a bitch, aren't you!"

I couldn't argue with that—not from inside a four-by-four cell.

"At least he's not old enough to be my grandfather!"

I wondered what she meant by that, but I didn't pursue it. Instead I got back to the task at hand.

"Your mother would like to see you. She needs you now."

"She'll be all right," she said. "She can just take a couple of Valium and wash them down with some expensive vodka."

In spite of a perverse impulse to leave this spoiled teenybopper to roost in Jed Kimball's lunatic henhouse, I felt I had to try to talk sense. She was, after all, a sixteen-year-old who had made a dubious life choice by almost any standards. And my job was to bring her home.

"Linda's been pretty tough—and sober—since David died. I think you'd like her the way she is."

"I know what I'm doing," Jennifer said.

"Lots of people who know what they're doing at sixteen sure wish they hadn't at eighteen," I said. "How many wives does Jed Kimball have?"

"I've got to go now," Jennifer said. "I hope you like what I've brought you to eat." She slapped the wooden square back into the hole and thumped it into place. I sat back and ate a rather good roasted rabbit, some mashed potatoes, and a generous helping of canned green beans. The food tasted very good. Then I lay down and went to sleep, contemplating Jennifer Peterson and just how the hell I was going to get out of here.

I didn't sleep well that night—at least I assumed it was night. My watch had stopped and there wasn't enough light to see it anyway. Even if it had been running and I could see it, I wouldn't know which end of the day it was pointing to. By now I was smelling so bad I was having trouble tolerating myself. And I hadn't been very successful in hatching an escape plan, not even for myself, let alone Jennifer. When the by-now-familiar rattle that signaled feeding time began to happen, it seemed a little louder this time. But I attributed that to something inside my head rather than something outside the door.

The light around the human form was gray again, but a different gray from the first—brighter. And the form was different—bigger. It wasn't Jennifer. It was a man.

"All right. You can come out now!" Beautiful words from an unbeautiful voice. It was Jedediah Kimball. He was backing away into the gray, so I crawled out through my two-by-two door. I was in another room with a slightly larger opening that seemed to lead out into daylight.

I was indeed in daylight, gray morning daylight, gray because the sky was almost black with clouds. It wasn't raining just then but the smell was in the air, lightning flashes sparked periodically, and distant thunder rolled. I was emerging from a small stone room that was part of numerous small stone rooms that all together made up a medium-size complex of Anazasi cliff dwellings, cruder and likely more ancient than those in Mesa Verde but similar in design and function.

After I crawled out into the open air I tried to stand, and immediately fell to the ground. I had been bent over so long I couldn't straighten up—not all at once. On the second try, with the help of the side of the little dwelling, I made it and found myself staring into the face of Jed Kimball, a clean-shaven Jed Kimball.

He appeared to be at least mildly amused at my plight. "Well, if it isn't the city boy. You do get around. Been a lot of very good trackers try and find me in here. None of them ever did." Then Jed Kimball opened out his arms. "Look, Utley, no weapons. I have no desire to shoot you dead. No desire at all."

"Your hospitality leaves a little to be desired," I said, as I rubbed the back of my legs.

"Let's just call that a little softening-up period. I mean, you are intruding here."

"These are public lands," I said.

"Well, maybe so. Public for whoever has the guts to come in." And Jed Kimball brushed back his thinning hair in a graceful gesture. Everything the man did was graceful, except maybe kill people. "But what say we cut that nonsense. You didn't come here to talk about trespassing on public lands . . . or did you come here to talk at all?"

"I don't mind talk," I said. "You must spend long evenings."

"The talk is a little limited," he said. "Heber there ain't much of a talker." He pointed a hundred feet across the ledge toward the beefy young man with the dumb eyes I'd seen in Rattlesnake Valley. He was still holding a rifle, as if it were epoxied to his hands. "Mostly the rest is just women talk." He smiled knowingly at me. "Why don't you come on down in the kiva with me, maybe get to know each other better." And he smiled again. It wasn't easy to tell when the man was serious.

"Ellen, dish up some lunch for Brother Utley and me! We're going to have a little talk!" he bellowed up the cave.

A haggard-looking woman emerged from the largest of the cliff dwellings—Ellen, I presumed. She was wearing jeans and a man's plaid shirt. Her gray hair was pulled back in a bun. She was sunburned, a little plump, and looked as if she'd had many children.

"Give us a few minutes, Jed. It's on the stove." I could see the smoke curling out a hole in the roof. She ducked back in the door immediately. No hellos for me.

Jed Kimball led me down a short ladder into the kiva, a circular well about seven feet deep and maybe ten feet across that had been the center of the religious lives of the original inhabitants. We sat down opposite each other.

"I like it down here," Jed announced. "Gets me in touch with the ancient people. Sometimes I think lately they're about the only friends I have. They won't turn on you. They're safely dead." And he reared back his head and laughed. His laughter echoed in the narrow canyon as if two dozen hysterical ghosts were in full agreement with his observation. His mood changed abruptly—he was hard to keep up with—and he stared hard across the circular space at me.

"You like what you see?" I said.

He went on staring.

"You don't remember me, do you?" I said.

"Where do I know you from?"

"Years ago? Back in Salt Lake City?"

Slowly recognition dawned in his eyes. "Good Lord. Now I remember. And the name . . . Utley . . . skinny kid. Used to live above the store. Right?"

I smiled. "Right. On both counts."

"Hard to believe," he said, "after all these years." Then he leaned over and stared even harder at me. I noticed that his blue eyes were not quite as cold as they'd been a few days ago. "You don't look too bad. Don't think Heber did any permanent damage."

"Nasty reception you give people," I said.

He laughed mildly. "We tend to be suspicious of anybody comes up here. Especially people with pistols. Especially when it ain't hunting season." Then the laughter cut off fast, as though it had been sliced with a knife. He shifted position and put his elbows on his knees. "Now, before we eat, suppose you tell me just why you came down here." And he waited for an answer. His eyes were very cold again.

I, of course, tried to fashion some red herring, but nothing credible came to mind. I really had nothing to tell him but the truth. I next turned to strategies of how to approach that. Nothing better there. "Well, I can't imagine you'll buy any bullshit," I said.

"Don't imagine I will," he said, his eyes not leaving me for an instant.

"I came up here to find Jennifer Peterson."

He paused, shifted his weight, and smiled grimly. "What makes you think you'll find her here?"

"I already did," I said.

"Mr. Utley . . . Gabe. Jennifer is my wife." He let that sink in a moment. "And you're trying to tell me that you've come all the way in here to take my wife away from me? Some folks would find that real amusing, Gabe."

"All I want is to take Jennifer back to her mother. That's all. What she does when she's older is her business."

"You really don't get it do you, Gabe. You really don't get it. Well, let me try and explain it to you so you won't misunderstand the situation . . . God has anointed me his Prophet on the earth. He has given me the keys to the Kingdom. He has commanded me to keep his law, his law that says I must take unto me good women to help me in my mission. And what God has given me, no man better try and take away. Jennifer Kimball is mine and I'll kill any jack rabbit tries and takes her away from me."

I figured from Jed's tone of voice and from the nervous way he was fingering the bowie knife strapped to his leg that this subject had been quickly exhausted. Our respective positions on Jennifer Peterson Kimball were clear.

I didn't say anything, and Jed didn't look as if he expected me to. He motioned to the woman Ellen. She came to the kiva carrying a plate of food for each of us. Heber was still down the way, still stroking his rifle, still looking dumb and hostile, as if he'd like to finish what he'd started a day or so ago. The sky was still dark, lightning still flashing. It hadn't started to rain.

We ate our dinner in silence, closely attended by Ellen, who appeared to carry most of the burdens of the world. As I looked more closely at her, it was clear that she had been a lovely woman and still ought to be. She looked fifteen years older than her husband.

When we had finished and Ellen had cleared the dishes, Jed Kimball stood and climbed out of the kiva. "Come on, I want to show you something." I went up after him. "Ellen!" he called. "Bring everybody on out here!" Ellen ducked into her place, and soon people started emerging from doors, windows, cracks in the wall. It seemed Jedediah and Aaron had trained their families similarly, to hide silently and to appear on call. This tableau was spectacular. There must have been fifty people in all—six or seven women, children ranging in age from a few weeks to fifteen or sixteen. Few mature men, I noticed.

"Take a good look, Gabe. This is my family. These are God's chosen. This is what it's all about, what I fight for. God has set this family here as an example of his Kingdom."

Jed saw me searching the faces. "I know who you're looking for." And he turned and beckoned with his arm. "Jennifer! There's a man here looking for you. Why don't you come on down and meet him!"

From the side of one of the buildings stepped a young girl who walked slowly the seventy-five feet to where Jed and I were standing. She had on a long dress, done up tight at the neck, with long sleeves buttoned at the wrist. Her hair hung loosely down to her shoulders. It looked as if it hadn't been combed for days. As she got closer there was no mistaking that she was Linda's daughter. Her looks startled me, as had her voice. The daughter, young and beautiful, was sculpted like her mother. She took her place by Jed and stood staring boldly at me. Jed put his arm around her.

"This is my wife, Gabe. Jennifer Kimball. Look at her, she's a lovely girl, and she's where she belongs now. This is her home, this is her family, these are her people."

He stopped and gave me time to look at her. He looked at her, obviously enjoying it immensely. "Now, Gabe, Jennifer came to me of her own free will. I didn't take her from anybody. She just got tired of living in a wicked and corrupt world. She got tired of being destroyed by those people who call themselves Latter-day Saints, got tired of their money, their neglect, their hypocrisy. Jennifer can tell you a few things about their hypocrisy."

I looked at Jed and Jennifer. For some reason I thought first what a handsome couple they made. Then I looked back beyond them to the rest of the family. It wasn't the same experience as looking at Aaron's pathetic little entourage. These people were clean, well fed, and cleareyed. They were proud and carried themselves as if they were God's chosen, though the men stood a little straighter and looked happier about it all than did the women. I found myself almost buying it—almost.

"Sounds good, Jed. It even looks good. That is, until I remember where we are down here at the end of the world because you have nowhere else to go. How long can your family live like this, cowering down in a canyon, fearing every minute of their lives?"

Jed was not at all hostile in his response. I'd given him fuel for his rhetorical fires, it seemed, and off he went. "It's a violent world, Utley. Violence all around us. God's people have always fired violence. The righteous have always been persecuted. God never makes it easy for his people. Christ said he came to bring the sword, to set brother against brother. There's violence because people know they're an abomination before God and they can't look the truth in the face. We take strength from our persecution because God is speaking to us. When you know that, petty and wicked people—liars—don't matter. God simply washes them away in a sea of their own blood!"

Jed was on a roll, and I had no hopes of matching him. I was much out of practice, and besides, I doubted I believed anything strongly enough to talk that well. I didn't even try to respond. I began concentrating instead on how I was going to take Jennifer Whatever-her-last-name-was away from all this. I was also worrying about how I was going to keep from getting killed.

Jed seemed to read my mind again. "Tell you what I'm not going to do, Gabe. I'm not going to kill you, not just yet. You aren't worth it, tenacious bastard that you are." And he laughed. So did his echoes. "I'm just going to keep you locked up a few more days, give you time to think things over. Then I'll decide what to do with you, whether to put you out of your misguided misery."

Then he laughed again. He was being very affable through all his threats. Even now I was finding it hard to dislike the man. I had no doubt about why these people followed him, nor about why Jennifer was here. The schoolboys who dated her had to be pretty tame stuff in comparison to this charismatic maniac. But I also found it easy to remember that this latest wife of God's anointed Prophet was a mixed up sixteen-year-old girl who ought to be with her mommy and I was being paid—I hoped I was being paid—to take her home.

"And, Gabe," Jed zeroed in on me with his penetrating blue eyes.

"Yeah?"

"I didn't kill Susan Whitesides. So cross that off your list of grievances against me, all right?"

"Maybe," I said.

"And one other thing you can count on, city boy. And soon!"

"What's that?"

"You can count on a major sign to the Mormon people, a sign that will show these deluded sinners that things are not as they seem—that their leaders are liars . . . You remember that."

"I'll remember that," I said.

Jed Kimball gave a signal and suddenly the family portrait burst into life. The children started playing, shouting and running about as though they'd been doing it all day. The women began moving busily about their tasks. I watched Jennifer walk back up to the top of the complex and go in a door. I noted carefully which door. Heber stayed right where he was. Did he bathe with that rifle?

Jed personally escorted me back to my cell and secured my trapdoor. I was back in the dark, back to the life of contemplation. But I had two advantages I hadn't had before. I knew how the wooden plug was secured in place, and I had squirreled away a table knife from supper.

It took me about three hours to scrape the ancient mortar from around the stone bricks to the right of the wooden plug until I had a hole I could put my arm through. I could then, in the middle of the night—and I thought I had a pretty good sense of time now—creep up the hill to Jennifer's door and carry her away. Easy? Sure. At least four contingencies that could get me killed on the spot popped into my mind, the most vivid being that Jennifer probably would scream her lungs out the moment she saw me. Why, after all her rhetoric, was I banking on a hunch that she would come quietly? Maybe it was the frightened little girl I saw behind those rebellious eyes. Still, I was willing to stake a lot on the assumption that right now in her heart of hearts she would rather have her teddy bear next to her in her bed than Jedediah Kimball.

I put all that out of my mind for the present, replaced the rocks, and sat back and waited for dinner. It wasn't Jennifer this time, nor Jed. It was Ellen, who still didn't say a word to me and who simply plopped my food into the cell and closed me back up again. It was beans. The quality of the fare was in definite decline. I ate and decided to wait another five or six hours until everybody was asleep.

I guessed it was about midnight when I first heard peculiar sounds outside—shouts, mumbled angry words, all women's voices. I waited a while until they died down. I didn't want to meet Jed Kimball or Heber face-to-face while crawling out of my hole. I'd rather be shot on the run. When all was quiet, I removed the stones and reached around and pounded the wooden crossbar out of its iron mooring, not as quietly as I would have liked. But nothing happened; there was no response from outside. I removed the wooden door very quietly and crawled out of my smelly cell. There was light from a fire flickering through the other entrance. I inched my way over and looked out.

What I saw was amazing. It was a big bonfire, with three women taking part in an intense melodrama. One of the women was Jed's wife Ellen. She was on the opposite side of the fire from me, kneeling, a look of anxiety on her face. A second woman, younger, whom I recognized from Jed's presentation of his family, was cowering on the ground like a frightened animal. The third woman was standing holding an old twelve-gauge shotgun on the second woman—it was Adrene Snow Kimball dressed in overalls and a man's shirt, looking very ornery and determined. I could see no sign of Jed or Heber or anyone else.

The words had not stopped. They were merely being uttered in hushed malevolent shades, whispers of determination on the one hand, whispers of fear on the other. I waited in the door and listened. Adrene Kimball was doing the talking.

"I've give ya all the chance I'm gonna, Allison. Now you tell me where Jed is or I'll blow ya all over the ground."

The woman—Allison apparently—crouched closer to the ground and whimpered out her answer. "I tell you, Addy . . . for the hundredth time. I don't know. They just up and left."

"You gotta know, Allison, this is all your fault. If you'da stayed with Aaron, not gone traipsin' off with Jed, none a this woulda happened. Now you and Jed's gotta pay." And the big woman shifted the shotgun to one hand and with the other smashed Aaron's former wife savagely across the face, knocking her over and into the fire. Allison scurried back quickly, her skirt on fire, and rolled frantically in the dirt. Ellen jumped around to help, but Adrene warned her off.

"You just stay out of this, Ellen. This is between us." Ellen backed off slowly. Allison had succeeded in putting out the fire and had gotten up to an elbow when Adrene turned back to her. "Now I'm gonna start to count—just like Jed did with Aaron—and I'm gonna count to twenty, and if ya haven't told me where he is by then I'm gonna shoot." And she started to count, shotgun poised and ready to fire.

Allison looked frantically around, mainly at Ellen, who was in no position to help. In fact, Ellen would likely kill her if she did tell. It went through my mind that Allison was indeed pretty, just as Aaron had said, in a coy, spoiled kind of way. It was clear though that none of her coquettishness was helping her out tonight, and she was long past even trying. The counting continued—fifteen, sixteen. Adrene aimed the shotgun at Allison's eyes. This might all be family business, but it was getting hard to tolerate.

I shouted out the door. "Adrene! Put down the gun!"

As expected, I became the object of the big woman's anger. The shotgun turned toward me, toward my voice, anyway. I waited a second until her trigger finger settled, then I stepped out into the firelight. Allison scampered around the fire and clung to Ellen, still afraid to take her eyes off Adrene.

"Maybe there's a better way to do this," I said, as I walked carefully down the path to the fire. The big woman looked hatefully at me. All three of them looked hatefully at me. I chose to talk to Ellen.

"Has Jed gone?"

She looked at me sullenly. "Yes, he has."

"Is Jennifer still here?"

"He's taken her with him."

"And you won't say where they've gone."

"It's none of your business. It's nobody's business."

Adrene, angry at my interruption, broke into our conversation—not politely. She aimed the gun at Ellen this time. "I've no quarrel with you, Ellen. But if yer gonna glue yourself to Allison there, I'd as leave blast you both into hell as spit on ya." And she aimed the gun at a spot of ground two feet from Allison and let go a blast that echoed for thirty seconds through the narrow canyon. Jed's ghosts didn't laugh. That shot was apparently enough for Allison. She scrambled back around the fire on her knees to Adrene and embraced the woman around her big thighs. "Don't kill me, Addy, please don't kill me. I don't want to die. I'll tell you where Jed's gone."

Ellen rose to her feet, anger in her eye, but Adrene stopped her in her tracks with a warning thrust of the gun. She froze in place.

"Where's he gone?" Adrene asked.

"He's gone north, Addy! He's took Jennie with him! He's

gone up to Salt Lake! He's gone up there to kill Amos Jensen!"

Ellen let herself down to the ground, releasing a weary sigh as she did so. Adrene pushed the younger woman, Allison, contemptuously away from her.

"I'm not gonna kill ya, Allison. Ya ain't good enough to die yet. Anyway, I reckon Ellen here will take care of ya, give ya what ya deserve." Then Adrene turned to me.

"You gonna help me get to Salt Lake, Utley?"

#

Adrene and I finally arrived in Escalante after a very difficult day hiking up out of the wilderness. I bought a newspaper immediately to see if Jed had succeeded in killing Amos Jensen, or in getting himself killed. But there was nothing. I also bought my second .38 of the week. Before long I'd have a six-pack, and I bought each of us a motel room and let Adrene settle in. I don't think she'd ever been in a motel before. Her eyes were as big and round as a child's as she sat on the clean bed and gazed around the rather tacky little room. Escalante was not a big tourist center.

I went to my room next and gave Arvin Smith IV a call, collect.

"Where the hell are you Utley? Nobody's been able to find you for days."

"Well, I'll be damned. Finally got away from you folks. Isn't easy, you know . . . 'Course you know."

"This a business call," Arvin asked, "or did you just want to gloat? Uncle doesn't like paying for social calls."

"It's something you might be interested in."

"What?"

"From what I can gather down here where I am, Jed Kimball's on his way to Salt Lake to kill Amos D. Jensen."

Arvin paused on the other end of the line. I could hear the engine start. "Where are you?"

"Southern Utah. Escalante. Kimball shouldn't be more than a few hours ahead of me. Nothing's happened there?"

"Not like that," he said. "Are your sources reliable?"

"I think so."

"Well, who the hell is it?" Arvin was manic, gearing for action.

"One of Jed Kimball's wives," I said. "The one he stole from his brother Aaron. The pretty one."

"My God, but you do get around." I think it was a compliment.

"I assume you folks can take care of security," I said.

"There are seldom complaints, Utley. We take care of our own."

"Good, I'm tired. I plan to sleep the clock around. I'll leave it all in your capable hands."

"I'm flattered you trust us. But there is maybe something of a problem in the next few days."

"Oh?"

"Yeah. It's General Conference up here. Half the Mormons in the world are arriving in town. It makes security a lot harder. The Brethren are bopping around all over the place, attending meetings, shaking hands, giving interviews. It's an assassin's paradise."

"Good God," I said. "Well, can you keep the silver-tongued devil under special wraps? For a few days?"

"We'll have to, I guess. But he loves these conferences. It's his chance to shine. He talks better, he looks better, and he wheels and deals better than anybody. It's his party, and he really loves it. I'm afraid it'll be a lot like telling the Pope to keep a low profile at a nuns' convention."

"Well, I'm sure you and yours can handle it. I'm going to get some rest—it's been a hell of a few days—then I'll be up in your neighborhood tomorrow sometime. Maybe you can get me some good seats to Conference."

"I'm afraid the choice seats are reserved for the faithful, Utley. People like me. You may have to catch it on TV."

I rang off, satisfied I'd done my duty, hit the sack, and slept for nine straight hours. I'd surely have done another nine, but Adrene Snow Kimball roused me at five in the morning—my God, these farmers—wanting to be off to Salt Lake.

I guided Adrene sleepily to Escalante's café, praying that I wouldn't fall dead asleep in the middle of the street before I got my coffee. She did give me a disapproving look as I grabbed the coffee cup with both hands and inhaled it. I was getting too old to disturb my morning ritual. Adrene was not concerned with my vices for long, however. She was too engrossed in the supersize breakfast special I had ordered for her. She looked as if she had never seen anything so wonderful in her life. I suspected she'd never eaten in a restaurant. My suspicion was confirmed when she started to eat. She ate it all—eggs, potatoes, hotcakes, bread, and ham—with her knife. Just how she did it, I'll never know—it all disappeared so fast—but I think it was through some ingenious interrelationship between the knife and her fingers. She was almost in tears by the time she finished, she was so full and happy.

She wasn't happy for long, however, and she grabbed me almost before I could pay the check and all but carried me out to the Jeep. She was in a great hurry to get to Salt Lake.

On the trip north, I discovered that Adrene wasn't much of a conversationalist. She sat like a large stone, staring forward, seeing nothing. Seeing nothing, I suspected, except the face of Jedediah Kimball. I wouldn't want to be Jed when this woman found him. I tried to talk about things she was interested in.

"You have any idea where Jed would go first in Salt Lake City?"

"He and his people have a house," she said.

"You know where?"

"Yup."

"Will you let me take you there, Mrs. Kimball?"

Finally I got a response from her. She turned toward me, making a judgment, I felt. That apparently accomplished, she turned back front and said, "It's family."

"You have to know, Mrs. Kimball, that every policeman in the state is looking for your brother-in-law."

"I reckon."

Another pause.

"Will you let me take you to the house?" I said.

"You ain't police?"

"No, I'm not."

She turned and looked at me again. "I reckon you can," she said.

Adrene Kimball directed me to a big frame farmhouse at the end of a dirt road in the south end of the Salt Lake Valley. No one seemed to be about, but I had learned that that meant nothing in a typical Kimball household. I pulled out my .38 and attempted to persuade Adrene to leave her shotgun in the Jeep. She demurred, and we were well armed as we walked up the sidewalk. But there was still no sign of trouble.

I knocked on the door several times and got no response. "Who lives here?" I said.

"The mother," Adrene responded.

"Jed's and Aaron's mother?"

"Yup."

"Their father's dead?"

"Yup. Got killed down in Mexico. Lotsa folks think Jed done it."

"Does the old woman live here alone?" I asked.

"Yup. S'far as I know. Her and Eliza. She's a little deef. They're both a little deef."

I took that as a cue to go on in. The door wasn't locked.

We stepped into the front hall and still hadn't been shot at, which I took to be a good sign.

"Mom!" Adrene shouted.

In response to this, a very large girl appeared in the doorway to what I assumed was the living room. She looked to be retarded and stared at us with great, uncomprehending eyes. She had a big friendly grin set on her face and a hearing aid in each ear. She was holding a glass of milk in her right hand. Adrene appeared to know her.

"Hello, Eliza."

"Hello," Eliza said happily, through a cleft palate. She was gripping the bottom of her short gray sack of a dress in her left hand, like she was trying to wring herself out.

"Is your grandma here?" Adrene said with more tenderness than I would have thought possible.

"She right here," said the girl as she backed into the room, which was indeed the living room. She lumbered over to a far corner and handed the milk to a very tiny old woman sitting in an ancient wooden wheelchair. She couldn't have weighed more than ninety pounds and had the aspect of a wizened mummy. She obviously couldn't see through the bad cataracts that shrouded her eyes, though she seemed to sense that something was wrong in the room. She tried to peer through the cloudy blue lenses of her eyes. She reached out a brown, bony caricature of a hand toward us, dropping the glass of milk on the floor. She didn't seem to notice. Her extended hand betrayed a terrible case of palsy and shook in time with her head, which she was also extending toward us.

Eliza, frightened by me and startled by the breaking glass, backed a couple of steps away into a corner and put the hem of her dress in her mouth, exposing her overweight nakedness to us.

"Git yer dress down, Eliza," Adrene Kimball snapped at the girl. Eliza did as she was told. Then Adrene turned to the old woman and shouted a question at her.

"Do you know where Jed's gone, Mother Kimball?"

"What?" Mother Kimball said, cupping her ear.

"Do you know where Jed's gone?" Adrene repeated, louder this time.

"Jed? . . . Did you say, Jed?" At least she knew the subject matter.

"Yes. Jed. I'm lookin' for him."

The old lady didn't hear the second question but that didn't appear to matter to her. She had her subject, and she started to talk. "Jed. Jeddie. Little Jeddie. A good boy. Always good to his mama. Made me proud of him. Good to Eliza baby here. Always good to Eliza."

"Was Jed here?" Adrene asked, trying to penetrate. She was shouting so loudly I thought she would deafen those of us in the room who weren't already deaf. "Was Jed here?" she repeated.

"Jed's gone away. He's gone away. But he'll be back. He's a good boy. He'll come back to his old mama." This antediluvian old woman was straining hard; the tendons in her neck were taut as ropes. She was breathing heavily. Her sightless eyes were scanning everywhere, trying to see something.

"Where has Jed gone?" Adrene persisted. "Where has Jed gone?"

"Jed's gone. Jed's gone. Gone to the city. Gone to give a sign from God. Gone to take the sword against the wicked. The sword of righteousness. Jed'll destroy the wicked. He's his daddy's boy!"

Then the old woman stopped speaking. She gasped for air two or three times. I feared for a moment that she might die on the spot. But she recovered, sank back in her chair with a contented smile on her face, and dozed off, still muttering about daddy's boy.

Eliza, poor frightened girl, had recovered the hem of her dress and had it back in her mouth, her ample charms bared again before all in the room. Adrene Kimball chose to

ignore it this time—maybe she'd figured I was a big boy—
and stalked out of the room and out the front door. I said
good-bye to Eliza, who was cringing in the corner, and followed Mrs. Kimball out to the Jeep. As I followed, I had a
strong feeling I ought to give Arvin Smith another call.
Mother Kimball had made a kind of zany sense.

Finding a telephone was another matter. It took ten minutes to find a booth in front of a second-class shopping center. And the phone was in use by a gangly teenage girl with
fluffy hair, braces, and a bad case of acne. Adrene clearly
was not charmed by her tight short-shorts or the long cigarette in her mouth. Since the girl was behaving as if she was
talking to her boy friend, I asked politely if I could use the
phone. I had an emergency. The girl looked at me as if I
were the village idiot and let forth a stream of obscenities
that turned my lived-in ears blue. When I saw that Adrene
was about to fetch her shotgun—probably she wasn't, but I
wasn't betting on it—I got in the Jeep and drove to find
another phone, this time at a service station a couple of
blocks up the road.

It took three calls to get Arvin. This was a busy day for
him. But I finally did. "Arvin, when is Amos Jensen scheduled to speak in the Tabernacle?"

"Why? You know something?"

"Let's say I have an educated intuition."

"About Jed Kimball."

"Yeah. About Jed Kimball."

"He's on for this afternoon," Arvin said. "The session
starts in an hour."

"When will Jensen arrive?" I said.

"He'll be here five minutes before two."

"Well, keep watch," I said. "I wouldn't be surprised if
Kimball shows up at Conference today."

Adrene was still beside me as I drove up to the city, the

shotgun in her lap. "Mrs. Kimball," I said. "If you're coming with me, you can't take that. You're likely to be shot on sight."

"Don't worry 'bout me," she said. "I'm goin' my own way."

I started to argue, but I was in a hurry and I figured she was Jed's problem. It was about a quarter to two when we arrived.

The inside of the big oval Tabernacle was filled long before I arrived, as was the smaller granite Assembly Hall to the south. Still, the grounds were practically wall-to-wall with people. It was a cloudy day, but it hadn't started to rain yet. The faces were bright and happy. The men were all in suits, the women all in frilly dresses; at least it seemed that way to me. Jed Kimball would surely stick out, certainly he would if he had on his red and black shirt.

I pushed my way through the crowd to the west entrance of the Tabernacle, where the dignitaries arrived. Big limo after big limo deposited old men in dark suits. The area was cordoned off and an army of security people was keeping the crowd at bay. A big guy was arguing very physically with me when I caught Arvin Smith's eye. Arvin appeared to be the field general today. The big man was not happy to let me through. He could see I wasn't dressed right.

"Any sight of Kimball?" I asked Arvin.

"Nope. Not yet. I hope this isn't just some big practical joke, Utley."

"Yeah, I plan to jump out and pop a paper bag when Amos Jensen steps out of his car." I looked around for myself. It would be hard for anybody to get within fifty feet of the door. But maybe fifty feet would do. I looked up and saw men discreetly set on rooftops, rifles obviously at their fingertips. I couldn't imagine this would be a problem place. "You got the inside covered this well?"

"That's a little harder, Gabe. There are ten thousand faithful Saints in there."

"Do your men have a good description of Kimball?"

"They know he's very tall, has blue eyes, and can wrestle a bull to the floor. There've been a lot of tall, blue-eyed Brothers very pissed the last half hour. We've tried to check everybody," Arvin said, with a twinkle in his eye.

"Mind if I go inside and have a look?" I said.

"Help yourself. Better take this, though." And he handed me a security card.

I wandered in the back door and up onto the back of the stand. The Tabernacle Choir was symmetrically set in place, singing a standard Mormon hymn, their voices and the great organ filling the big hall with music. I checked out every male face close enough to do any damage and didn't see Jedediah Kimball.

I went back outside and watched Amos D. Jensen arrive in a big black Cadillac. As he got out, the militia got especially alert. The rooftop rifles emerged, ready to fire. A girl scout couldn't have gotten anywhere near Amos Jensen. He walked past me to the door. If he recognized me, he didn't say hello. He looked like a great old warrior marching on into battle, looked as if he was having a good time through all this. He seemed to enjoy the special attention.

I followed the Jensen entourage into the Tabernacle and stood off to the side as he walked to his seat on the top row behind the speaker's podium. He shook hands with his colleagues and then sat down in a big soft wingback chair. Security men placed themselves discreetly at every possible avenue to Jensen. Other of Arvin's men were within easy reach of everyone in the crowded auditorium. The operation was all very smooth, very thorough, and very subtle. I didn't see Abe Lewis or his goons anywhere in sight.

The conference session began with a piece by Handel sung by the choir. The television cameras were rolling. It was a great public spectacle, and that was what worried me. I'd have preferred that Jed Kimball had made a move outside, where he could be taken and quietly carried away by

Arvin's army. But a sign from God would be much less effective out in the parking lot.

A prayer, another song—"We Thank Thee, Oh God, for a Prophet"—a hymn in which the audience joined. Then the speakers started. I remembered how bored I'd gotten as a child. I couldn't tell any difference in the message now, thirty years later. But I was grateful just for the boredom. So was Arvin Smith.

Amos D. Jensen was to be the last speaker. After another Tabernacle Choir number, the aging President of the Mormon Church—Arvin's uncle—walked very slowly to the podium and introduced Amos Jensen. He used few words —partly because Amos Jensen needed no introduction, and partly because the ailing old man seemed to have trouble getting out any words at all.

Amos D. Jensen walked proudly and aggressively to the podium—and took over. He was in good form today and launched quickly into an attack on the Fundamentalist cults. Great, I thought, well timed. This polygamist nut has sworn to kill you today, and you charge into the fray with a verbal broadside. I was expecting a bullet fusillade in response, from Jed and Heber and the other guys. But in my calmer moments I thought that was probably a little melodramatic, even for them.

Amos Jensen was getting set to roll into his conclusion now. It had been almost twenty minutes and nothing had happened.

"And I tell you, Brothers and Sisters, that these people come among you spreading falsehood and wickedness, bringing violence into our lives. And they bring you a living lie. They would have you believe that your leaders have gone astray, that your leaders have betrayed the faith, that your leaders have lost the mantle of Joseph and of Brigham! Well, let me tell you, your leaders have not betrayed the Covenant. But look around at those who call themselves Fundamentalists, look at the ragged little bands of gypsies with their unwashed babies and their cunning wicked eyes. They will lead you to hell!"

He was certainly primed today, letting it all loose. Very few speeches like this come over the Conference podium anymore. Several of Jensen's colleagues among the Apostles were decidedly uncomfortable, decidedly annoyed, that good Brother Jensen was dignifying the Fundamentalists with all this rabid attention. The first counselor to the Church president had his head in his hands. The president didn't, however. This frail little man was watching Amos D. Jensen very intently with shrewd opossum eyes. His eyes were not pleased with what was going on.

Then it happened. And I could not have written a more unlikely scenario had I been writing an absurdist play.

Four enormous women charged, as if from nowhere, up the steps leading to the speaker's platform. It took a second to dawn on me, but the first of the bunch had Jed Kimball's blue eyes. In his hand was a .38 pistol. My God, my pistol, I thought as one of a dozen thoughts that invaded my brain at that instant. The pistol was being aimed at Amos D. Jensen, who had just noticed the invaders out of the corner of his eye.

I had barely reached into my jacket for my gun when the first shot rang out, the crack of the .38 pistol. The second shot came only an instant later. It was a much louder report—a twelve-gauge shotgun.

Amos Jensen clutched his lower abdomen but stayed standing at the podium, a look of bewilderment on his face. Jed Kimball in his women's clothes had lurched ahead, as if he were going to tackle the amazed Apostle. But he wasn't going to tackle anybody; he was lurching only to the floor. The back of his dress was wet with blood. He collapsed face down at the feet of the president of the Mormon Church—dying.

Before anything else happened, the alert Mormon security men were all over the other three women and had their faces pressed into the plush carpet of the Tabernacle platform.

Then I saw who'd fired the second shot. It had been one of Arvin's sharp-eyed security men, wearing a black suit with a white shirt and black tie. He had on big mirror glasses and a black hat. He just stood there, the smoking shotgun in his hand, breathing heavily.

Then it began to dawn on me what I was seeing. Three other security men rushed to this man's side as if they were ready to take him into custody. I knew for sure when they took off his hat and all the scraggly hair tumbled out—it was Adrene Kimball. Adrene Kimball had waylaid one of Arvin's security men and heisted his clothes. "Goin' my own way" indeed.

The men took her shotgun away from her, but she didn't seem to care. Her face looked relaxed for the first time since I'd met her. Jedediah had finally messed with the wrong woman.

Everyone in the Tabernacle was in a state of shock, but the security men quickly and efficiently evacuated the building. Amos Jensen was still standing when the stretcher was brought for him. Jed's three companions were disarmed and literally dragged outside. I picked up the .38 from the rug behind the podium. It was mine all right, my little toy gun. And I walked down to where the security men were set to lead Adrene Kimball away. They were gentler with her than with the others. They likely had figured out that she'd done their work for them.

"How did you know, Mrs. Kimball?"

"The clothes," she said simply. "The dress was my sister's." And a smile crossed her face for the first time— maybe ever. "And could be it was just my nose."

"Your nose?"

"Yup. I could smell Jed a mile away. Ya kin do that when ya hate bad enough."

When I turned to watch Jed Kimball's body being taken

away, I saw Arvin Smith deep in conversation with his uncle, the president of the Church. The old man was talking, giving instructions it seemed. Arvin smiled his little wry grin, nodded, shook hands with the old man and walked down to talk with me.

"I guess we have you to thank for the alert," he said. "You didn't tell me we should watch out for women, though."

"I hadn't heard it was going to be a fashion show," I said.

"Who was the woman? The real one."

"Adrene Kimball, Jed's sister-in-law, Aaron's first wife. She got very angry at Jed for killing her husband."

As I watched the press and the police swarm onto the scene, it occurred to me that for all the grand pyrotechnics I still hadn't any idea where Jennifer Peterson was. I hadn't long to think, however. One of the reporters was buzzing over towards me—the ubiquitous Ramona McKinley.

"Well, well, Gabriel Utley, intrepid sleuth, always right there on the scene."

"See what you miss by not coming to church?" I said.

"Were you here all through this?" Mona asked. She sounded like a reporter.

"Let's say I even helped set it up. But let's not say it publicly." I paused for effect. "I drove the murderer up from southern Utah."

"Who was the murderer? I haven't been able to get anything out of anybody."

"You probably have fewer problems with access to information when you deal with the police, Mona. But on the other hand, the police often don't know anything. Mormon cops aren't so fussy about the First Amendment," I said.

"Are you going to play games with me, Gabe, or are you going to tell me what happened?"

"What would you like first? How about an official statement? Jedediah Kimball, gunman, prophet, polygamist, and
all-around nasty fellow met his end today. He lived by the
gun and he died by the gun. Just what is the meaning of
this for society? Will men no more shoot each other? Will no
one prophesy? Will men no longer marry more than one
woman? Only the press can know that for sure."

"Goddamn it, Gabriel, come off it. I've got a story to do
and you feel like clowning around. I'll go to Arvin!"

"Go ahead. He'll round out the story nicely for you. I
think his uncle had started to color in the edges before
Amos D. hit the ground." I paused and stared into her darting, frustrated eyes. "Besides. You're attractive when you
don't get what you want."

She gave me a fishy look. Got her. I had a presentiment
that I might spend a lot of my time in the near future trying
to get one up on her. I would if I didn't get my ass immediately back to New York once I found Jennifer Peterson.
And I would be a damn fool if I didn't go—on the next
plane.

"Well, in a nutshell," I said, "Jed Kimball and his cronies
got dressed up as tall women and sauntered up on the platform here and shot Amos D. Jensen. That's it in a nutshell."

"But who shot Jed Kimball? . . . And what do you mean
you drove the murderer up from southern Utah?"

"Adrene Snow Kimball, widow of the late Mr. Kimball's
dead brother—you got that?—took her trusty shot gun and
dressed herself in men's clothing and followed Jedediah
into the Tabernacle here, and not quite in the nick of time
shot her intended target in the back, thereby rendering him
dead. And maybe your lead on all this can be something
about the sexual identity problems of Mormon Fundamentalists."

Mona continued her fishy look while she wrote up what I
was saying. I saw that we were about to have a visitor. It was

Dale Olander. I was getting very tired of this Mona-Dale team.

"Hello, Utley," Dale said, not too brightly. He had his notebook out, too. Suddenly I was a popular source.

"Hello, Dale. Nice to see you. Didn't get much of a tan on your vacation south."

"Sure didn't get as much as you, it seems."

"Been talking to Arvin?" I said.

"Yeah."

"I promised I'd find Jed Kimball for you, didn't I, Dale."

"You going to let me have the murder weapon or am I going to have to take it from you, Utley?"

"I was afraid you'd ask," I said, as I handed him the gun. "Thought it might just slip by you."

"We're not quite as cow hick as we first appear."

"I'll give you that," I said. "You work better than I would've given you credit for." And I smiled at Mona, who ignored me and turned to talk with a man who was taking photos of the blood spot on the floor.

"You stay in touch, Utley," Dale said officiously as he left me to join Mona. I stood where I was, feeling lonely and searching my brain for a clue what to do next. Where had Jed Kimball deposited Jennifer?

I was about out the main front door of the Tabernacle to phone Linda when Mona called to me. The acoustics are wonderful in the Tabernacle. I waited while she walked up the aisle, wondering what exquisite Chinese torture she had for me this time. She had that kind of look on her face, fully recovered from her frustration. She got right to the point.

"You found Jennifer Peterson yet?" She said it like she knew I hadn't.

"No. Still got that one to do."

"Want some help?" she said slyly.

Jesus, getting one on her sure didn't last long. "Why not?"

I said. "We detectives are trained to accept help wherever it comes from. Even smart-ass broads."

"Why don't you give Jerry Romero a call?"

"Jerry Romero? What does Jerry have to do with this? What would he know about Jennifer Peterson?" I had a whole mass of questions, questions I felt I'd appear brighter not asking.

"Jennifer called him this morning."

It was my turn for the fishy look. Was she just getting even for a few minutes ago? But then she'd take at least as much satisfaction from solving my main problem for me than from putting me on, so I stayed with her. "How does Jerry know Jennifer?"

"If you'd have been straighter with us from the beginning you might have solved your problem sooner."

I looked at her dubiously.

"Well, maybe not solved it sooner. Maybe just had more information." At least she was being honest.

"So? You still haven't told me how Jerry knows her," I said.

"She was one of Jerry's girls—before she found religion." Mona was enjoying telling me this. Why hadn't she told me before? Probably because she wouldn't have enjoyed it as much. And, I thought in all fairness, it probably wouldn't have done any good for me to know it—then. She went on, "She was the agency's top young model. She did a lot of work for Jerry. Jerry did a lot for her."

"Like what?" I said.

"Like introducing her to nice rough boys, and getting her good drugs. He even introduced her to Jed Kimball. Jerry's a hell of a matchmaker. She's never been an easy kid to take, Gabe. If I'd have been the Petersons, I'd have probably shipped her away a long time ago, whether she wanted to go or not. In fact, I'm a little surprised they wanted her back."

"I don't think Daddy did, much," I said, and I started out the door.

Mona caught my arm. "Aren't you even going to thank me?"

"Thanks."

"Some thanks," she said.

"We've each won one. What's to thank?"

"Will you give me a call later, Gabe?"

I looked at her but didn't say anything. I was very suspicious. I had decided that there was nothing more to be done or said between us, at least privately.

"Maybe," I said, and turned and trotted out to the parking lot and my waiting Jeep. I wanted to get to Jerry Romero's fast. And I wanted to get away from Mona equally as fast.

XXXI

When I saw the big black Lincoln parked in front of Jerry's apartment, I knew that some other folks had gotten there before me. I knew who by the red mud on the hubcaps. Hadn't these guys been called off yet? I had seen the car in time to park around the corner and sneak up on it. I had a pistol pressed against the driver's head before he had time to radio a warning that I was on my way. The driver was the man who had had his foot on my LeBaron's bumper in Pipe Springs. I took his pistol and put it in my pocket then told him to lay face down on the floor of the car, and that if I were to see so much as the tip of his ear, I would dispatch him into eternity. They usually leave the callow types in the car.

I went to a telephone booth on the corner and put in a dime. I felt I'd better call Arvin Smith IV before I charged into Jerry's apartment. I found it interesting I called Arvin rather than Dale. It took three dimes in all to reach him. Finally I caught him at the Church public relations office— these folks get right to the important things.

Something was going on in Jerry's apartment as I paused outside the door. I decided to just burst in and hope that some of Arvin's good guys would get here fast. Of course, I still wasn't absolutely sure that these weren't Arvin's guys.

I kicked through the door and charged into the room, knowing I'd at least have surprise on my side. It turned out that that was about all I had on my side.

The tall gray-haired man in the blue pin-stripe suit was standing over Jerry, who was on his knees, kept there by the man in the dark suit from Pipe Springs. The gray-haired man had a long thin knife set just below Jerry's right eye as if he was priming to shove it into his brain. As I burst in, Abe Lewis, who was over in the corner presiding over a semiconscious Jack Vigo, turned toward the door, a .45 magnum ready to shoot me.

Having the advantage of surprise, I was able to shoot first, barely. Lewis went staggering back into one of Jerry's bookcases. The gray-haired man pulled the knife away from Jerry's eye, none too gently, and started toward me. But he had no doubts that I had the drop on him, so he let it slide limply to his side. He obeyed my little signal to let it drop all the way. It stuck up in the pine floorboard. The other man had both his hands busy holding Jerry and hadn't time even to reach for his weapon.

I told Jerry to pick up Lewis's magnum and keep the young guy guarded, and then I put my .38 back inside my coat and started toward the gray-haired man. I hit him first in his flaccid stomach, pushing him back against a desk. I smashed him three or four times at the side of his face with my fist and then kneed him in the groin.

Then I grabbed his right arm, twisted it behind him, and shoved his face against the wooden floor. I was twisting hard. He had to know I was indifferent whether I broke his arm. I took out my .38 and pressed it against the back of his head.

"Now talk to me, tall man, and talk fast. I don't have a lot of time. And I've seen as much of you as I ever intend to."

"Wh-wh-what do you want?" he said in a muffled voice into the hardwood floor.

"Did you kill Orson Kimball?"

He didn't reply, only grunted into the floor.

I increased pressure on his arm. I twisted until his arm snapped like a number two pencil. He let out a great howl of pain. I didn't let the rest of him move. I pressed the pistol harder into his skull.

"Now let's try again. Did you kill Orson Kimball?"

"Yes!" he cried through his agony.

"Who told you to kill Orson Kimball?"

There was a slight hesitation. I put a little pressure on the broken arm. He howled in pain again.

"I'll make it easier—a yes or no question . . . Was it David Peterson?"

"No!"

"Was it Amos Jensen?"

He didn't say anything. He simply started to bawl in great, heaving sobs. I pressed the gun harder into his head, warning him he'd better cut that out. "It's past the time to cry, killer." When he quieted some, I asked my next question.

"Did you kill Susan Whitesides?"

He went entirely limp, his blubbering was very soft now. He didn't fight giving me an answer. "No. I didn't kill her. I was just cleaning up. I cut her throat. But she was already dead."

"Who killed her?"

"David Peterson killed her."

Arvin Smith IV charged into the room with a squad of men

behind him. I let go the slack pin-stripe sleeve, holstered my gun, and stood up to greet the man who had to be Porter Rockwell's favorite descendant.

"You into torture, Gabe? I'm surprised. You seemed the gentle type."

"Just a couple things I wanted to know," I said.

"You sure seemed determined to find out," he said, as he surveyed the room.

"These guys have been bugging me something fierce, Arvin. And they just had a good friend of mine on his knees."

"Well, suppose you let me take over and handle this. I want to find out a few things myself." And he looked sardonically at me. "If we need you to come in and run the rack, I'll give you a call."

Then Arvin Smith and his very efficient crew cleaned up the mess and marched and carried the remains of the over-the-hill gang down to a waiting unmarked green van with a big antenna on top.

Jerry had very willingly surrendered his magnum, had helped a stunned Jack Vigo into the bedroom, gotten himself a very big glass of Scotch, and was popping something into his mouth. He was sitting on his couch, shivering.

"Rough bunch," I said. "They the ones who took care of you before?"

Jerry nodded yes.

"What did they want?"

He gulped down a couple of ounces of Scotch. "They wanted Jennifer Peterson real bad."

"Why would they think you might know where she is?"

"I guess they knew Jennifer called me this morning."

"How would they know that?"

Jerry just smiled at me. His good humor was returning. "I've learned never to initiate anything on the telephone in this town, Gabe. Not anything sexy, illegal, or damaging to the Mormon Church. I think the Mormon Mafia wires sea gulls. Those damned birds have to be good for something other than shitting on people's heads."

"And Jennifer called you, right?"

"That's right, blurted out her name and everything before I could utter the shadow of a warning . . ." He took a big drink and poured another. "You've been talking to Mona, have you?"

"Yeah. Saw her in the Tabernacle. She's over there sniffing out the goodies. Big story for her. She had Pulitzer written all over her face."

"She couldn't have choreographed the ending better, could she?" Jerry said.

I was getting restless. I wanted to find Jennifer. "Do you know where Jennifer is, Jerry?"

"No. Didn't have a chance to find out. I didn't want her to blurt that to the sea gulls."

"Well, I guess I'd better be on my way. Mind if I use your phone?"

"Go ahead. But be careful. If you trust Arvin Smith, you're a lot braver man than I."

I picked up the phone and dialed Linda's number. I didn't have many other possibilities just now.

"Hello, Linda?"

"Yes . . . Gabe?"

"Yeah."

"My God, what's been happening downtown? I've had the TV on. You were there, weren't you?"

"I was there. Right in the middle, you might say. I'll tell you all about it later. Right now I'm still trying to track down your daughter."

"You are?" She sounded surprised.

"Yes, I am. That's what you're paying me for. All the other crap's just extra."

"But she's right here, Gabe. With me. She came home three hours ago."

Terrific, I thought. Gone was my fantasy of delivering the wayward daughter proudly to her mother's door, the hero come home with his prize; home from the battle, home to win the fair maiden. The damned kid had just decided to schlump home on her own. Why did I feel cheated?

A radiant Linda let me in the front door. She had on expensive pink slacks and a matching sweater, and her hair was tied carelessly back by a scarf. She was barefoot. She gave me the ritual hug and led me into the living room.

And there she was. Jennifer Peterson was sitting Indian fashion on the white leather couch, wearing a pair of cut-off jeans and a T-shirt that said, "Go Utes!" She was on her third can of Coke and was stuffing her face hungrily with a big hamburger with all the trimmings. Her face was thin and pale, and the strain of the past weeks was evident. But she was much more believable as the casual teenager than she'd ever been as the obedient polygamist wife. She was smoking a cigarette.

Linda introduced us properly. It was Jennifer Peterson this time, and she didn't seem to mind. I could detect no sign that she was mourning her dead husband. Neither of them looked much to be mourning.

"Hello, Jennifer," I said. "I've been down quite a winding trail after you."

"Yeah." She didn't look up from her hamburger. "I guess they got Jed, didn't they."

"I guess they did. But it all seems senseless. It was a crazy stunt."

"He figured if he could get away with it, it would let a lot of people know he was the Prophet."

"But why Amos Jensen?" I said.

"You don't know?" she asked, a little incredulously.

"No, Jennifer, I don't know." Déjà vu—hadn't we been down this path before?

"Come to think of it, I guess almost nobody knows. Except me." And she giggled slightly, as if she just realized she had a secret.

I sat down opposite her and accepted the beer Linda offered. "You want to tell me, Jennifer?"

She looked distrustfully at me.

"I'm not the cops," I said. "I'm not the Mormon Mafia. I'm just a friend of the family who's worked very hard trying to find you."

"And you figure that gives you the right to know," she said, a little insolently.

I looked over at Linda, who was still smiling her concerned-mother smile. I noticed that the smile had slipped a little, was a little icy. "Jennie, dear. Gabe is right. He has gone to a lot of trouble. He has a right to know."

Jennifer looked at her mother like a cougar getting ready to pounce. "He may have a right to know, Mother, having worked so hard and all, but are you sure *you* want to know?" She finished her statement with a superior smile. I'd never been much into spanking as a parent, but I was sorely tempted.

A look of apprehension chased the ice from Linda's eyes. Jennifer sat tall. I felt a sense of two women engaged in some sort of primal dominance game. Linda's voice got very quiet. "Jennifer, dear. Whatever it is, I want to know it. I've been in the dark quite long enough about your affairs."

"You've always been in the dark about my affairs, Mother."

Before it got any nastier, I felt I'd better jump in. From my question, it was probably clear whose side I was on.

"David left something for your mother," I said. "Did you take it?"

Jennifer bit a fingernail, inhaled deeply from her Virginia Slim, and said, "I'd kill right now for some good grass." It did cross my mind that she'd been running with people who killed for a lot less. Linda and I both kept looking at her, waiting. Finally she realized we weren't going to give up.

"Oh shit, what's the difference? It's all over now." And she licked the remains of her hamburger off her fingers and got up and walked towards the hall. "All right. I'll get it."

She returned in a minute with a mangled piece of paper that looked like it had been dragged through a rabbithole. Probably it had. Without a word, she handed it to me and sat back down and unscrewed the cap from a bottle of bright red fingernail polish she'd brought out with her.

I took the ragged piece of white Xerox paper, a copy of a handwritten note, and read aloud, so Linda could hear:

> This is to certify that on this date Elder David Peterson was given Susan Whitesides as a wife in the Holy Covenant of Celestial Marriage.
>> Lawrence Alger, Prophet, Seer, and Revelator,
>>> Church of the Covenant.
>> Amos D. Jensen, President, Quorum of the
>> Twelve Apostles, Church of the Covenant.

I read the document over again, making sure I comprehended what it said. I noticed it was dated during the time Jennifer had supposedly gone to Las Vegas with Susan Whitesides. I started over. Linda looked as though she'd been struck by lightning. I turned to Jennifer, who was smoking away and starting to paint her toenails.

"Your father was married to Susan Whitesides?"

"That's what it says, doesn't it?" She said, finishing her big toe and moving on to the next.

"Is that where you and Susan were?"

"We went south to Covenant City. All in the same big van."

"Why did you go?" I asked, still trying to stop my brain from exploding out my ears.

"Amos Jensen wanted to marry me," she said simply. "David tried to get me to go along—said we could have a jolly double wedding."

"You say Amos Jensen wanted to marry you?" I said, trying to make sure I was hearing what I was hearing.

"Yep. He'd kind of made a deal with Dad. He'd see that David got Susan if he got me. Said it would be good for David's advancement in the Church."

"Jesus," I said, as I watched Linda, white as paste, staring at her daughter as if she was a visitor from Venus.

"Elder Amos D. Jensen had the hots for me since I was nine."

"Seems a precocious observation," I said.

"I was a precocious kid—had to be. Besides, girls know those things. The horny old bastard was still bouncing me on his knee when I was fifteen, trying to cop a peek up my dress. I knew he wanted me. That's why it didn't really surprise me when David got me involved. He always was scared shitless of Amos Jensen."

Linda finally got hold of herself enough to say something. She addressed herself to Jennifer, who was just finishing up her left foot. "So you knew all that time David had taken another wife."

"Yep."

"And you didn't tell me."

"Why should I? It wouldn't have done any good. Dad was too busy burying his nose in Amos Jensen's ass to pay attention to you. And besides, you didn't need that. You already had enough problems. One more might have been more than the pills and booze could handle."

Linda winced and struggled to drive the pain from her face. I was surprised how quickly she was able to—a good sign. Then she just sat and stared at her daughter as if she was priming to give her a sound, motherly spanking. I empathized. In fact, I almost slapped Jennifer across the room for that crack, but I restrained myself. This kid would get hers. It might take years. But she'd get hers. Besides, there was more I wanted to know.

"What about Jed?" I said.

"What about him?" Jennifer said, picking at a toenail on her right foot.

"How did you get mixed up with him?"

"Jerry introduced him to me. They'd been friends since childhood." I made a mental note to confront Jerry with his lies about Jed Kimball. But then again, it wouldn't do any good. Jerry had a lot of friends, and he was loyal to them all in his own way. At least he talked to all segments of this crazy society . . . and he had led me to Jennifer in a daft, roundabout way.

"Why did you go off with him?" I said.

She was now trying to dig out a hangnail on her right big toe. That accomplished, she lit another cigarette and answered. "David and Susan got me really believing that stuff—about more than one wife and all. I was a real convert."

"So why not Amos Jensen?" I said. "He may not be a maiden's dream, but anyone who married him would have a leg up into heaven."

She turned up her nose into a sneer—at Jensen, not heaven, I assumed. "I got real pissed at David for trying to shove that dirty old man on me. He wouldn't let me alone about it. Said it was my duty to marry him, that he would be the Prophet before long."

"So you just went off and found yourself another Prophet," I said.

She looked over at me. Her eyes got hard. "I guess I did. Someone I could really believe was a Prophet." She paused and shot me a furtive grin. "And he was the sexiest man I ever met."

I chose to ignore that comment and went on. "So you stole the paper from David's folder and took it with you."

"Yep. Jed wanted to have it." Her eyes got coy. "But I wouldn't give it to him."

"Why not?"

"Because it kept him coming back more often. He knew I

kept it hidden. I kept telling him that next time, if he was really nice to me, I'd give it to him. But I never did."

"Didn't you worry that he might just come in and take it from you—with a knife?"

Her eyes aimed defiant darts at me. "Jed would never hurt me. He was a very gentle man—with his women. And he loved me best. He told me that . . . and I think he kind of liked the game."

"But he knew what was on the paper," I said.

"Sure he did."

"I guess that's another reason Jed would want to kill Amos Jensen," I said.

"Yep. Amos was the Prophet now. Of the Church of the Covenant. He got insane about other people who claimed to be Prophet."

I figured I had learned about all I could from Jennifer—certainly all my overloaded brain could handle for a while—and my thoughts turned back to Linda, who was sitting listening to all this with a very tough look in her eyes. I had just decided not to tamper with her new strength by telling her any more bad news about David when she reached over and took my hand and said, "David killed Susan Whitesides, didn't he, Gabe?"

"How did you know?"

"I didn't know. Not until now. I just knew something was terribly wrong. The worst of it started the night she died."

"Why do you think he did it, Linda?"

"All the guilt," she said simply. "All the guilt."

I stood up and walked quietly to the door. I thought I'd better give Arvin Smith another call. I had some real goodies for him this time. Linda was sitting quietly, allowing the tumblers inside her head to come into new and proper places. I recognized the look from twenty years before. She was very beautiful just then. Jennifer was absently lighting another Virginia Slim off her last, wishing even harder, I suspected, for some good dope.

"I'll call tomorrow, Linda."

"Gabe." She looked over at me.

"Yes, Linda."

"It's astonishing how you can live with someone for twenty years and not know anything about what makes them work inside. And the tragic thing is that when you allow that to happen, you can never really know anything about what makes *you* work inside."

"It's dangerous, letting yourself know someone too well . . . especially if you're married to him."

"Thanks, Gabe."

"Good-bye, Jennifer."

"Bye." She was deeply engrossed in painting the middle toe on her right foot.

Arvin set up our meeting at the fancy restaurant on top of the Hotel Utah—a late supper. He said we could have it both ways there; he'd be on home ground and I could have a drink. When I walked in about ten he was already there, nursing a 7-Up, popping jellybeans, and looking out over Temple Square, which was lovely, peaceful, and deserted in the night. I slid into the chair opposite him. He had already ordered a split of good German wine for me.

"Bitch of a day," he said. And he looked tired, his brown eye in ascendancy.

"Kept you and yours busy."

"Wish we could have been just a little faster. Weren't expecting women."

"How's Amos Jensen?" I said.

He looked out at the Temple spires. "Well, I guess it sort of depends on how you look at it. But first, why don't we talk about what you have to show me?"

I pulled out the piece of Xerox paper and handed it to Arvin. His expression didn't change as he examined it. "Um-hm . . . Interesting."

He shot me his engaging sly smile. "It's not a big surprise, not what it says. What is a little surprising is that any paper exists at all."

"It's a copy. Looks like David made it."

"Maybe I underestimated David," Arvin said. Then he did an extraordinary thing. He took the rumpled sheet of paper and held a corner over the candle on the table. He watched it burn. I sat like a dummy and watched it burn. He dropped it into the ashtray before it singed his hand.

"It's all right," he said. "It doesn't matter."

"What do you mean it doesn't matter? That piece of paper could turn the Mormon Church upside down."

"Exactly," he said.

"Seems to me it'll be pretty hard for you folks to keep this one out of the papers. I mean, my God, you've got a spectacular shooting in the middle of General Conference with one Prophet trying to kill another Prophet while your Uncle Prophet sits and watches it all. That's a *Newsweek* cover if ever I saw one."

"Oh, it'll make *Newsweek,* all right, maybe even the cover. But it won't read quite as you describe it."

I wasn't ready for this, not just yet. I took a good, healthy slug of wine and sat staring out into the night for a few minutes while I sorted out what to say next. Arvin seemed content to sit and look at me. I seemed to amuse him. He performed the ordering chores when he saw I was off in cloud-cuckoo land and had started on his soup when I finally came around.

"Is there anything you don't know about all this, Arvin?"

"Probably not," he said. "You kind of filled in the missing link with your piece of paper; I mean, about David Peterson. It sort of makes sense out of the Whitesides killing. A kind of bizarre sense."

"You never did tell me who the man in the blue pin-stripe suit is, Arvin."

"Didn't I?" he said, smiling. "I guess I thought it was a little touchy."

"You know he murdered Orson Kimball."

"Yes I do. I found something at the trailer."

"What?"

"A Fundamentalist tract."

"Why would that be surprising?"

"The kind of Fundamentalist tract Amos Jensen's son hands out on streetcorners."

"My God. You mean . . ."

"You're a smart detective. Got it on the third try."

"Amos Jensen's son."

"Rulon Jensen, his daddy's heir apparent since Amos Junior got sent to Fresno."

"I'm beginning to get the picture," I said.

"I was afraid you might," Arvin said as he began his salad. I still hadn't touched my soup. I was well into the wine, however.

"I don't suppose Rulon or any of them will be prosecuted, will they."

"I don't suppose. They'll have a nice big sunny room for Rulon in Fresno."

"Why did Amos even bother to stay with the Mormon Church? Seems he had his own kingdom nicely carved out. He was even Prophet."

"You have to understand, Gabe, that the major thing the Mormon Church has that the Fundamentalist sects don't have—besides several billion dollars and respectability—is access to the Temple. They want that so they can perform their marriages there. Amos Jensen gave that to them. He got them in late at night. Besides, a lot of those folks have no qualms at all about playing both sides of the fence. Why should they?"

"You will tell me one thing, though, won't you?"

"Not if I can help it."

"David Peterson. How did he die?"

He pondered how to answer this, then seemed to decide maybe I had a right to know. "Rulon—crazy Rulon—met both Orson Kimball and David out in Magna. Took care of them both on one hysterical bloody binge. I found this in the trailer, too." And he handed me a gold cuff link molded into a question mark. "I got nosing around, found that David had gone into Amos Jensen the day before he died, determined to confess something publicly. Old Amos apparently told David to go home and think it over. But before he could think too hard, the old man had him sent out to Magna to have a talk with Orson Kimball."

"Poor David," I said. "Seems not everybody can play both sides of the fence."

"Let's just say, Gabe, that schizophrenia is an occupational hazard in a society like this."

"But why poor dumb old Orson?" I said.

"I guess you could say it was getting a little out of hand by the end. Goes back to the big man."

"Amos Jensen."

"That's right. Seems he got abnormally preoccupied with your little runaway. Went wild when she ran off with Jed Kimball. Devoted the entirety of his considerable resources to tracking her down."

"He could have hired better guys," I said.

"Better guys would know better. And Abe Lewis and his little band aren't bad at what they do. Not if what they do has to do with guns and beating up sexual deviants." Arvin stopped and smiled conspiratorially at me. "Old Amos got real angry when they couldn't keep up with a New York City slicker in the Utah desert."

I smiled back. "Somebody should have told them about my survival merit badge."

Arvin raised his 7-Up glass in a toast. "Here's to your survival in the desert." I joined him.

"What now, Arvin. Tell me what I'll read in *Newsweek* Monday."

He leaned over the table. For some reason, he enjoyed confiding secrets that I couldn't do anything about. "Well, unofficially, Amos Jensen is in fine shape. The slug from your gun missed anything vital. Mostly, it's just the shock, though there is some question whether the old bull will ever be able to properly service any of his nine wives again.

"You'll read in the *Tribune* tomorrow morning that Amos D. Jensen suffered a stroke as a result of that traumatic incident in the Tabernacle. You'll read that he will have to retire from the Quorum of Twelve Apostles. Go Emeritus, as we say."

"Simple."

"Well, not exactly simple, Gabe. But tidy. And the Church goes on."

"And yesterday's shooting will be recorded as an aberration perpetrated by a fringe loony from out of the nineteenth century. Nothing to do with what the Mormons are today."

Arvin simply smiled at me.

"Your uncle's not as feeble as he looks," I said.

"Uncle may be old, Gabe, but Uncle's jungle instincts are still intact. He takes the survival of the Church very seriously. And when it gets to the point that one of his Twelve Apostles starts sending the Avenging Angels scrambling all over the territory after a sixteen-year-old honeypot he has a crush on, Uncle loses patience."

"Don't imagine your uncle would be amused by Jensen's claim to be Prophet, either."

"There certainly is that to be said. You might think both Jed and Amos felt strongly about their prophetic callings. But compared to Uncle they're in the bush leagues. Uncle is the Prophet and he never forgets it and he doesn't want anybody else to forget it. He has a very low tolerance for rivals."

"Well, thanks for the dinner," I said, getting up.

"No problem. It's on the Church. You kind of did us a favor."

"I'll be in touch."

"Not soon, I hope. I trust you'll be on that plane tomorrow. I don't think Uncle would like to see you around the day after."

"And Uncle gets anything he wants?"

"Usually," Arvin said, "usually. And I'd hate to be in the way when he doesn't."

"Good-bye, Arvin."

"Good-bye, Gabe. See you around. If I ever get to New York."

I walked to the elevator, got on it, and rode down to the lobby. As I stepped out, I saw Mona sitting on a couch. I went over and sat down beside her. "Hi, Mona. You lost your way?"

"Arvin said you'd be here."

I didn't say anything.

"Are we friends?" she asked. "I wouldn't want to part and not be friends."

"We're friends. At least we're two people with a potent professional respect for each other."

"Jesus, Gabe. That's pompous."

I didn't say anything—again.

"You want to come over to my place?"

I paused, pondering. But there really wasn't anything to ponder. Walking out with this woman would be a risk. But then, if you don't take risks, you never really learn anything, do you?

"Sure," I said. And we walked out the door together into a stormy Salt Lake evening.